THE CABALA
and
THE WOMAN OF ANDROS

BY THORNTON WILDER

NOVELS

The Cabala

The Bridge of San Luis Rey

The Woman of Andros

Heaven's My Destination

The Ides of March

The Eighth Day

Theophilus North

COLLECTIONS OF SHORT PLAYS

The Angel That Troubled the Waters

The Long Christmas Dinner & Other Plays in One Act

The Collected Short Plays of Thornton Wilder Vol. 1

The Collected Short Plays of Thornton Wilder Vol. 2

PLAYS

Our Town

The Merchant of Yonkers

The Skin of Our Teeth

The Matchmaker

The Alcestiad

The Beaux' Strategem (with Ken Ludwig)

A Doll's House

ESSAYS

American Characteristics & Other Essays

The Journals of Thornton Wilder, 1939–1961

The Selected Letters of Thornton Wilder

The Letters of Gertrude Stein and Thornton Wilder

A Tour of the Darkling Plain: The Finnegans Wake Letters of Thornton Wilder and Adaline Glasheen

Thornton Wilder

THE CABALA

and

THE WOMAN

OF ANDROS

FOREWORD BY PENELOPE NIVEN

HARPER**PERENNIAL** ● MODERN**CLASSICS**

NEW YORK ● LONDON ● TORONTO ● SYDNEY ● NEW DELHI ● AUCKLAND

HARPER**PERENNIAL** ● MODERN**CLASSICS**

A hardcover edition of this book was published in 1958 by Harper & Row Publishers, Inc. It is reprinted here by arrangement with the Wilder Family LLC.

THE CABALA. Copyright © 1926 by Albert & Charles Boni. Copyright renewed © 1954 by Thornton Wilder. Copyright © 2002 by the Wilder Family LLC. THE WOMAN OF ANDROS. Copyright © 1930 by Albert & Charles Boni. Copyright renewed ©1958 by Thornton Wilder. Copyright © 2002 by the Wilder Family LLC. Foreword copyright © 2006 by Penelope Niven. Afterword Copyright © 2006, 2022 by Tappan Wilder. All rights reserved. Printed in the United States of America. No part of this book may be used or reproduced in any manner whatsoever without written permission except in the case of brief quotations embodied in critical articles and reviews. For information, address HarperCollins Publishers, 195 Broadway, New York, NY 10007.

HarperCollins books may be purchased for educational, business, or sales promotional use. For information, please email the Special Markets Department at SPsales@harpercollins.com.

First Harper Perennial Modern Classics edition published 2006.
Reissued in 2022.

Library of Congress Cataloging-in-Publication Data is available upon request.

ISBN 978-0-06-309785-8 (pbk.)

22 23 24 25 26 LSC 10 9 8 7 6 5 4 3 2 1

*To my friends at the American Academy
in Rome, 1920–1921*

T.W.

FOREWORD BY PENELOPE NIVEN *xi*

THE CABALA
BOOK ONE: FIRST ENCOUNTERS *1*
BOOK TWO: MARCANTONIO *28*
BOOK THREE: ALIX *60*
BOOK FOUR: ASTRÉE-LUCE AND THE CARDINAL *95*
BOOK FIVE: THE DUSK OF THE GODS *124*

THE WOMAN OF ANDROS *135*

AFTERWORD BY TAPPAN WILDER *205*
ACKNOWLEDGMENTS *261*
ABOUT THE AUTHOR *265*

FOREWORD

From boyhood Thornton Niven Wilder devoted every scrap of time he could spare or steal to creating plays, poems, and stories. Endowed with an intense imagination, boundless curiosity, and an affinity for vivid stories, he dreamed about the books he would write. As a teenager he began composing a series of three-minute playlets for three characters. ("Authors of fifteen and sixteen years of age spend their time drawing up title-pages and adjusting the tables of contents of works they have neither the perseverance nor the ability to execute," he wrote years later in the foreword to an edition of his short plays.) The young Wilder possessed the ability and the perseverance as well as the dreams, and as a college student frequently saw his work in print, usually in undergraduate publications.

From 1920 until 1926, when his first novel, *The Cabala,* was published, Wilder was a graduate student and a school master, earning his bread-and-butter income teaching prep-school French and tutoring on the side. In the coveted leftover hours, he poured himself into the reading and writing that had always been his primary occupation. He also gravitated to the theaters from New York to Philadelphia, for he had fallen in love early with the magic of the stage.

Wilder was twenty-nine when *The Cabala* appeared on the American literary scene, earning good reviews and modest royalties. It was followed in 1927 by a spectacular popular and critical success—the bestselling Pulitzer Prize–winning novel *The Bridge of San Luis Rey,* hailed internationally as an overnight sensation. In reality, it had been a fifteen-year-long overnight—a persistent apprenticeship of reading, writing, thinking, imagining, and experimenting, often while "caught," as Wilder said, "in the quicksands of Teaching." *The Bridge of San Luis Rey* brought honors, celebrity, and fortune—and for decades its vast shadow would overwhelm and even obscure the significance of *The Cabala* and *The Woman of Andros,* the novels that immediately preceded and followed it. This new volume sheds light on Wilder the novelist and on the two novels standing on either side of *The Bridge.*

In 1920, twenty-three years old and fresh out of Yale College, Thornton Wilder booked passage on the French ocean liner *Providence,* bound for Italy and the future. He embarked with great excitement and very little money on what he later called his "Italian year," becoming a visiting student in the School of Classical Studies at the American Academy in Rome.

Isabella Thornton Niven Wilder, his mother, had always nurtured his imagination, his dreams and his artistic sensibilities. She was particularly pleased with her son's plans to travel to Italy, where she and other family members spent time over the years. She translated the poems of Giosué Carducci from Italian into

English, wrote poems of her own, introduced her children to classical literature and Greek drama, took them to the theater to see the plays of Ibsen and Shaw as well as stock company plays, and awakened in Thornton his lifelong love of music and of European literature and culture. He took with him to Italy a grounding in classical mythology, history, and literature, including Dante's work. It is no wonder that in the fall of 1920 he was captivated by the treasures of Rome—art, architecture, music, literature, and his new enthusiasm, archeology.

"After I'd graduated from college I was sent to Europe to study archeology," Wilder recalled decades later. "One day our class in Rome was taken out into the country to dig up a bit of the Etruscan world, a street. Once thousands of people had walked it. The rut was very deep. Those who have uncovered such a spot are never the same again." He wrote that each of us possesses "something of the mind of an archeologist" and that while people in previous centuries knew "that many people had lived and died a long while ago" and that "there were many people living on the earth," the modern mind grasps the reality that

> millions and billions have lived and died, and that probably billions and billions (let us not despair of the human race) will live and die. The extent of this enlarged realization alters the whole view of life.

Wilder's pivotal Italian year helped to forge his vision of the individual's relationship to the universe, the infinite permutations and combinations of the basic life events, or plots—birth, struggle, love, aspiration, defeat, transcendence, death.

"How perfect it is, my being here!" he exulted in a letter home from Italy in 1920. "How much happier a chance has fallen than a year in Paris or London or New York. Rome's antiquity, her variety, her significance swallow these others up, and I feel myself being irresistibly impelled toward saying of her that she is the Eternal City." He wrote to his father that he wanted to develop a literary consciousness that took into account "the artistic anxiety of the European" and a "new abundance and range of America." He said that his foray into ancient Rome evoked in him a new appreciation for the American experience.

Amos Parker Wilder, father of Thornton and four other precocious children, was a journalist, consular official, and platform lecturer, with ambitious yet practical dreams for his sons and daughters. He deplored the fact that four of them seemed bent on becoming "'artistic' writers, that is to say unmarketable." Many years later, Wilder wrote that his father "had read my numerous works with deep concern; they appeared to him to be—borrowing a phrase he had picked up in China—'carved cherry stones.'" The Wilder children were well acquainted with this metaphor, for their father used it often when he sought to discourage their interest in writing.

Amos Wilder hoped that Thornton would return from Italy in a year's time "uncorrupted" and equipped to earn a living. He worried about his son's seeming inability to concentrate and persevere, his tendencies toward woolgathering and dilettantism. Amos concluded that teaching was the best fit for Thornton's temperament, and with the help of strong references from two of his son's Yale professors, secured a teaching post for Thornton. By the autumn of 1921, the traveler was settling into his job as assistant housemaster for Davis House and French teacher at Lawrenceville School, a few miles from Princeton, New Jersey.

At night, his duties done—lessons prepared, papers graded, and young charges asleep—Wilder turned to his reading and writing. Years later, former students in Davis House recalled hearing Wilder's footsteps tracing a steady pattern across the floorboards as he worked on the novel and the plays he was writing after hours. He had rejoiced in his sojourn in the land of Virgil, Cicero, Tasso, and

Dante. It was enough, he said, "to set the imagination racing." As he worked on his first novel in his spare time, he was transmuting the Italian experiences, real and imagined, into art.

Wilder's papers reveal some of the winding pathway from conception to completion of the novel, an imaginary memoir of a young American mingling with a small clique of privileged, eccentric residents of early-twentieth-century Rome. He referred to his story variously as "Notes of a Roman Student," "Roman Memoirs," "The Trasteverine," and "The Memoirs of Charles Mallison: The Year in Rome," among other titles. Along the way Wilder experimented with characters and structure, with voice and style, even momentarily groping, like other writers of the time, for a literary response to World War I. "The whole memoirs are to be a sort of adieu to the romance and medievalism that barely survived the war," he wrote to his mother.

As was his habit, Wilder was deeply influenced by his reading—the plays of French dramatist Paul Claudel, for instance, especially *Le Père Humilié* (1920), depicting the decline and dissipation of noble families; Pierre Champagne de Labriolle's *Histoire de la Littérature Latine Chrétienne;* and Ernest Renan's *Souvenirs d'enfance et de jeunesse.* In July 1922, temporarily free of his teaching and house-parenting duties, Wilder rented a room on the top floor of the YMCA in Newport, Rhode Island, set up his Underwood typewriter and spent several hours a day typing the book he was composing in longhand. He wrote to his father that he had "carved some cherry stones," and was working on "a type of sentence, on a hint from Lytton Strachey, wherein you crowd under *one* trait in common a host of disparate details, in order to give an impression of rich complicated life."

As always, Wilder entrusted his dreams and his work-in-progress to his mother, who took a keen interest in her son's reading and writing. "Just as soon as I get a fair copy made of BOOK ONE," he wrote to her, "I look it over and with my blue pencil start indicating alterations; within an hour the whole script is unsightly. My only consolation is that every touch has been an improvement." He was weaving an intricate tapestry of comedy, satire, irony and tragedy, and by August 1922, he sent his manuscript to the editors of *The Dial,* then one of the prestigious literary journals in the United States. "I am submitting under separate cover the MSS of a series of imaginary memoirs of a year spent in Rome, entitled 'The Trasteverine,'" Wilder wrote. "These give the appearance of being faithful portraits of living persons, but the work is a purely fanciful effort in the manner of Marcel Proust, or at times, of Paul Morand. Attached hereto find return postage. Very truly yours, Thornton N. Wilder."

The Dial declined the manuscript, but expressed an interest in seeing more when the book was further along. *The Double Dealer,* a monthly magazine in New Orleans, published an excerpt from the novel. (This journal published other fledgling writers— Ernest Hemingway, William Faulkner, Jean Toomer, Edmund Wilson, and Amos Niven Wilder, Thornton's older brother, who wrote poetry.) Wilder's journal of that time reveals his continual experimentation and his struggles with form and direction. On September 9, 1922, he wrote,

> There is a great book in the idea; I have fertility of inven-
> tion, but I soon tire of the clumsiness of my phrasing.
> I think my reluctance to go on with it is not mere lack
> of perseverance, but a consciousness of the real difficulty
> of combining the real and the fantastic; it must be long
> brooded.

The conscientious if somewhat unorthodox schoolmaster created a flamboyant cast of characters in the five sections of the book. The members of the Cabala are introduced to the reader by James Blair, a young American scholar in Rome, and friend of the novel's narrator, another young American, nicknamed Samuele. The Cabalists, says Blair, are "Fierce intellectual snobs" who are "very rich and influential," so much so that everyone else fears them and suspects them of "plots to overturn things." Furthermore, they are "so wonderful that they're lonely," and they derive "what comfort they can out of each other's excellence." Soon we meet the energetic Miss Grier, wealthy American spinster, Vassar College trustee, and a dominant force in the Cabala; Her Highness Leda Matilda Colonna duchessa d'Aquilanera and her young son, the doomed, handsome prince Marcantonio, who has "fallen on bad ways"; the cultured French woman Alix, Princess d'Espoli, unhappily married to her Italian prince; ancient, wise Cardinal Vaine, who has spent his life in the mission fields of China; and the fervently devout Mlle. Astrée-Luce de Marfontaine. There is even a cameo appearance in the novel by John Keats. Wilder's lodging in Rome in 1920 had been a stone's throw from the house where Keats died in 1821. Wilder wrote to his mother about his character's "bored attendance at the sick-bed of a not very likable poet, a faithful description of his tubercular symptoms day by day, his terror and weakness, and finally his funeral in the Protestant Cemetery—the death of Keats faithfully documented and seen through the veil of 'my' dislike and revulsion."

The young American narrator of *The Cabala*'s interwoven stories calls himself "the biographer of the individuals" in the novel, not "the historian of the group." He is also sometime-mentor, would-be savior, and occasional perpetrator of events—a character device Wilder would use in future fiction. He sought to evoke in the novel both the Rome he experienced and the Rome he imagined:

> From all these eccentrics and madmen and scoundrels—
> thousands of portraits—is supposed to arise the hot breath
> of life more romantic than Jules Verne—an escape from

routine and weariness and stenographer's anaemia, and
a reproduction of the feeling that Rome gives you when
you're no longer in it.

"Of course it is only written to please myself," Wilder wrote
to his mother. "There is nothing in it except what I am madly
curious about; no compromise made for people who do not like the
particular forms of strangeness and disorder that I like."

Wilder observed in later years that *The Cabala* "presumes to
give a picture of contemporary life among the highly privileged
members of Roman society. That picture is almost entirely
imagined." He had met very few members of the aristocracy,
he said, and "no members of the ecclesiastical hierarchy." He
noted that the book's sources could be found "in the reading of
Marcel Proust, the memoirs of the Duke of Saint-Simon, and the
characters of La Bruyère. These works I devoured rapturously in
the reading-room of the Princeton University Library on the free
evenings afforded me by my first job—teaching eight miles away
at The Lawrenceville School."

The Cabala was published by Albert & Charles Boni in 1926.
The New York Times Book Review hailed the "debut of a new
American stylist," and called Wilder's novel "a literary event."
According to the *Saturday Review of Literature,* the novel was a
"sophisticated extravaganza." Critics admired the novel's charm,
its irony, and its elements of comedy and satire. But it would soon
be dwarfed by *The Bridge of San Luis Rey,* which followed in 1927
and quickly brought Wilder international fame, as well as his first
Pulitzer Prize.

As he was finishing the second book, Wilder had written in
a 1926 journal entry, "Some day someone will discover that one
of the principal ideas behind my work is the fear of catastrophe
(especially illness and pain), and a preoccupation with the claims of
a religion to meet the situation." That same year, in a later journal

entry pocked with words blotted out, Wilder had this to say about his novels:

> The Cabala was written because I brooded about great natures and their obstacles and ailments and frustrations. The Bridge was written because I wanted to die and I wanted to prove that death was a happy solution.
>
> The motto of The Bridge is to be found in the last page of The Cabala: Hurry and die!
>
> In The Cabala I began to think that love is enough to reconcile one to the difficulty of living (i.e. the difficulty of being good); in The Bridge I am still a little surer. Perhaps some-day I can write a book announcing that love is sufficient.

There are riddles woven into these lines that a biographer works hard to unravel. And there is this question: What would Wilder's third novel have to say about the sufficiency of love?

"Had a fine month at Peterborough," Wilder wrote to his brother Amos in August of 1929. He had traveled to the MacDowell Colony that summer to work on *The Woman of Andros,* and he found "the long solitary hours in the Studio fine. Lots more Andros done but confused about the direction to take in the fourth quarter of it. No hurry, and no worry." He described *The Woman of Andros* as his first novel, "in the sense," he said, "that the others were collections of tales, novelettes, bound together by a slight tie that identified them a belonging to the same group."

By the time Wilder finished his third novel, he had enjoyed a wealth of new experiences and friendships, as well as international celebrity and enough of a fortune to build a house for his family and otherwise support his parents and sisters. He had seen the first New York production of one of his plays, *The Trumpet Shall Sound*; had published *The Angel That Troubled the Waters,* a collection of short plays; and had toured the country as a platform lecturer with resounding success, speaking to full houses on "The Relation of Literature and Life," "The Future of American Literature," "Enthusiasms and Disappointments of Play-Going," and other topics. He had bought his first automobile, had struck up friendships with two other young novelists making their mark, Ernest Hemingway and Scott Fitzgerald, and had taken an internationally publicized "walking tour" in Europe with world heavyweight boxing champion Gene Tunney ("as fine a person as you'd want to meet," Wilder wrote to Hemingway before the trip). When Fitzgerald wrote to Wilder about *The Bridge of San Luis Rey,* Wilder answered with an autobiographical snapshot:

> I have been an admirer, not to say a student, of the Great Gatsby too long not to have got a great kick out of your letter. It gives me the grounds to hope that we may sometime have some long talks on what writing's all about. As you see I am a provincial school-master and have always worked alone. And yet nothing interests me more than thinking of our generation as a league and as a protest to the whole cardboard generation that precedes us from Wharton through Cabell and Anderson and Sinclair Lewis. . . . I like teaching a lot and shall probably remain here for ages; a daily routine is necessary to me. I have no writing habits, am terribly lazy and write seldom.

With typical self-deprecation, Wilder underplayed his discipline as a writer, for his journals and letters testify to his habitual absorption in his work. As he wrote *The Woman of Andros,* based in part, he said, on a Greek comedy by Terence, Wilder was immersed in

Greek drama and philosophy, spending time in ancient Greece in his imagination, his reading, and his preparations for lectures he would give at the University of Chicago, when he became a part-time faculty member in 1930. On a trip to England, in September 1929, he sketched ideas for the lectures in his journal: What fifth century Greece thought of itself; how it was viewed by successive ages and by modern archeology; how it was viewed by "specific great authors." He wanted to learn Greek, and he was rereading Aeschylus and Euripides.

When asked why he chose remote ages and settings for his early novels, Wilder answered "Because I am not yet ready to do something modern. I cannot yet reconcile a philosophic theme with the ringing of doorbells and telephones." Actually, in Wilder's novels as well as his plays, literal setting and time are almost incidental—embroidery rather than scaffolding. He experimented with setting in fiction just as he experimented with sets on stage. The "sets" of his novels are draped in richer detail than the minimalist sets for his plays, but in Wilder's fiction as in his drama, time and place are not fundamental to the story. Character and theme dominate.

This is especially the case in *The Woman of Andros,* set on Brynos, an imagined Greek island, before the birth of Christ. (One interviewer reported that Wilder said the novel was set in 400 BC, but he commonly wrote that it was "about 200 BC—that is, in the decline of the Great Age of Greece.") Wilder's major character, the woman of Andros, is Chrysis, a beautiful, intelligent *hetaira*, or highly cultured courtesan, who is the benefactress of a household of dependent "stray human beings," misfits, outsiders like herself, whose physical and/or emotional needs Chrysis seeks to fulfill. She and her younger sister Glycerium love the same god-like young man. Throw into the brew two worried fathers, a contemplative priest of Apollo, some suspicious islanders, a battle-worn sea captain, and an avaricious pimp, and you are in for a compelling concoction of myth, fable, and fantasia, laced with memorable aphorisms. ("The loneliest associations are those that pretend to intimacy," for example. "It is true that of all the forms of genius, goodness has the longest awkward age." "Stupidity is everywhere and invincible.")

Wilder draws his readers into the interior lives of some of the inhabitants of Andros, especially lovely, alluring Chrysis. His 1929 journal reveals that she was his frequent imaginary companion as he worked on the book at the MacDowell Colony and on a trip to England with his mother. Revelations and lines of dialogue came to him as he took long walks, or rode the train, or spent hours at night copying the book by hand on the sea voyage from England to New York, beset by his habitual doubts. "From time to time the whole book seems mistaken," he fretted in his journal in October 1929:

> Have I let myself go again to a luxury of grief? I remember this haunted me through the writing of the Bridge and I am still not sure whether *that* is the way the world is. Already I have begun to reduce some of the expressions. This perpetual harping on the supposition that people suffer within. Am I sufficiently realist?

He indicated that there were autobiographical traits in three characters—Chremes, one of the fathers of Brynos, this "happiest, and one of the least famous of the islands"; Chrysis, the Woman of Andros herself; and the young priest of Aesculapius and Apollo. Space here does not permit an exploration of Wilder's life to illuminate that intriguing premise. There is, however, a prophetic, life-affirming scene in the novel that points us toward pivotal themes in Wilder's future work. If you have seen or read *Our Town,* which appeared eight years after *The Woman of Andros,* you will recognize the story Chrysis tells her banquet guests about the Greek hero who begged Zeus to permit him to return to earth for just one day. Granted his dangerous wish, the hero, like Emily in Wilder's play, discovers that "the living too are dead and that we can only be said to be alive in those moments when our hearts are conscious of our treasure." He kisses "the soil of the world that is too dear to be realized."

From the earliest pages of his first novels and plays, Wilder examined the universal quandaries encapsulated in the questions the young man Pamphilus asks in *The Woman of Andros*: "How does one live? What does one do first?" In March 1930, Wilder wrote to Norman Fitts, then the *Boston Evening Transcript* critic, "It seems to me that my books are about: What is the worst thing that the world can do to you, and what are the last resources one has to oppose it? In other words: When a human being is made to bear more than a human being can bear, what then?" Wilder's novels and plays pose evocative questions about spiritual belief and the mysteries of the mind and the spirit. He came to believe that the questions about the "vast themes" took precedence over the answers, contending that writers "have only one duty, namely to pose the questions correctly."

This challenge absorbed and tantalized him. Wilder's first two novels and his early plays oscillated between story lines and search for meaning, between fable and examination of faith–but the emphasis rested on story and style rather than on substance and revelation. His focus changed with *The Woman of Andros,* however. Here the story is driven by the characters and their multifaceted search for meaning, including Wilder's ongoing examination of the "sufficiency of love." The young man Pamphilus, for instance, perceives in many of his fellow islanders "a sad love that was half hope, often rebuked and waiting to be reassured of its truth." He asks, "But why then a love so defeated, as though it were waiting for a voice to come from the skies, declaring that therein lay the secret of the world." The islanders in *The Woman of Andros* struggle with the nature of the "perpetual flames of love" that burn in the human heart—romantic love, especially first love; love for family; love of wisdom; even love for the unlovable in society. "If I love them enough, I can understand them," Chrysis reflects. She believes that life's most difficult burden is " the incommunicability of love." Ultimately Chrysis comes to the encompassing love of life itself: "Remember me," she says, "as one who loved all things and accepted from the gods all things, the bright and the dark."

In *The Woman of Andros* Wilder was still probing other questions he had parsed in *The Cabala* and *The Bridge of San Luis Rey,* such as "whether the associations in life are based upon an accidental encounter or upon a profound and inner necessity." The characters in *The Woman of Andros* also grapple with the enigma of suffering, the mystery of death, the understanding of the "highest point towards which any existence would aspire." As the omniscient narrator, Wilder reflects that "the most exhausting of all our adventures is that journey down the long corridors of the mind to the last halls where belief is enthroned." Chrysis epitomizes that journey, ultimately concluding that "It is the life in the mind that is important." When external events defy her power to shape or control, she relies on the interior harmony of mind, heart and spirit for ballast and refuge.

As you will discover in the afterword to this volume, *The Woman of Andros* set off an obstreperous critical controversy. Still the novel pleased many critics and Wilder fans, and became a bestseller, although not of the magnitude achieved by *The Bridge of San Luis Rey,* for so long the yardstick by which all of Wilder's other novels would be measured.

Thornton Wilder spent all of his literary life perpetually evolving—becoming a playwright of bolder innovation and theme, becoming a novelist of deepening vision and complexity. And how did he write what he wrote? Slowly. Painstakingly. In seclusion, when he could, in remote places in his own country, in favorite habitats in Europe. Part-time, while juggling professional, personal, and family obligations. In longhand, with pen or pencil, a unit of three pages at a time. He believed that the "mechanical flavor" of the typewriter interfered with the clarity of his thought and his work. He carved those cherry stones—elegant sentences, fluid paragraphs, pages infused with irony, verve, wisdom, and beauty. He found in the act of writing not so much pleasure as "a deep absorption." And there was the alluring power and possibility inherent in the process of "imaginative narration." In his notes for a lecture on the novel as a literary form, Wilder wrote, "Consider the story-teller: Out of his head he invents souls and destinies." Wilder went on to say, "There seems to be some kind of law deep down in human nature whereby the most compelling means of communicating ideas about the nature of what it is like to be alive is to ENWRAP one's illumination in a STORY."

Welcome to the worlds that Thornton Wilder, the storyteller, created in *The Cabala* and *The Woman of Andros,* to the invented souls that inhabit them, and to the illuminations enwrapped in the stories. In these two novels Wilder gives us the questions, sharp and clear, and leaves it to us to find the answers.

— PENELOPE NIVEN

THE CABALA

BOOK ONE

FIRST ENCOUNTERS

The train that first carried me into Rome was late, overcrowded and cold. There had been several unexplained waits in an open field, and midnight found us still moving slowly across the Campagna toward the faintly-colored clouds that hung above Rome. At intervals we stopped at platforms where flaring lamps lit up for a moment some splendid weather-moulded head. Darkness surrounded these platforms, save for glimpses of a road and the dim outlines of a mountain ridge. It was Virgil's country and there was a wind that seemed to rise from the fields and descend upon us in a long Virgilian sigh, for the land that has inspired sentiment in the poet ultimately receives its sentiment from him.

The train was overcrowded, because some tourists had discovered on the previous day that the beggars of Naples smelt of carbolic acid. They concluded at once that the authorities had struck a case or two of Indian cholera and were disinfecting the underworld by a system of enforced baths. The air of Naples generates legend. In the sudden exodus tickets for Rome became all but improcurable, and First Class tourists rode Third, and interesting people rode First.

1

In the carriage it was cold. We sat in our overcoats meditating, our eyes glazed by resignation or the glare. In one compartment a party drawn from that race that travels most and derives least pleasure from it, talked tirelessly of bad hotels, the ladies sitting with their skirts whipped about their ankles to discourage the ascent of fleas. Opposite them sprawled three American Italians returning to their homes in some Apennine village after twenty years of trade in fruit and jewelry on upper Broadway. They had invested their savings in the diamonds on their fingers, and their eyes were not less bright with anticipation of a family reunion. One foresaw their parents staring at them, unable to understand the change whereby their sons had lost the charm the Italian soil bestows upon the humblest of its children, noting only that they have come back with bulbous features, employing barbarous idioms and bereft forever of the witty psychological intuition of their race. Ahead of them lay some sleepless bewildered nights above their mothers' soil floors and muttering poultry.

In another compartment an adventuress in silver sables leaned one cheek against the shuddering windowpane. Opposite her a glittering-eyed matron stared with challenging persistency, ready to intercept any glance the girl might cast upon her dozing husband. In the corridor two young army officers lolled and preened and angled for her glance, like those insects in certain beautiful pages of Fabre, who go through the ritual of flirtation under futile conditions, before a stone, merely because some associative motors have been touched.

There was a Jesuit with his pupils, filling the time with Latin conversation; a Japanese diplomat reverently brooding over a postage-stamp collection; a Russian sculptor sombrely reading the bony structure of our heads; some Oxford students carefully dressed for tramping, but riding over the richest tramping country in Italy; the usual old woman with a hen and the usual young American, staring. Such a company as Rome receives ten times a day, and remains Rome.

My companion sat reading a trodden copy of the London *Times*, real estate offers, military promotions and all. James Blair after six years of classical studies at Harvard had been sent to Sicily as archaeological adviser to a motion picture company bent on transferring the body of Greek mythology to the screen. The company had failed and been dispersed, and Blair thereafter had roamed the Mediterranean, finding stray employment and filling immense notebooks with his observations and theories. His mind brimmed with speculation: as to the chemical composition of Raphael's pigments; as to the lighting conditions under which the sculptors of antiquity wished their work to be viewed; as to the date of the most inaccessible mosaics in Santa Maria Maggiore. Of all these suggestions and many more he allowed me to make notes, even to the extent of copying some diagrams in colored inks. In the event of his being lost at sea with all his notebooks—a not improbable one, as he crosses the Atlantic on obscure and economical craft, not mentioned in your paper, even when they founder—it would be my confusing duty to make a gift of this material to the Librarian of Harvard University where its unintelligibility might confer upon it an incomputable value.

Presently discarding his paper, Blair decided to talk: You may have come to Rome to study, but before you settle down to the ancients you see whether there aren't some interesting moderns.

There's no Ph.D. in modern Romans. Our posterity does that. What moderns do you mean?

Have you ever heard of the *Cabala*?

Which one?

A kind of a group living around Rome.

No.

They're very rich and influential. Everyone's afraid of them. Everybody suspects them of plots to overturn things.

Political?

No, not exactly. Sometimes.

Social swells?

Yes, of course. But more than that, too. Fierce intellectual snobs, they are. Mme. Agaropoulos is no end afraid of them. She says that every now and then they descend from Tivoli and intrigue some bill through the Senate, or some appointment in the Church, or drive some poor lady out of Rome.

Tchk!

It's because they're bored. Mme. Agaropoulos says they're frightfully bored. They've had everything so long. The chief thing about them is that they hate what's recent. They spend their time insulting new titles and new fortunes and new ideas. In lots of ways they're medieval. Just in their appearance for one thing. And in their ideas. I fancy it's like this: you've heard of scientists off Australia coming upon regions where the animals and plants ceased to evolve ages ago? They find a pocket of archaic time in the middle of a world that has progressed beyond it. Well, it must be something like that with the Cabala. Here's a group of people losing sleep over a host of notions that the rest of the world has outgrown several centuries ago: one duchess' right to enter a door before another; the word order in a dogma of the Church; the divine right of kings, especially of Bourbons. They're still passionately in earnest about stuff that the rest of us regard as pretty antiquarian lore. What's more, these people that hug these notions aren't just hermits and ignored eccentrics, but members of a circle so powerful and exclusive that all these Romans refer to them with bated breath as the Cabala. They work with incredible subtlety, let me tell you, and have incredible resources in wealth and loyalty. I'm quoting Mme. Agaropoulos, who has a sort of hysterical fear of them, and thinks they're supernatural.

But she must know some of them personally.

Of course she does. So do I.

One isn't afraid of people one knows. Who's in it?

I'm taking you to meet one of them tomorrow, this Miss Grier. She's leader of the whole international set. I catalogued her library for her,—oh, I couldn't have got to know her any other way. I lived in her apartment in the Palazzo Barberini and used to get whiffs of the Cabala. Besides her there's a Cardinal. And the Princess d'Espoli who's mad. And Mme. Bernstein of the German banking family. Each one of them has some prodigious gift, and together they're miles above the next social stratum below them. They're so wonderful that they're lonely. I quote. They sit off there in Tivoli getting what comfort they can from one another's excellence.

Do they call themselves the Cabala. Are they organized?

Not as I see it. Probably it never occurred to them that they even constituted a group. I say, you study them up. You ferret it out, the whole secret. It's not my line.

In the pause that followed, fragments of conversation from the various corners of the compartment flowed in upon our minds so recently occupied with semi-divine personages. I haven't the slightest desire to quarrel, Hilda, muttered one of the Englishwomen. Naturally you made the arrangements for the trip as best you could. All I say is that that girl did *not* clean off the washstand every morning. There were rings and rings.

And from an American Italian: I says it's none of your goddam

business, I says. Take your goddam shirt the hell outta here. He
run, I tell you; he run so fast you don't see no dust for him he
run so.

The Jesuit and his pupils had become politely interested in the
postage stamps and the Japanese attaché was murmuring: Oh,
most exclusively rare! The four-cent is pale violet and when held
up to the light reveals a water-mark, a sea-horse. There are only
seven in the world and three are in the collection of the Baron
Rothschild.

Symphonically considered, one heard that there had been no
sugar in it, that she had told Marietta three mornings running to
put sugar in it, or bring sugar, although the Republic of Guate-
mala had immediately cut them, a few had leaked out to collectors,
and that more musk-melons than one would have thought possible
were sold annually at the corner of Broadway and 126th Street.
Perhaps it was in revulsion against such small change that the
impulse first rose in me to pursue these Olympians, who though
they might be bored and mistaken, had at least, each of them, "one
prodigious gift."

It was in this company then, and in the dejected airs of one in
the morning that I first arrived in Rome, in that station that is
uglier than most, more hung with advertisements of medicinal
waters and more redolent of ammonia. During the journey I had
been planning what I should do the moment I arrived: fill myself
with coffee and wine, and in the proud middle of the night, run
down the Via Cavour. Under the hints of dawn I should behold
the tribune of Santa Maria Maggiore, hovering above me like the
ark on Ararat, and the ghost of Palestrina in a soiled cassock
letting himself out at a side door and rushing home to a large
family in five voices; hurry on to the platform before the Lateran
where Dante mixes with the Jubilee crowd; overhang the Forum

and skirt the locked Palatine; follow the river to the inn where Montaigne groans over his ailments; and fall a-staring at the Pope's cliff-like dwelling, where work Rome's greatest artists, the one who is never unhappy and the one who is never anything else. I would know my way about, for my mind is built upon the map of the city that throughout the eight years of school and college had hung above my desk, a city so longed for that it seemed as though in the depth of my heart I had never truly believed I should see it.

When I arrived finally, the station was deserted; there was no coffee, no wine, no moon, no ghosts. Just a drive through shadowy streets to the sound of fountains, and the very special echo of travertine pavements.

During the first week Blair helped me find and fit out an apartment. It consisted of five rooms in an old palace across the river and within stone's-throw of the basilica of Santa Maria in Trastevere. The rooms were high and damp and bad Eighteenth Century. The ceiling of the salone was modestly coffered and there were bits of crumbling stucco in the hall, still tinted with faint blues and pinks and gilt; every morning's sweeping carried off a bit more of some cupid's curls or chips of scroll and garland. In the kitchen there was a fresco of Jacob wrestling with the angel, but the stove concealed it. We passed two days in choosing chairs and tables, in loading them upon carts and personally conducting them to our mean street; in haggling over great lengths of gray-blue brocade before a dozen shops, always with a view toward variety in stains and unravellings and creases; in selecting from among the brisk imitations of ancient candelabra those which most successfully simulated age and pure line.

The acquisition of Ottima was Blair's triumph. There was a

trattoria at the corner, a lazy casual talkative wine-shop, run by three sisters. Blair studied them for a time, and finally proposed to the intelligent middle-aged humorous one that she come and be my cook "for a few weeks." Italians have a horror of making long-term contracts and it was this last clause that won Ottima. We offered to take on any man she recommended to help her with the heavier work, but she clouded at that and replied that she could very well do the heavier work too. The removal to my rooms must have arrived as a providential solution to some problem in Ottima's life, for she attached herself passionately to her work, to me, and to her companions in the kitchen, Kurt the police dog and Messalina the cat. We each winked at the others' failings and we created a home.

The day following our arrival, then, we called upon the latest dictator of Rome and found a rather boyish spinster with an interesting and ailing face, fretful bird-like motions and exhibiting a perpetual alternation of kindness and irritability. It was nearly six when we walked into her drawing-room in the Palazzo Barberini and found four ladies and a gentleman seated a little stiffly about a table conversing in French. Mme. Agaropoulos gave a cry of joy at seeing Blair, the absent-minded scholar to whom she was so attached; Miss Grier echoed it. A thin Mrs. Roy waited until something had been dropped into the conversation about our family connections before she could relax and smile. The Spanish Ambassador and his wife wondered how on earth America could get on without a system of titles whereby one might unerrably recognize one's own people, and the Marquesa shuddered slightly at the intrusion of two coarse young redskins and began composing mentally the faulty French sentence with which she would presently excuse herself. For a time the conversation blew fitfully about, touched with the formal charm of all conversation conducted in a language that is native to no one in the group.

Suddenly my attention was caught by a tension in the room. I sensed the tentatives of an intrigue without being able to gather the remotest notion of the objectives. Miss Grier was pretending to babble, but was in reality quite earnest, and Mrs. Roy was taking notes, mentally. The episode resolved itself into a typical, though not very complicated, example of the Roman social bargain, with its characteristic set of ramifications into religious, political and domestic life. In the light of information received much later, I call your attention to what Mrs. Roy wanted Miss Grier to do for her; and what Miss Grier asked in return for her services:

Mrs. Roy had narrow eyes and a mouth that had just tasted quinine; while she spoke her ear-pendants rattled against her lean clavicles. She was a Roman Catholic, and in her political activity a Black of the Blacks. During her residence in Rome she had occupied herself with the task of bringing the needs of certain American charitable organizations to the attention of the Supreme Pontiff. Slander attributed a diversity of motives to her good works, the least damaging of which was the hope of being named a Countess of the Papal States. The fact is that Mrs. Roy was pressing audiences in the Vatican with the hope of inducing His Holiness to commit a miracle, namely to grant her a divorce under the Pauline Privilege. This consummation, not without precedent, depended upon a number of conditions. Before taking any such step the Vatican would ascertain very carefully how great the surprise would be in Roman Catholic circles; American cardinals would be asked in confidence for a report on the matron's character, and the faithful in Rome and Baltimore, without their being aware of it, would be consulted. This done it would be well to gauge the degree of cynicism or approval the measure would arouse in Protestants. Mrs. Roy's reputation happened to be above reproach, and her right to a divorce indisputable (her husband had offended under every category: he had been unfaithful; he had lapsed from a still greater faith; and he had become an *animae periculum*, that is, he had tried to draw her into an irreverent argument over the liquefaction of the blood of St. Januarius); but the Protestant *imprimatur* was needed. Whose opinion would be more valuable for this purpose than that of the austere directress of the American Colony? Miss Grier would be approached—and both women knew it—through channels exquisite in their delicacy and resonance; and if an uncertain note were sounded from the Palazzo Barberini, the familiar verdict Inexpedient would be returned to the petitioner, and the question never reopened.

Mrs. Roy having so much to ask from Miss Grier, wanted to know if there were any service she could render in return.

There was.

No Italian work of art of the classic periods may leave the country without an enormous export tax. How then did Mantegna's "Madonna between St. George and St. Helen" ever arrive at the Alumnae Hall of Vassar College without passing through the customs? It was last seen three years before in the collection of the poor Principessa Gaeta; it was so ascribed in the reports of the Minister of Fine Arts for the following years, in spite of the rumor that it was being offered to the museums of Brooklyn, Cleveland and Detroit. It changed hands six times, but the dealers, savants and curators were so taken up with the problem as to whether or not St. Helen's left foot had been retouched by Bellini (as Vasari affirms) that it had never occurred to them to ask if it had been registered at the border. It was finally bought by a mad old Boston dowager in a lavender wig who, dying, bequeathed it (along with three spurious Botticellis) to that college with which her vicious spelling alone would have prevented her association in any capacity save that of trustee.

The Minister of Fine Arts at Rome had just heard of the donation and was in despair. When the thing became known his position and reputation would be gone. All his vast labors for his country (*exempli gratia:* he had obstructed the disinterment of Herculaneum for twenty years; he had ruined the façades of twenty gorgeous Baroque churches in the hope of finding a Thirteenth-Century window; etc., etc.) would avail him nothing in the storms of Roman journalism. All loyal Italians suffer at the sight of their art treasures being carried off to America; they are only waiting for some pretext to rend an official and appease their injured honor. The Embassy was already in agonies of conciliation. Vassar could not be expected to give up the picture, nor to pay a smuggler's duty. Tomorrow morning the Roman editorials would picture a barbarous America stealing from Italy her very children and references would be made to Cato, Aeneas, Michelangelo, Cavour and St. Francis. The Senatus Romanus would sit on every bit of delicate business that America was endeavoring to recommend to Italian favor.

Now Miss Grier, too, was a trustee of Vassar. She had a flattering position in the long processions that formed in June among the sun-dials and educative shrubs. She was ready to pay the fine, but not until she had placated the city fathers. This could be done by obtaining the favorable votes of the committee that was to sit that very evening. This committee was composed of seven members, four of whose votes she already commanded; the other three were Blacks. For the matter to be dropped in the interest of the Princess Gaeta a unanimous verdict was necessary.

If Mrs. Roy descended at once to her car, she would have time to drive to the American College in the Piazza di Spagna and confer with dear omniscient Father O'Leary. Marvellous are the acoustics of the Church! Before ten that evening the three Black votes would be decently cast for conciliation. It was Miss Grier's task over the tea-table to convey this long exposition to Mrs. Roy and to intimate the ineffable return she, Miss Grier, would be able to make for any favors. This was complicated by the necessity of making sure that neither Mme. Agaropoulos nor the Ambassadress (men don't matter) suspected the least collusion. Fortunately the Ambassadress could not understand rapid French, and Mme. Agaropoulos, being sentimental, could be continually distracted from the main issue by little sops of prettification and pathos.

Miss Grier played these several cards with the economy and precision of a faultless technique. She had that quality which is a peculiar part of the genius that invests great monarchs, and which we see notably in Elizabeth and Frederick, the power of adjusting threats to just the degree that stimulates, yet does not antagonize. Mrs. Roy understood at once what was expected of her. She had been packing committees and conciliating soured Papal chamberlains and Italian political *dévotés* these many years; trading in influence was her daily portion. Moreover joy can exert the happiest sort of influence on the intelligence and she felt her divorce was at hand. She rose hastily.

Will you excuse me if I run? she murmured. I told Julia Howard I would call for her at Rosali's. And I have an errand in the Piazza di Spagna.

She bowed to us and fled. What emotion is it that lends wings to such matter-of-fact feet and blitheness to such thin dispositions? The next year she married a young French yachtsman, half her age; she settled down in Florence and gave birth to a son. The Blacks no longer talked votes when she entered their drawing-rooms.

Vassar retains the painting and in its archives a letter from the Italian Secretary for Foreign Affairs which reads like a deed of gift. The influence of a work of art upon the casual passerby is too subtle for determination, but one has faith to believe that the hundreds of girls who pass beneath the Mantegna daily draw from it impulses that make them nobler wives and mothers. At least that is what the Ministry promised the College.

When the others had gone, Miss Grier made a face after them, lowered the lights and bade us talk about New York. She seemed to take some pleasure in such exotic company as ourselves, but her mind strayed until suddenly jumping up, she smoothed out the folds of her gown and bade us hurry off, dress, and come back to dinner at eight. We were surprised but equal to it, and dashed off into the rain.

At once I harried Blair for more facts about her. He could give me little; the portrait of her mind and even of her features lies in the following account of her ancestry that I made out for myself by reading between the lines and by studying the photographs of a history of the Griers, written by a second cousin, for considerations.

It seems that her great-grandfather had gone to New York in 1800, suffering from ill-health. He took an old house in the country and intended spending his days like a hermit, studying the prophetic passages of the Bible and encouraging the multiplication of four pigs that he had brought across the water in a basket. But his disposition improving with his affairs, he soon discovered himself to be married to the heiress of Dawes Corners, Miss Agatha Frehestocken, the death of whose parents, ten years later, united two farms of considerable extent. Their children, Benjamin and Anne, were brought up with such education as fell to them on rainy afternoons at the caprice of their father. Our Miss Grier's grandfather, a crafty single-minded country boy, disappeared for many years into a whirlpool of obscure activity in town, becoming in turn potboy, newspaper devil and restaurant manager. At last he revisited his parents and forced them to permit his using their land as security for some railroad investments. We have his picture at this stage: the daguerreotype of the Dutch yokel with the protruding lower lip and grinning pugnacious eyes is reproduced in any history of the great American fortunes. Probably the gentle art of horsewhipping one's parents was revived that Sunday evening at Dawes Corners for Anne intimates that she was directed to take her knitting into the feed-house and sit on sacks until she was recalled. The old father cursed the son roundly from the imprecatory psalms and had his curious revenge: the worm of religious introspection was stirred in the brain of Benjamin Grier and a strain of ill-health in his body. Success came of it: he became a deacon and a millionaire at about the same time; he was presently directing five railroads from a wheel-chair. His parents died in a Washington Square mansion, unforgiving to the end.

Benjamin married the daughter of another magnate, a girl who in another age and faith would have retired to a convent and eased the poverty of her mental and spiritual nature in a perpetual flow of damp unexplainable tears. She bore a sickly son to the world of brownstone, a son in whom the esthetic impulse, stifled during so many generations of Griers and Halletts, attained a piteous flowering, a passion for the operas of Rossini, and for things he fondly took to be Italian, garish rosaries, the costumes of the peasants of Capri, and the painting of Domenichino. He married a firm sharp woman, older than himself, who had deliberately chosen him in the vestry of the Presbyterian Church. They were incredibly wealthy, with that wealth that increases in the dark and, untended, doubles in a year. With the affiliation of this determined Grace Benham one last offspring was made possible to the Grier line,—

our Miss Grier. To the score of governesses that trod sobbing on one another's heels, she appeared a monster of guile and virulence. She was dragged without rest from New York to Baden-Baden, from Vevey to Rome, and back again; and she grew up without forming any attachment to place or person. Her parents died when she was twenty-four and finally sheer solitude did what exhortation could not do: her character softened in an attempt at piteously luring people to talk to her, live with her, to fill somehow the moneyed emptiness of her days.

Such an account of her extraction, if she read it, would have neither interested her nor embarrassed her. Her mind lay under the hot breath of a great fretfulness; she lived to ridicule and insult the fools and innocents of her social circle. In this fretfulness floated all the enthusiasms and frustrations of her line: her great-grandfather's gloom, her grandfather's whip and his dread of the Valley of Bones, her grandmother's red eyes and her father's repressed loves for the Normas and Semiramides of the Academy of Music. She was restless too, with the masculine capacities inherited from her grandfather, the capacities of a business magnate, that given her sex and situation could find their only outlet in a passion for making women tremble and a mania for interfering in the affairs of others. She was with all this a woman of intelligence and force; she ruled her eccentric and rebellious parish with acrid pleasure and at her death the drawing-rooms of Rome resounded with a strange wild murmur of muted joy.

Her portrait is not complete without an account of her strangest habit, due partly to the sleepless nights of a lifetime of illness, and partly to the fear of ghosts instilled in her by governesses when she was a girl. She was never able to sleep until the coming on of dawn. She feared to be alone; toward one in the morning she could be found urging her last callers to stay a little longer; *c'est l'heure du champagne,* she would say, offering them that untimely inducement. When finally they went away she would devote the rest of the night to music, for like the German princes of the Eighteenth Century she maintained her own troup of musicians.

These sessions before dawn were not vaguely and sentimentally musical; they were to the last degree eclectic. In one night she would hear all the sonatas of Scriabin or the marches of Medtner; in one night both volumes of the Well-Tempered Clavichord; all the Handel fugues for organ; six Beethoven trios. Gradually she won away from the more easily appreciated music altogether and cultivated only what was difficult and cerebral. She turned to music that was interesting historically and searched out the forgotten rivals of Bach and the operas of Grétry. She paid a group of singers from the Lateran choir to sing her endless Palestrina. She became prodigiously learned. Harold Bauer would listen meekly to her directions on phrasing Bach—he averred that she had the only truly contrapuntal ear of the age—and the Flonzaleys acceded to her request to take certain pages of Loeffler a little faster.

In time I encountered a number of people who for one reason or another were unable to sleep between midnight and dawn, and when I myself tossed sleepless or when I returned late to my rooms through the deserted streets—at the hour when the parricide feels a cat purring against his feet in the darkness—I pictured to myself old Baldassare, in the Borgo, former Bishop of Shantung, Apostolic Visitor to the Far East, rising at two to study with streaming eyes the Church Fathers and the Councils, marvelling he said, at the continuous blooming of the rose-tree of Doctrine; or of Stasia, a Russian refugee who had lost the habit of sleeping after dark during her experience as nurse in the War, Stasia playing solitaire through the night and brooding over the jocose tortures to which her family had been subjected by the soldiers of Taganrog; and of

Elizabeth Grier listening the length of her long shadowed room to some new work that d'Indy had sent her or bending over the score while her little troup revived the overture to *Les Indes Galantes*.

When we remounted the steps an hour later, then, we found the guests already arrived and awaiting their hostess. Among other privileges Miss Grier had long reserved to herself a prerogative of royalty, that of being the last arrival at one's own parties. In the hall the maître-d'hôtel gave me a note reading: Please take in Mlle. de Morfontaine, a high Merovingian maiden who may invite you to her villa at Tivoli. In a few moments Miss Grier had slipped in and was greeting her guests in a hurried zigzag across the room. She was dressed after a costume-plate by Fortuny, conceived in salamander red and black. About her neck hung a rare medal of the Renaissance, much larger than any other woman would have ventured to wear.

As this woman wanted to be in a position to hear every word spoken at her table Rome had long had good reason to complain of the crowded arrangements of her dinners; we were packed together like the hurried diners at Modane. But she had still other conventions to challenge: she discussed the food; she reversed the direction of conversation from the right to the left hand at the least convenient opportunities; she talked to the servants, chattily; she shifted the conversation from French to English or Italian capriciously; she referred to guests who had been invited but had not been able to come. One suddenly became aware that she was not eating the courses that were served to us. She began with a little bowl of breadcrumbs and walnuts; to this she added later— while we confronted a *faisan Souvaroff* dressed with truffles and *foie gras* and graced with that ultimate dark richness which it is the privilege of Madeira to confer on game—an American cereal,

soaked in hot water and touched with butter. Nor could she re-
strain herself from teasing her guests in a dangerous way, and with
almost inspired precision: a political Duke on his dull speeches;
Mrs. Osborne-Cady on the career as a concert-pianist that she had
sacrificed to a more than usually disappointing home-life. For a
moment at the beginning of the meal her electric eyes paused at my
place and she began to murmur ominously, but thinking better of
it she ordered the servant to offer me some more *oeufs cardinal*
adding with a sort of insolence that they were the only *oeufs
cardinal* that one could eat in Europe and that Mémé (the elder
Princess Galitzine) was a little fool to vaunt her chef, who had
received his training in railway-stations, etc., etc.

The high Merovingian maiden at my left was Mademoiselle
Marie-Astrée-Luce de Morfontaine, daughter of Claude-Elzéar de
Morfontaine and Christine Mézières-Bergh; her grandfather Comte
Louis Mézières-Bergh had married Rachel Krantz, the daughter of
the great financier Maxi Krantz, and had been the French ambassador to the Vatican in 1870. She was then, excessively rich, for
she owned, they said, more shares in the Suez Canal than the
Rothschilds: She was tall, large-limbed and bony, without somehow being too thin. Her high white face, framed between two
carnelian ear pendants, recalled some symbolical figure in a frieze
of Giotto, out of drawing, but radiating gaunt spiritual passions.
She had a hoarse voice and a rapt manner, and for the first ten
minutes said many foolish things because her mind was afar off;
one felt vaguely that it would come around in its own time. This it
presently did and with considerable impact. She outlined to me the
whole Royalist movement in France. She seemed to believe as
passionately in its aim as she depised its practice. There can be no
king in France, she cried, until catholicism has had a great revival

there. France cannot be great save through Rome. We are Latins; we are not Goths. They are forcing alien systems upon us. Eventually we shall find ourselves, our kings, our faith, our Latin hearts. I shall see France return to Rome before I die, she added clasping her hands before her chin. I replied faintly that both the French and Italian temperaments seemed to me singularly unrepublican, whereupon she laid her long pale hand upon my sleeve and invited me to come that week-end to her villa.

You will hear the whole argument, she said. And the Cardinal will be there.

I asked which Cardinal? The pain on her face showed me that at least for the circle in which she moved there were not seventy cardinals, but one.

Cardinal Vaini, of course. The College at present is singularly free of uninteresting priests, but surely the only cardinal with learning, with distinction, with charm, is Cardinal Vaini.

I had so often encountered learning, distinction and charm (to say nothing of piety) in the lower reaches of the Church that I was shocked to learn that these qualities were so rare higher up.

Besides she added, what other is friendly to France, the rebellious daughter? You have not yet met the Cardinal? Such knowledge! And to think that he will not write! If I may say it without disrespect His Eminence is afflicted with a sort of—inertia. The whole world is waiting for an explanation of certain contradictions in the Fathers; he is the only man who can do it; yet he remains silent. We beg him with prayers. It is in his power to effect the re-entry of the Church into literature. Perhaps he might single-handed carry through the cause we all have so at heart.

I asked shyly what cause this might be.

She turned toward me with some surprise. Why, the promulgation of the Divine Right of Kings as a dogma of the Church. We hope to have an Ecumenical Council called for that purpose within the next twenty-five years. I thought that of course you knew; in fact I assumed that you were one of our workers.

I replied that I was both an American and a Protestant, an answer that I felt relieved me of the burden of being a catholic royalist.

Oh, she said, we have many adherents who at first glance would appear to have no interest in the movement: we have Jews and agnostics, artists, and, yes, even anarchists.

I now felt quite sure that I was sitting beside an insane person. They don't lock you up when you have millions, I said to myself. The idea of trying to collect a Council, in the Twentieth Century, to give crowns a supernatural sanction and to enroll the sanction among the articles of obligatory belief, was no mere pious revery; it was lunacy. We were prevented from returning to the subject that evening, but several times I found her spacious half-mad glance resting on me with greater implication of intimacy than I was quite ready to acknowledge.

I will send the car for you at eleven, she murmured as she passed me in leaving the table. You must come. I shall have a great favor to ask of you.

On returning to the drawing-rooms I found myself beside Ada Benoni, daughter of a popular senator. Although she seemed almost too young to go out in the evening, she had that soft cautious sophistication of well-brought-up Italian girls. I asked her almost at once if she would tell me about the Cabala.

Oh, the Cabala's only some people's joke, she answered. There is no Cabala, really. But I know what you mean. And the young girl's eyes carefully estimated the distance between us and the company on all sides. By Cabala they mean a group of people that are always together and have a lot in common.

Are they all rich? I asked.

No . . . she answered thoughtfully. We mustn't speak so loudly. Cardinal Vaini can't be rich, nor the Duchess d'Aquilanera.

But they're all intellectual?

The Princess d'Espoli isn't intellectual.

Then what have they in common?

Oh, they haven't anything in common, except . . . except that they despise most people, you and me and my father and so on. They've each got one thing, some great gift, and that binds them together.

Do you believe that they work together and plan trouble here and there?

The girl's forehead wrinkled and she reddened slightly. No, I don't think they mean to, she said softly.

But they *do?* I insisted.

Well, they sit over there in Tivoli and talk about us and somehow, without knowing it, they then *do* something.

How many of them do you know?

Oh, I know all of them a little, she replied quickly. Everybody knows all of them. Except, of course, the Cardinal. I love them all, too. They're only bad when they're together, she explained.

Mlle. de Morfontaine has asked me to spend the week-end at her villa in Tivoli. Will I see them there?

Oh, yes. We call that the hotbed.

Is it all right? Have you any advice to give me before I go?

No.

Yes, you have.

Well, she admitted, drawing her eyebrows together, I advise you to be . . . to be stupid. It's hard. You must expect them to be very cordial at first. They have a way of getting very excited about people and then getting tired of them and dropping them. Except every now and then they find someone they like and they adopt him or her for good, and there's a new member of the Cabala. Rome's full of people who went through the rapids and didn't stick. Miss Grier's especially that way. She's just met you lately, hasn't she?

Why, yes,—just this afternoon.

Well, she'll have you around every minute of the day for a while. She's coming over in a minute to ask you to stay to her midnight supper. She has famous midnight suppers.

But I can't. I was here to tea and immediately asked to dinner. It would be ridiculous to stay to midnight. . . .

It's not ridiculous in Rome. You're just getting into the rapids, that's all. Everybody cultivates their friendships in rushes. It's very exciting. Don't try and fight against it. If you do that you lose the best of everything. Do you want to know how I know about your being in the rapids? Well, I'll tell you. My fiancé was to have come to the dinner tonight, and an hour before, a note was brought to his house asking him to come next Friday instead and go to the Opera also. She does that often and it only means that she has found some new friend she insists on keeping by her that evening. Of course the second invitation, the consoling one, is always bigger and more showy than the first, but we get angry.

I should say so. I'm sorry I was the one to prevent . . .

Oh, that's all right, she answered. Vittorio's out waiting for me in the car now.

So it was that when Blair and I presented ourselves before Miss Grier to take our leave, she drew me aside with an irresistible vehemence and standing against my ear said: You are to come back here tonight. There will be some people in to a late supper whom I want you to meet. You can, can't you?

I made some show of protest, and the effect was appalling. But, my dear young man, she cried, I'll have to ask you to trust me. There is something of the first importance that I want to put to you. The fact is I have already telephoned a very dear friend of mine. . . . Please now, just as a favor to me, put off what you had planned. There's a very great service we want to ask you.

Of course with that I fairly folded up, as much with surprise as compliance. Apparently the whole Cabala wanted me to do favors.

Thank you, thank you so much. About twelve.

It was then about ten. Two hours to kill. We were about to go to the Circus, when Blair exclaimed:

Say, do you mind if I drop in and see a friend of mine for a minute. If I'm going Tuesday I ought to say goodbye and see how he is. Do you hate sick people?

No.

He's a nice fellow, but he hasn't long to live. He's published some verse in England; one of the thousand, you know. It got an awful rap. Maybe he's quite a poet, but he can't get over that diction. He's awfully adjectival.

We climbed down the Spanish Steps and turned in at the left. On the stairs Blair stopped and whispered: I forgot to tell you that he's watched over by a friend, a sort of water-colourist. They're dead-poor and it's all they can do to get a doctor. I meant to lend them some more money—what have you with you?

We assembled a hundred lire and knocked at the door. Receiving no answer we pushed it open. There was a lamp burning in the further of two mean rooms. It stood beside a bed and cast its light on the remorseless details of a barricade built during the last stages of consumption against a light vaulter; bowls and bottles and stained cloths. The sleeping invalid was sitting high in bed, his head turned away from us.

The artist must have gone out for a minute to look for some money, said Blair. Let's stay around a bit.

We went into the other room and sat in the dark looking at the moonlight that filled the Fountain of the Boat. There were fireworks on the Pincian Hill in memory of some battle on the Piave and the tender green of the sky seemed to tremble behind the Chinese blooms that climbed the night. A friendly tram entered the square at intervals, stopped inquiringly, and bustled out again. I tried to remember whether Virgil had died in Rome . . . no, buried near Naples. Tasso? Some piercing-sweet pages of Goethe, the particular triumph of Moissi who brings to them his wide-open eyes and elegiac voice. Presently we heard a call from the next room: Francis. Francis.

Blair went in: I guess he's gone out a minute. Can I do something for you? I'm going in a day or two and I called around to see how much better you are. Would it tire you if we sat with you a bit? . . . Come on in, say!

For the moment Blair had forgotten the poet's name and our introduction was slurred over. The sick man looked his extremity, but his fever gave to his eyes an eager and excited air; he seemed willing to listen or to talk for hours. My eye fell upon a rough pencilled note that lay on the table beyond the invalid's reach: Dear Dr. Clarke: he spat up about two cupfuls of blood at 2 P.M. He complained so of hunger that I had to give him more than you said. Be back at once. F.S.

Have you been able to write anything lately? Blair began.

No.

Do you read much?

Francis reads to me. He pointed to a Jeremy Taylor on his feet. You're Americans, aren't you? I have a brother in America. In New Jersey. I was to have gone over there.

The conversation lapsed, but he kept staring at us, smiling and bright-eyed, as though it were swift and rare.

By the way, are there any books you'd like us to lend you?

Thank you. That would be fine.

What, for instance?

Anything.

Think of one you'd like especially.

Oh, anything. I'm not particular. Only I suppose it would be hard to find any translations from the Greek?

Here I offered to bring in a Homer in the original and stammer out an improvised translation.

Oh, I should like that most of all, he cried. I know Chapman's well.

I replied, unthinking, that Chapman's was scarcely Homer at all, and suddenly beheld a look of pain, as of a mortal wound, appear upon his face. To regain control of himself he bit his finger and tried to smile. I hastened to add that in its way it was very beautiful, but I could not recall my cruelty; his heart seemed to have commenced bleeding within him.

Blair asked him if he had almost enough poems for a new book.

I don't think about books any more, he said. I just write to please myself.

But the insult to Chapman had been working in him; he now

turned his face away and great tears fell upon his hands. Excuse me. Excuse me, he said. I'm not well, and I seem to . . . to do this about nothing.

There was a search for a handkerchief, but none being found he was persuaded to use mine.

I don't want to go away without seeing Francis, said Blair. Do you know where I might find him?

Yes, yes. He's around the corner at the Café Greco. I begged him to go and get some coffee; he'd been here all day.

So Blair left me with the poet, who seemed to have forgiven me and was ready for the hazards of further conversation. Feeling it was better I did the talking, I began to discourse upon everything, on the fireworks, on the wildflowers of Lake Albano, on Pizzetti's sonata, on a theft in the Vatican library. His face showed clearly what matter pleased him; I experimented on it, and discovered that he was hungry for hearing things praised. He was beyond feeling indignant at abuses, beyond humor, beyond sentiment, beyond interest in any bits of antiquarian lore. Apparently for weeks together in the wretched atmosphere of the sick-room Francis had neglected to speak highly of anything and the poet wanted before he left the strange world to hear some portion of it praised. Oh, I laid it on. His eyes glowed and his hands trembled. Most of all he desired the praise of poetry. I launched upon a history of poetry, calling the singers by name, getting them wrong, assigning them to the wrong ages and languages, characterizing them with the worn epithets of an encyclopedist, and drawing upon what anecdotage I could,—all bad, but somehow marshalling the glorious throng. I spoke of Sappho; of how a line of Euripides drove mad the citizens of Abdera; of Terence pleading with audiences to come to him rather than to the tight-rope walkers; of Villon writing his mother's prayers before the great picture-book of a cathedral wall;

of Milton in his old age, holding a few olives in his hand to remind himself of his golden year in Italy.

Quite suddenly in the middle of the catalogue he burst out fiercely: I was meant to be among those names. I was.

The boast must have revolted me a little and my face have shown it, for he cried again: I was. I was. But now it's too late. I want every copy of my books destroyed. Let every word die, die. When I'm dead I don't want a soul to remember me.

I murmured something about his getting well.

I know more about it than the doctor, he replied, staring at me with stern fury. I studied to be a doctor. And I watched my mother and brother die, just as I am dying now.

There was no answer for that. We sat silent. Then in a gentler voice he said:

Will you promise me something? My things weren't good enough; they were just beginning to be better. When I am dead I want you to make sure that Francis does what he promised. There must be no name on my grave. Just write: Here lies one whose name was writ in water.

There was a noise in the next room. Blair had returned with the water-colourist. We withdrew. The poet was too sick to see us again and when I came back from the country he had died and his fame had begun to spread over the whole world.

BOOK TWO

MARCANTONIO

La Duchessa d'Aquilanera was a Colonna and came from the conservative wing of a family that cannot forget its cardinalitial, royal and papal traditions. Her husband had come of a Tuscan house that had received its illustration by the Thirteenth Century, was praised in the histories of Machiavelli and execrated in Dante. Neither family had counted a misalliance in twenty-two generations, and even in the twenty-third incurred only such stigma as attaches to marriage with an illegitimate Medici or a Pope's "niece." The Duchess could never forget—among a thousand similar honors—that her grandfather's grandfather, Timoleo Nerone Colonna, Prince of Velletri, had carried many an insulting message to the ancestors of the present King of Italy, the old but apologetic house of Savoy; and that her father had refused a Grandeeship at the court of Spain because it had been withheld from his father; and that through herself she carried to her son the titles of Chamberlain of the Court of Naples (if there were one), Prince of the Holy Roman Empire (if that superb organization had only survived) and Duke of Brabant, a title which unfortu-

nately reappears among the pretensions of the royal families of
Spain, Belgium and France. She had the best of claims to an
Altesse, and even to an Altesse Royale; at least to the Sérénissime,
for her mother had been the last member of the royal family of
Craburg-Hottenlingen. She had the largest cousinage outside the
Buddhist priesthood. The heralds of the European courts bowed to
her with a particular distinction, realizing that by some accident
many diverse and lofty lines converged in her odd person.

She was fifty when I met her, a short, black-faced woman with
two aristocratic wens on the left slope of her nose, yellow, dirty
hands, covered with paste emeralds (an allusion to her Portuguese
claims; she was Archduchess of Brazil, if Brazil had only remained
Portuguese), lame with the limp that pursues the Della Quercia,
just as her aunt had been epileptic with the epilepsy of the true
Vani. She lived in a tiny apartment in the Palazzo Aquilanera,
Piazza Araceli, from the windows of which she watched the
sumptuous weddings of her rivals, ceremonies to which she had
been invited, but dared not attend, foreseeing that she would be
assigned to places that fell below her pretensions; to accept a
humble seat would be to admit that one had relinquished the
whole bundle of vast historic claims. She had left many a great
function abruptly on discovering that her chair was behind some of
those Colonna cousins who had cast away all right to aristocratic
distinction by marrying theatre women or Americans. She refused
to be seated behind pillars among dubious Neapolitan titles—in the
shadow of her own family tombs; to be left among the footmen at
the door of a musicale; to be invited at the eleventh hour; and to
be kept waiting in antechambers. For the most part she clung to
her ugly stuffy rooms, brooding on the disregarded glories of her
line and envying the splendors of her richer relatives. The fact is
that from the point of view of a middle-class Italian she was not

really poor; but she was too poor to afford the limousine and livery
and great entertainments; to be without these and yet invested with
her pretensions was to be poorer than the last nameless body fished
out of the Tiber.

Recently however she had begun to receive unexpected and
thrilling recognitions. Little though she went out, when she did
appear in society, her austere face, her majestic limp, and her
strange jewels carried conviction. People were afraid of her. The
arbiters of precedence in Rome dared at last to intimate to the
Odescalchi and Colonna and Sermoneta that this almost shabby
little woman whom they snubbed and shoved like some half-wit
poor relation, had every right to precede them at a formal function. French circles, such as had not lost all seigneurial deferences
under the sponge of republicanism, recognized her ultramontane
alliances. She was the first to notice the improvement in her reception, and if a bit bewildered it did not take her long to set her sails
to the unexpected breeze. She had a son and daughter to advance
and it was for them that she now resolved to immolate her pride.
From the earliest signs of her rehabilitation she forced herself to
sally out into the world, and finding that her stock was higher in
the international colony she stooped distastefully to call upon the
American peeresses and on the South American representatives.
Eventually she found herself at Miss Grier's midnight suppers.
The reflection of the consideration she received in such places
finally reached her own people and she was gradually spared the
more obvious humiliations.

It became necessary for her now to drop her former friends, the
dull soured old women, more plaintive than herself, and with less
reason, with whom she had been accustomed to fret away the long
afternoons and evenings behind the drawn blinds of the Piazza
Araceli. She was obliged likewise to abandon a sordid habit that

linked her no less surely to the previous centuries, namely that of rushing into law-suits. The innate capacity for affairs which abounded in this woman had found during the days of her obscurity this extraordinary outlet. She went about scenting out old claims and deeds, the slips of tradesmen and the subtle omissions of lawyers. She was always protecting her shyer friends from imposition, and she was always successful and often made a good deal of money. She employed obscure boy-lawyers and when she was called upon as a witness, relying on her distinctions to prevent her being interrupted, she used the occasion as an opportunity to sum up the whole case. The middle classes seeing in the morning paper that S. A. Leda Matilda Colonna duchessa d'Aquilanera was attacking the City of Rome over the valuation of property near a railroad, or contesting the bill of some popular stationer or fruiterer on the Corso, suffered willingly the inconvenience of holding a seat in court for hours in order to see the malignant resourceful woman and to hear her trenchant sarcasms and her irresistible accumulation of evidence. Yet her relatives had always sneered at this passion, failing to see that she represented more clearly than themselves the qualities that had always gone to characterize the aristocracy.

It was this woman then whom we confronted when we returned at midnight for our third engagement that day in the old palace. Supper was served in a larger, brighter apartment than I had yet seen. As I entered the huge doorway my eyes fell upon a strange figure that I knew at once must be a Cabalist. A short, dark, ugly woman, holding a cane between her knees was staring at me with magnificent fierce eyes. With the bodiced dress and eagle's head I became aware of her jewels, seven huge lumpy amethysts strung about her neck on a golden rope. I was presented to this witch who at once, and by the blackest art, made one like her. On hearing that Blair was leaving Rome shortly she centered her attention on me.

For a moment she sat before me, sliding the end of her stick nervously about on the floor, drawing in her upper lip, and gazing hard into my eyes. She asked me my age. I was twenty-five.

I am the Duchess d'Aquilanera, she began. What language shall we speak? I think we will talk English. I do not talk it good, but we must be plain. It must be so you must understand me quite perfectly. I am a great friend of Miss Grier. I have often talked over with her a great problem—a sorrow, my young friend—that is in my home. Suddenly tonight at seven o'clock she call me up on the telephone and told me she have found someone who could help me: she mean you. Now listen: I have a son of sixteen. He is important because he is somebody. How you say?—he is a personage. We are of a very old house. Our family has been in the front of Italy, everyone in her triumph and in her trouble. You are not sympathetic to that kind of greatness in America, not? But you must have read history, no? ancient times and the middle times and like that? You must realize how important the great families are . . . have always been to . . . countries . . .

(Here she grew nervous, and blew several bubbles and expended herself in those splendid Italian gestures denoting difficulty, perhaps futility, and resignation before the impossible. I hastened to assure her that I had great respect for the aristocratic principle.)

Perhaps you have and perhaps you haven't, she said at last. In all events, think of my son as a prince whose blood contains all sorts of kings and noble people. Well, now I must tell you he has fallen in bad ways. Some women have got hold of him and I do not know him any more. All our boys in Italy go that way when they are sixteen, but Marcantonio, my God, I do not know what is the matter with him and I shall go crazy. Now in America you are all descended from your Puritans, are you not, and your ideas are very different. There is only one thing to do, and that is: you must save my boy. You must talk to him. You must play tennis with him. I have talked to him; the priest has talked to him, and a good friend of mine, a Cardinal, has talked to him and still he does nothing but go to that dreadful place. Elizabeth Grier says that most boys in America at your age are just . . . naturally . . . good. You are *vieilles filles;* you are as temperate as I do not know what. It's very strange, if it's true, and I do not think I believe it; at all events it's not wise. At all events you must talk to Marcantonio and make him stay away from that dreadful place or we shall go mad. My plan is this: next Wednesday we are going for a week to our beautiful villa in the country. It is the most beautiful villa in Italy. You must come with us. Marcantonio will begin to admire you, you can play tennis and shoot and swim and then you can have long talks and you can save him. Now, won't you do that for me, because no one has ever come to you in such trouble as I have come to you in today?

Hereupon, in sudden fear that all her efforts had been in vain, she began waving her stick to attract Miss Grier's attention. That lady had been watching us from a corner of her eye and now came running up. The Duchess burst into a flood of tears, crying into her pocket handkerchief: Elisabetta, speak to him. Oh, my God, I have failed. He not want us and all is lost.

I was divided between anger and laughter and kept muttering into Miss Grier's ear: I'd be glad to meet him, Miss Grier, but I can't lecture the fellow. I'd feel like a fool. Besides what would I do with a whole week. . . .

She's put it to you wrongly, said Miss Grier. Let's not say anything more about it tonight.

At this the Black Queen began rolling about in her chair, the motions preparatory to rising. She rammed her stick against my shoe for leverage on the polished floor and stood up. We must pray to God to find another way. I am a fool. I do not blame the young man. He cannot realize the importance of our family.

Nonsense, Leda, said Miss Grier, firmly in Italian. Be quiet a moment. Then turning to me: Would you like to pass a week-end at the Villa Colonna-Stiavelli, or not? There's no stipulation about lecturing the Prince. If you like him, you'll feel like talking to him anyway, and if you don't like him, you're welcome to leave him alone.

Two Cabalists were begging me to take a glimpse of the most famous of Renaissance villas, one moreover that was obstinately closed to the public and that had to be peered at from the road half a mile away. I turned to the Duchess and bowing low accepted her invitation. Whereupon she kissed the shoulder of my coat, murmured with a beautiful smile: Christiano! Christiano! and bidding us goodnight, passed bowing from the room.

I shall see you Sunday at Tivoli, said Miss Grier, and tell you all about it there.

During the next few days my mind lay under the dread of the two engagements that lay ahead of me: the week-end at the Villa Horace and the missionary enterprise at the Villa Colonna. I stayed in my rooms, depressed, reading a little, or took long walks through the Trasteverine underworld, thinking about Connecticut.

The car that called for me Saturday morning already contained a fellow-guest. He introduced himself as M. Léry Bogard, adding that Mlle. de Morfontaine had offered to send for us separately, but that he had taken the liberty of requesting that we be called for together, not only because any company in crossing the Campagna is better than none, but because he had heard many things of me that led him to believe that we would not be uncongenial. I replied in that language wherein all courtesy sounds sincere, that the possibility of being congenial to so distinguished a member of the French Academy and to so profound a scholar was a greater honor than I dared hope for. These overtures did not tend to chill the encounter. M. Bogard was a fragile elderly gentleman, immaculately dressed. His face was delicately tinted by exquisite reading and expensive food, russet and violet about the eyes, his cheeks a pale plum from which rose the ivory-white of his nose and chin. His manner was soft and conciliatory, expressed for the most part in the play of his eyelids and hands, both of which fluttered in unison like petals about to fall upon the breeze. I spoke hesitantly of the pleasure I had derived from his works, especially from those pages, so faintly tinctured with venom, on Church History. But now he cried out at once: Do not mention them! My early indiscretions! Horrible! What would I not give to withdraw them. Can that nonsense have reached as far as America? You must let your friends know, young man, that those books no longer represent my attitude. Since then I have become an obedient son of the Church and nothing would give me greater comfort than to hear that they had been burned.

What may I tell my friends now represents your real views? I asked.

Why read me at all? he cried in mock grief. There are too many books in the world already. Let us read no more, my son. Let us seek out some congenial friends. Let us sit about a table (well-spread, pardi!) and talk of our church and our king and perhaps of Virgil.

My face must have shown a trace of the suffocation I experienced at this plan of life, for M. Bogard became at once more

impersonal. The country we are traversing now, he said, has
known stirring times . . . and he began an instructive travelogue,
as though I were some stupid acquaintance, his hostess' son, and as
though he were not, nor ever had been, a distinguished scholar.

On arriving at the Villa we were met by the steward and shown
to our rooms. The Villa had been a monastery for many years and
in purchasing it Mlle. de Morfontaine had obtained likewise the
adjoining church which still served the peasants of the hillside.
She claimed that the Villa was the very one that Maecenas had
given to Horace: local tradition affirmed it; the foundations were
of the best opus reticulatum; and the location fulfilled the rather
vague requirements of classical allusion; even onomatopoeia testi-
fied, declared our hostess, asserting that from her window the
waterfall could be literally heard to lisp

". . . domus Albuniae resonantis
Et praeceps Anio ac Tiburni locus et uda
Mobilibus pomaria rivis."

In furnishing her monastery our hostess had combined, as best
she could, a delight in esthetic effects and a longing for severity. A
long low rambling plaster building, without grace of line, was the
Villa Horace. Disordered rose gardens surrounded it, with intentionally neglected gravel paths, and chipped marble benches. One
entered a long hall at the end of which several steps descended to a
library. The hall was lined with doors at regular intervals on both
sides, doors to what had once been cells now thrown together into
reception rooms. Many of these doors stood open during the day
and the long corridor, paved with russet tile, was striped with the
sunshine that fell across it. The ceiling had been coffered, and like
the doors touched with dark green and gilt, and with that rich
wasted brick-red that is the color of Neapolitan tiles. The walls
were yellow white, of caked and crumbling plaster, and the beauty

of the view with the optical illusion of distance and the depth and the lightness of the library seen like some great green-golden well at the further end, appealed to that sense of balance and one's tactile imagination as do the vistas in the paintings of Raphael whose spell is said to reside in that secret. To the left lay the reception rooms, carpeted in one color, hung with tabernacles and Italian primitives, while huge candelabra, pots of flowers and tables covered with brocades and crystals and uncut jewels, relieved the severity of unfreshened walls. Towards the end of the hall at the right one ascended a few steps to the refectory, the barest room in the house. By day the refectory was a meaningless casual club-room. Luncheon was a negligible affair at the Villa; one's conversation must be saved for dinner; at luncheon one barely looked at one another, one talked about the last rains and the next drought, or any subject that did not faintly allude to the devouring passions of the house, religion and aristocracy and literature. The beauty of the refectory was purely a matter of lighting and at eight o'clock the greatness of the room lay in the pool of wine-yellow light that was shed on the red table cloth, the dark green crested plates, the silver and the gold, the wineglasses, the gowns and decorations of the guests, the ambassadorial ribbons, the pontifical violets, and the little army of satin-clad footmen that suddenly appeared from nowhere.

On the night of my arrival the Cardinal was the last to appear at dinner, and entered directly into the refectory where we stood waiting for him. His expression was benignant, even beaming. While he blessed the meal, Mlle. de Morfontaine knelt on her admirable yellow gown and M. Bogard dropped on one knee and shaded his eyes. The grace was in English, a strange affair discovered by our erudite guest among the literary remains of some disappointed Cambridge parson.

> Oh, pelican of eternity,
> That piercest thy heart for our food,
> We are thy fledglings that cannot know thy woe.
> Bless this shadowy and visionary food of substance,
> Whose last eater shall be worm,
> And feed us rather with the vital food of
> Dreams and grace.

The Cardinal, though unimpaired in mind and body, looked all of his eighty years. The expression of dry serenity that never left his yellow face with its drooping moustache and pointed beard gave him the appearance of a Chinese sage that has lived a century. He was born of peasants on the plain between Milan and Como, and had begun his education at the hands of the local priests who soon discovered in him a veritable genius for latinity. He was passed upward from school to school gaining in his progress all the prizes the Jesuits had to offer. The attention of a large body of influential churchmen was gradually drawn to him and at the time of his graduation from the great college on the Piazza Santa Maria sopra Minerva (presenting a thesis of unparalleled brilliance and futility on the forty-two cases in which suicide is permissible and the twelve occasions on which a priest may take up arms without danger of homicide) a choice between three great careers was offered to him. The details of each had been prepared under the highest patronage: he might become a fashionable preacher; or one of the courtier-secretaries of the Vatican; or a learned teacher and disputant. To the amazement and grief of his professors he suddenly announced his intention of following a road that to them meant ruin; he declared for Missions. His foster-fathers raged and wept and called on heaven to witness his ingratitude; but the boy would hear of nothing less than the Church's most dangerous post in Western China. Thither in due time he departed with scarcely a blessing from his teachers who had already turned their attention to more docile if less brilliant pupils. Through fire, famine, riots, and even torture, the young priest labored for twenty-five years in the province of Sze-chuen. This missionary fever however did not entirely spring from piety. The boy, conscious of the great powers raging within him, had been throughout his youth insolent, contemptuous of his teachers and of his companions. He knew and despised every type of a churchman to be found in Italy; never had he seen a thing adequately done by them, and now he dreamed of a field of work where he would be answerable to no fool. In the whole realm of the Church there was only one region that filled his requirements; a month's travelling by crude wagon separates one from the next priest in Sze-chuen. There, then, after a shipwreck, some months of slavery, and other experiences that he never related, but which reached the world from his native helpers, he settled in an inn, dressed as a native, grew a pigtail, and lived among the villagers for six years without mentioning his faith. He passed the time studying the language, the classics, the manners, ingratiating himself with the officials and so perfectly identifying himself with the daily life of the city that in time he all but lost the odor of foreignness. When at last he began to declare his mission to those merchants and officials in whose homes he had become an almost nightly visitor his work was rapid. Perhaps the greatest of all the Church's missionaries since the Middle Age, he turned many a compromise that was destined to shock Rome profoundly. He somehow achieved a harmonization of Christianity and the religions and accepted ideas of China that had its parallel only in those daring readings that Paul discovered in his Palestinian cult. So subtle were the priest's adaptations that it never occurred to his first converts to be even conscious of repudiating

their old faith until at last after twenty lectures he showed them
how far they had gone and how charred were the bridges that lay
behind them. Once he had them baptized however, he could give
them only the bitterest bread to eat: the foundations of his
cathedral lay squarely on a score of martyrs' graves, but once built
suffered no further assault and grew slowly and irresistibly. Finally
sheer statistics did what envy could not prevent and he was made a
bishop. At the end of his fifteenth year in the East he returned to
Rome for the first time and was received with cold dislike. His
health had been partly undermined, and he was granted a year's
repose, during which he worked in the Vatican library on a thesis
relative to nothing in China, the donation of Constantine. This
was considered shocking in a missionary and when it was published its learning and impersonality won it the neglect of the
ecclesiastical reviewers. He was treated with condescension by the
courtiers of the Palace; by implication they described to him their
idea of his great creation in Western China: a low mud-brick
meeting-house and a congregation of beggars who pretended to a
conversion in order to be fed. He did not trouble to describe to
them the stone cathedral with two awkward but lofty towers, the
vast porch, the schools and library and hospital; the processions on
Feast days carrying garish but ardent banners entering the great
cavern of the Church and singing the correctest Gregorian; nor of
the governmental honors, the tax-exemptions, the military respect
during revolutions, the co-operation of the city.

At last he returned, willingly enough, to sink himself for another ten years into the remote interior. His visit to Rome had
not altered his boyish attitude toward his fellowmen. He had heard
strange tales about himself,—how he had amassed a huge fortune
by taking bribes from the Chinese merchants, how he had inter-

preted the atonement in Buddhist terms and had allowed pagan symbols to be stamped upon the Host itself.

The ecclesiastical honors that eventually arrived must have been extravagantly deserved, for they came without his or any friend's negotiation. Sheer accomplishment must so have stared the Vatican in the face that it had felt torn from its hands the trophies it was accustomed to relinquish only on the receipt of petitions bearing ten thousand signatures or at the instance of wealth or power. To receive these new distinctions, the Bishop returned to Rome again after an absence of ten years. This time he meant to remain in Italy, having decided that henceforth his work would be better in the hands of natives. The ecclesiastics viewed this return with considerable trepidation, for if he returned as a scholar eager for doctrinal debates they dreaded seeing exposed their lack of interest or equipment; if he came as a critic of the Propaganda, they were all in danger. They watched him settle down with two Chinese servants and an absurd peasant woman whom he insisted on referring to as his sister, in a tiny villa on the Janiculum, join the Papal Archaeological Society and apply himself to reading and gardening. Within five years his retirement had become a greater embarrassment to the Church than his pamphlets might have been. His fame among Romanists outside Rome was unbounded; every distinguished visitor rushed from the station to get an introduction to the recluse of Janiculum; the Pope himself was a little tried by the zeal of visitors who imagined that His Holiness enjoyed nothing better than discussing the labors, the illness, and the modesty of the Cathedral Builder of China. English Catholics and American Catholics and Belgian Catholics who did not understand the exquisite subtlety of these matters and should let them alone, kept crying: Why isn't something being done for him? He humbly refused a high honorary Librarianship in the Vatican, but his refusal was not accepted and his name crowned the stationery; the same thing happened with the great committees on Propaganda; he did not appear at the meetings, but no speech was so influential as the report of chance words let fall in conversation with disciples at the Villino Wei Ho. His very lack of ambition frightened the Churchmen; they supposed it must arise from a similar emotion to that which kept Achilles sulking in his tent, and dreaded the moment when he would ultimately arise, swinging his mighty prestige and crush them for the honors they begrudged him; finally he was offered the Hat, by a committee from the College all in a perspiration lest he refuse it. This time he accepted their offer and went through the forms with a rigid decorum and with an observance of traditional minutiae that had to be elaborately explained to his Irish American colleagues.

It would be hard to say what his thoughts were those clear mornings as he sat among his flowers and rabbits, a volume of Montaigne fallen on to the gravel path from the tabouret beside him, what were his thoughts as he gazed at his yellow hands and listened to the hushed excitement of the Aqua Paola exclaiming in eternal praise of Rome. He must surely have asked himself often in what year his faith and joy had fled. Some said that he had become attached to a convert who had relapsed into paganism; some said that one day under torture he had renounced Christianity to save his life from the hands of brigands. Perhaps it was only that he had attempted the hardest task in the world and found it not so difficult after all; and reflecting that he could have built up a huge fortune in the financial world with half the energy and one-tenth the gifts; that he was the only person living who could write a Latin that would have entranced the Augustans; that he was the last man who would be able to hold in his head at one moment all the learning of the Church; and that to become a Prince of the Church required nothing but a devoted indifference to its workings,—reflecting on these things he may well have felt the world not to be worth the thunder of admiration and applause that was so continually mounting to Heaven in its praise. Perhaps one of the other stars is more worthy of one's best efforts.

Grace concluded, the meal could not be begun until the Cardinal was informed as to Alix. But where's Alix?

Alix is always late.

Are you sure she's coming?

She telephoned this afternoon, that . . .

Now isn't that too bad of her! She's coming in panting when the dinner's half over. Then apologies. Father, you're too kind to her. You always forgive her directly. You must act cross.

We must all act cross.

Everybody look angry when Alix comes in.

I had assumed that the conversation of the Cabala *in camera* would be vertiginous. If I anticipated the wit and eloquence of its table-talk I dreaded their gradual discovery that I was tongue-tied or doltish. When, therefore, the conversation at last broke forth I had the mixed sensation of discovering that it was not unlike that of a house party on the Hudson. Wait, I told myself, they will warm up. Or perhaps it is my presence here that prevents them from being at their best. I recalled the literary tradition that the gods of antiquity had not died but still drifted about the earth shorn of the greater part of their glory—Jupiter and Venus and Mercury straying through the streets of Vienna as itinerant musicians, or roaming the South of France as harvesters. Casual acquaintances would not be able to sense their supernaturalism; the gods would take good care to dim their genius but once the outsider had gone would lay aside their cumbersome humanity and relax in the reflections of their ancient godhead. I told myself that I was the obstacle, that these Olympians chattered and chaffed for a season until my departure, when the air would change,—what divine conversation. . . .

Presently in burst their Alix, the Princess d'Espoli, panting and a-flutter with apologies. She knelt to the Cardinal's sapphire. No one looked the least bit cross. The very servants beamed. We are to know a great deal about the Princess later; suffice it to say that she was a Frenchwoman of the utmost smallness and elegance, sandy-haired, pretty, and endowed with a genius for conversation in which every shade of wit, humor, pathos and even tragic power followed in close succession. Within a few moments she was enchanting the company with a lot of nonsense about a horse who had started talking on the Pincian Hill and the efforts of the Police Force to suppress such an aberration of nature. As I was presented to her she murmured quickly: Miss Grier told me to tell you that she will be here at about ten-thirty.

After dinner Mme. Bernstein played the piano for a time. She was still the power behind the great German banking house. Without ever venturing into her sons' offices or directors' meetings she yet disposed of all the larger decisions of the firm by curt remarks at their dinner tables, by postscripts to her letters and by throaty injunctions at the moment of saying goodnight. She wanted the sensation of having retired from its direction; her whole middle life had been expended in a magnificent display of generalship and financial imagination, yet she could not keep her mind off its problems. The friendship of the Cabala was beginning to reconcile her to advancing age, and drawing her further and further into her love for music.

As a girl she had often heard Liszt and Tausig in her mother's home; by dint of never playing Schumann or Brahms she had kept her fingers all silver and crystal, and even now, practically in her old age, she evoked the great era of virtuosi, a time when the orchestra had not led piano technique into a desperate imitation of brass and strings. Mlle. de Morfontaine sat holding in the cup of her hand the muzzle of one or other of her splendid dogs. Her eyes were filled with tears, but whether they were the facile tears of her half-mad nature or the witness of memories brought back on the tide of Chopin's sonata, we cannot know. The Cardinal had retired early and the Princess sat in the shadows, not listening to the music, but pursuing some of the phantoms of her most secretive mind.

Barely had the army with banners ceased drilling in the wintry sunlight of the last movement when a servant whispered to me that the Cardinal wished to see me.

I found him in the first of the two small rooms that had been set aside for him at the Villa. He was writing a letter, standing up to it at one of those high desks known to the clerks of Dickens and the illuminators of the Middle Age. I was later to receive many of those famous letters, never more nor less than four pages long, never falling short of their amazing suavity, never very witty nor vivid yet never untouched from beginning to end by the quality of their composer's mind. Whether he declined an invitation or suggested a reading of Freud's book on Leonardo, or gave suggestions on the feeding of rabbits, always from the first sentence he foresaw his last and always like a movement from Mozart's chambermusic the whole unit lay under one spirit and the perfection of details played handmaid to the perfection of the form. He seated me in a chair that suffered all the light that was in the room, treating himself to a fine shadow.

He began by saying that he had heard that I was to keep an eye on Donna Leda's son for a while.

I became warm and unintelligible in an effort at protesting that

I could guarantee nothing; that I was most reluctant; and that I still reserved the right to withdraw at any moment.

Let me tell you about him, he began. Perhaps I should say first that I am a sort of old uncle in the family, and their confessor for many years. Well,—this Marcantonio. What shall I say? Have you seen him?

No.

The boy is full of good things. He . . . he . . . Full of good things. Perhaps that's his trouble. You say you haven't met him yet?

No.

Everything seemed to start well. He was good in his studies. He made a lot of friends. He was particularly good in the ceremonial that his rank requires, his attendance at Court and at the Vatican. His mother was a little anxious about his boyish dissipations. She had his father in mind, I suspect, and wanted the boy to get over them as soon as possible. Donna Leda is a more than usually foolish woman. She was very pleased when he set up his own apartment off on the Via Po and became very secretive about it.

Here the Cardinal began to grope about again, perhaps surprised at his own awkwardness. Presently however he gathered up the reins with new determination and said: And then, my dear young man, something went wrong. We thought he would go through the usual experience of a Roman young man of his class and come out. But he has never come out. Perhaps you can tell me why this young fellow couldn't have had his five or six little affairs and gotten over it?

I showed myself as quite unequal to answering this question. In fact I was so amazed at the five or six little liaisons for a boy of sixteen, that it was all I could do to keep my face casual. I wanted badly not to appear shocked and endeavored by a lift of an eyebrow to imply that the boy might have a score if he liked.

Marcantonio, continued the priest, went around with a group of boys older than himself. His greatest wish was to be like them. You could see them at the races, in the music-halls, at Court, in the tea-rooms and hotel lobbies. They wore monocles and American hats, and all they talked about was women and their own successes. Euh . . . perhaps I should begin at the beginning.

There was a pause.

He was first initiated—perhaps I should use a stronger word— on Lake Como. He used to play tennis with some very warm little South American girls, heiresses from Brazil, I believe, from whom no secrets were hid. I fancy our Tonino merely meant to pay them a shy compliment or two, a sudden kiss under the laurel-bushes. But he soon found himself with a little . . . a sort of Rubens riot on his hands. Well, it began in imitation of his older friends. From imitation it went to an exercise of vanity. What was Vanity became Pleasure. Pleasure became a Habit. Habit became a Mania. And that's where he is now.

There was another pause.

You must have heard of how certain insane persons become enormously intelligent—that is, they become sly and secretive— trying to conceal their delusion from their guards? Yes; and I am told that vicious children perform feats of duplicity worthy of the most expert criminals, in an effort to conceal their tricks from their parents. You have heard of such things? Well, that is where Marcantonio is now. What can be done? Some people would say that we should let him go and make himself thoroughly sick. Perhaps they are right, but we should like to step in before that, if possible. Especially since there has come a new development into the story.

My mood at that moment was overwhelmingly against new developments. In the distance I could hear that Mme. Bernstein had resumed her Chopin. I would have given a lot for the power of being rude enough to leap for the doorknob and bid my host goodnight, a long goodnight to the wallowing little Prince and his mother.

Yes, continued the Cardinal, his mother has at last found a marriage for him. To be sure she does not believe there is a house in the world that can bring any new distinction to her own, but she has found a girl with an old name and some money and expects me to do the rest. But the girl's brothers know Marcantonio. They are in the group I described to you. They refuse to permit the marriage until Marcantonio has, well—been quiet for a while.

Now my face must have shown a rich mixture of horror and amusement and anger and astonishment, for the Cardinal became perplexed. You never can tell what will surprise an American, he probably said to himself.

No, no. Excuse me, Father. I can't, I can't.

What do you mean?

You want me to go to the country to hold him down to a few weeks of temperance. I don't understand how you can mean such a thing, but you do. He's a sort of Strassburg goose whom you want to stuff with virtue, don't you, against his marriage. Don't you see . . . ?

You exaggerate!

Excuse me if I sound rude, Father: No wonder you couldn't make an impression on the boy,—you didn't believe in what you were saying. You don't really believe in temperance.

Believe in it. Of course I do. Am I not a priest?

Then why not make the boy . . . ?

But after all, *we are in the world*.

I laughed. I shouted with a laughter that would have been insulting, if it hadn't contained a touch of hysteria. Oh, I thank thee, dear Father Vaini, I said to myself. I thank thee for that word.

How clear it makes all Italy, all Europe. *Never try to do anything against the bent of human nature.* I came from a colony guided by exactly the opposite principle.

Excuse me, Father, I said at last. I can't go on with it. Under any conditions I should feel an awful hypocrite talking to the boy. But if I knew it were only a measure to keep him good a month or two I should feel ten times more so. It can't be argued; it's just a matter one feels. I must tell Miss Grier I cannot visit her friend. She is driving out here at ten-thirty. If you will excuse me I shall go and find her in the music-room now.

Do not be angry with me, my son. Perhaps you are right. Probably I do not believe these things.

Hardly had I re-entered the music-room with my revolt written all over me when the Princess d'Espoli came forward. By that telepathy which the Cabala employed in its affairs she already knew that I had to be persuaded all over again. She made me sit down beside her and with the briefest outlay of those gifts of suppliance and enchantment of which she held the secret, she won my promise. In two minutes she had made it seem the most natural thing in the world that I should play stern older brother to a gifted drifting friend of hers.

As by the click of some invisible stage-manager Miss Grier entered.

How are you, how are you? she said, trailing her russet draperies across the tiles toward me. You can't guess who drove me out. I must hurry back. The Lateran choir is coming to sing Palestrina to me about twelve,—perhaps you know the motets from the Song of Songs? No? Marcantonio brought me here. He loves high-powered cars, and as his mother can't give him one I let him play with mine. Can you come out and meet him now? You'd better get your coat. Do you like night rides?

She led me out to the road where behind two blinding headlights a motor was humming impatiently. Antonino, she called.
This is an American friend of your mother's. Do show him the car
for half an hour, will you? Don't kill anybody.

An incredibly slight and definite little elegant, looking exactly
his sixteen years, with spark-like black eyes bowed stiffly to me in
the faint light over the wheel. Italian princes do not rise at the
approach of ladies.

Don't hurt my car or my friend, Marcantonio.

No.

Where are you going?

But he did not choose to answer and the aroused motor drowned
out the lady's questions. For ten minutes we sat in silence while the
road rose to the headlights. After a harrowing struggle with his
own selfishness Don Marcantonio asked me if I wanted to take the
wheel. Assured that nothing would alarm me more, he settled
down to driving with an almost voluptuous application. He made
nice distinctions with grades and corners, took long descents
cantabilemente, and played scherzi on cobblestones. The outlines of
the Alban hills stood out against the stars that like a swarm of
golden bees recalled that haughty Barberini who had declared that
the sky itself was the scutcheon of his house. All lights were out on
the farms, but occasionally we passed through a village whose
francobollo shop showed a lantern and a group of card players.
Many a wakeful soul in those enormous family beds must have
turned over, crossing himself, at the sighing whistle of our flight.

Presently however the driver wanted to talk. He asked a great
many questions about the United States. Could one plunge into the
life of the Wild West any minute? Were there many big cities as
big as Rome? What language was spoken in San Francisco? in
Philadelphia? Where did our athletes train for the Olympic
Games? Was the public allowed to watch them? Did I know about

such things? I replied that at school and college one couldn't help picking up hints on form and training. He then disclosed the fact that at the Villa Colonna he had directed the gardeners to make a running-track, cinders and hurdles and pit and shed and embanked corners. And that we were to use it every morning. He dreamed of himself doing incredible distances in incredible time. He outlined a plan to me whereby under my direction he would begin by running a mile every morning, and should add a half-mile daily for weeks. This would go on for years and then he would be ready to enter the Paris Olympics of 1924.

In my head the nerves of astonishment had been a little fatigued lately, what with Mlle. de Morfontaine and her Ecumenical Council, the Cardinal and his tolerances, Miss Grier and her cereals. But I confess they received no small twinge when this frail and emptied spirit announced his candidacy for a world's record in long runs. Not without sly intention I began to outline the sacrifices that such an ambition would entail. I touched on diet and early hours and early rising; he accepted them eagerly. I then skirted those self-denials that would touch him more particularly, and now with a mounting exaltation, with an almost religious fire, he pledged himself to all temperance. The fact that I was astonished shows my immaturity. I thought I was witness to a great conversion. I told myself that he wanted to be saved; that he was rolling up outside forces that might protect himself from his weakness; and that he hoped to find in athletics a deliverance from despair.

Returning to the Villa we found the company still listening to music. As we entered the room all eyes were turned towards us and I knew that for the present the Cabala had laid aside all activity and was brooding over one thing, the rescue of Donna Leda's son.

On arriving at my rooms in Rome I found several notes from a

Mr. Perkins of Detroit, a successful manufacturer who had crossed with me. Mr. Perkins, descending upon Italy for the first time, was resolved to see it at its best. There were no collections so private but that he was able to secure letters of admittance; no savants too occupied but that he obtained their services as ciceroni; audiences he obtained with the Pope were, as he called them, "super-special"; excavations not yet open to the public suffered his disappointed peerings. Some secretary at the Embassy must have mentioned that I had already made some Italian acquaintances, for there were these notes from him reminding me that he wanted to know some real Italians. He wanted to see what they were like in their homes, and he expected me to show him some. Mind, real Italians. I wrote him at once that all the Italians I knew were half French or half American, but assured him that when I had actually isolated a native I would bring them together. I added that I was leaving for the country, but would return in a week or two and see what could be done.

To the country then I went, being driven for the greater part of a day by Marcantonio himself. His enthusiasm for running had by no means abated; in fact it seemed to have gone from strength to strength, probably because of some lapses from strict training in the interval. It was late afternoon and a red sunset was filtering through a blue dusk when we entered the great gates of the park. There was first a forest of oaks; then a mile of open lawn with some hurrying sheep; then a pineta with a brook; the farmhouses in a cloud of doves; the upper terrace with a perspective of fountains; and at last the casino with the Black Queen trailing her garments of dusty serge across the driveway of powdered shell. There was little time to admire the orange-brown front of the villa roughened with wreaths and garlands that were crumbling away before the sun and rain, or the famous frieze of the women in Ariosto's poems, recalling the days when Pope Sylvester Lefthand held here his academy and invented the Sylvestrian sonnet-form. All I could do was to conceal my pleasure at the discovery that I was to live by candle-light in rooms that though the originals of hundreds of bad copies on Long Island, were here the secret shame of their owners. My hosts' ideal of residence was a hotel on the Embankment and they all but breathed an apology for the enormous rooms to which I was conducted, and in which I stood transfixed, lost in antiquarian dreams until Marcantonio knocked on the door to call me to supper.

At table I was presented to Donna Julia, Marcantonio's half-sister, and to a spinster cousin of the family, always present, always silent and whose lips never ceased moving, as solitaries' must, to the measure of her inner thoughts. Like all girls of her class Donna Julia had never been alone for more than a half-hour in all her life. Her immense talents for being bad had been balked at every turn; they had been forced to take refuge in her eyes. She had never even been allowed to read anything more inflammatory than the comedies of Goldoni and I Promessi Sposi, but she guessed at a criminal world and presently when marriage suddenly opened up to her every freedom she played her part in it. Donna Julia was a little stiff, almost ugly with her level baleful regard. She kept silent most of the time, was utterly incurious of me, and seemed chiefly occupied in angling for her brother's evasive glance so as to plant into it a triumphant significant idea.

One retired early at the Villa Colonna. But Marcantonio, for whom my simplest remarks were astonishing, would stop in at my room and talk for hours over some glasses of Marsala. No doubt his mother, noting the visits through her half-opened door down the hall, assumed with great satisfaction that I was reading lectures on hygiene. But, especially as the week advanced, we were chiefly taken up with a diagram that showed day by day how the little champion had run and in what time.

It must have been at the end of a week of this that in one of our late conversations his friendliness suddenly turned into contempt. A week's preoccupation with unsentimental matters now took its revenge. Back into his mind flooded the images of passion, and he wanted to boast. Perhaps he saw that prowess on the field was not to be his, and his egoism being athirst for all possible superlatives, he must replace it with a catalogue of the first prizes he had won in another arena. He recalled the Brazilian girls under the arbors of Como. He described how he had returned to Rome after that initiation bent on seeing whether the game was as easy as it had seemed. Suddenly his eyes had been opened to a world he had not dreamed of. So it was true that men and women were never really engaged in what they appeared to be doing, but lived in a world of secret invitations, signals and escapes! Now he understood the raised eyebrows of waitresses and the brush of the usher's hand as she unlocks the loge. It is not an accident that the wind draws the great lady's scarf across your face as you emerge from the door of the hotel. Your mother's friends happen to be passing in the corridor outside the drawing-room, but not by chance. Now he discovered that all women were devils, but foolish ones, and that he had entered into the true and only satisfactory activity in living— the pursuit of them. One minute he was exclaiming at the easiness of it; the next he described its difficulties and subtlety. Now he sang the uniformity of their weakness and now the endless variety of their temperaments. Next he boasted of his utter indifference and his superiority to them; he knew their tears but he did not believe they really suffered. He doubted whether they had souls.

To incidents that were true he added others that he wished had been true. To his acquaintance with a corner of Rome he added a fourteen-year-old's vision of a civilization where no one thought about anything but caresses. This fantasy took him about two hours. I listened without a word. It must have been this that undermined his exhilaration. He had been talking to impress me. Impressed I certainly was; no New Englander could help it; but I knew that a great deal depended on my not showing it. Perhaps it was his sudden realization that, seen through my eyes, these adventures were not enviable; perhaps it was that the black tide of reaction licked close on the heels of such pride; perhaps it was just truth finding room for utterance in his mounting fatigue,—at all events, there was strength left for one more outburst: I hate them all! I hate it. There's no end to it all. What shall I do? And he fell on his knees beside the bed and buried his face in the side of the mattress, his hands feverishly pulling at the cover.

Priests and doctors must often hear the cry Save me! Save me! I was destined to hear it from two other souls before my Roman year was over. Who now thinks it uncommon?

I scarcely know what I said when my turn at last came around. All I know is that my mind whipped up to its subject with a glee. Heaven only knows what New England divines lent me their remorseless counsels. I became possessed with the wine of the Puritans and alternating the vocabulary of the Pentateuch with that of psychiatry I showed him where his mind was already slipping: I pointed out wherein he already resembled his uncle Marcantonio, no mean warning; I made him see that even his interest in athletics was a symptom of his distintegration; how that he was incapable of fixing his mind on the general interests of man, and how everything he thought and did—humor, sports, ambition—presented themselves to him as symbols of lust.

My little tirade was effective beyond all expectation and for a number of reasons. In the first place, it had the energy and sincerity which the Puritan can always draw upon to censure those activities he cannot permit himself,—not a Latin demonstration of gesture and tears, but a cold hate that staggers the Mediterranean soul. Again, all my words had already their dim counterpart in the boy's soul. It is the libertine and not the preacher who conceives most truly of the ideal purity and soundness, because he pays it out, coin by coin, regretfully, knowingly, unpreventably. All my words went to rejoin their prototypes in Marcantonio's mind. Again, how could I know that he had arrived but recently at that stage of failure when one's whole being reverberates, as with some bell of despair, with the words: I shall never get out of this. I am lost. Again, I found out later that Marcantonio had a streak of religious frenzy in him, that for a year he had watched himself alternating communion and dissipation, the exaltation of the former itself betraying him into the latter and the despair of the latter driving him in anguish to the former. At last in sheer cynicism, after watching himself fail so often, he had missed Mass for several months. All these reasons go toward explaining the prostrating effect my brief and vindictive speech had. He cowered against the carpet, begging me to stop, gasping out his promises of reform. But having brought him to a conviction he might never attain again, I thought it unwise to let go. I had reserves of indignation left. But now he knelt crying on the carpet, covering his ears with his hands and shaking his wet face at me with all its terror and suppliance. I stopped and we stared at one another, darkly, trembling under our several headaches. Then he went to bed.

The next morning he seemed etherialized, made almost transparent by his new resolutions. He walked lightly and with an air of humility. No reference was made to the scene of the evening before, but his glances over the tennis net implied an obedience and a deference that were more annoying than impudence. After two sets we wandered over to the lower fountain and here stretched out on the semi-circular bench he slept for three hours. It seemed to me as I watched morning advance to noon and the sun penetrate his thin body in the delicious fatigues that follow hysterical outbursts, it seemed that it would not be rash to wonder if possibly we may have succeeded. I day-dreamed. From the formal terrace below the casino came the click of topiary shears; from the field where the ancient altar had been placed, drum-shaped and bearing an almost effaced frieze, came the shouts of some divinity students (to whom a little villa on the estate had been offered as a vacation house) playing football, their cassocks tucked up about their knees; from the pine wood the exclamations of two shepherds who sat whittling while their flock drifted almost imperceptibly to the road beyond. The fountain before me gave forth its varied sounds: the whir of its initial jet and the tinkle as it fell back into the first bowl; the drumtaps as this overflowed and slipped into the second; and the loud loquacity with which the lowest basin received all that came to it from every level. Tacitus lay unread upon my knee while my eyes followed the lizards that flashed in and out of the brilliant sunshine on the gravel, noting their confusion when a sudden breeze bent the poised veil of the fountain and swept us all with a fine mist. The monotony of light and the noise of water, of insects, and of doves in the farmhouses behind me, combined to recall those tremulous webs of sound that modern composers set shimmering above their orchestra, to draw across it presently on the oboes their bleating melody in thirds.

While I sat there a note was brought me from the house. Mr. Perkins of Detroit had heard I was at the Villa and from the hotel in the nearby town announced his intention of calling on me,—

lucky in having a pretext for entering the most inaccessible villa in Italy. I scribbled on the back of his envelope that an unfortunate event in the family prevented my asking him to the house at present.

The hot sunlight of the morning had gathered its storm and all afternoon we sat indoors. Marcantonio and Donna Julia attempted teaching me the Neapolitan dialect, while the silent cousin sat by, deeply shocked. But my lesson soon descended into a subtle and barbed quarrel between the teachers. It was conducted for the most part in rapid and hate-laden parentheses, far above my head, in their thick *argot*. What she taunted him about I can only guess. He was invariably beaten; he grew loud and angry. Twice he leaped around the table to strike her; she waited for the blow, stretching herself sleekly and looking up at him from her magnetic eyes. At length he urged me to come away from her and to go upstairs, and the two parted much as children of seven would with a bout of grimaces and a competition to have the last ugly word.

After dinner the war was resumed. The Duchess was nodding by the fire; the cousin was mumbling opposite her. And the two children sat in the shadows exchanging invective. I was made strangely uneasy by their curious quarreling. I excused myself and went to bed. The last thing I saw was an infuriated blow that Marcantonio directed at his sister's shoulder and the last sound I heard was the tremolo of her provocative laughter as they tussled on the carved wooden chest in the corner. I debated with myself on the stairs: surely I had imagined it; my poor sick head was so full of the erotic narratives of the week; surely I imagined the character of mixed love and hate in those blows that were savage caresses, and that laughter that was half sneer and half invitation.

But I had not imagined it.

At about three I was awakened by Marcantonio. He was still

dressed. He poured at my drowsy head a torrent of whirling words in which I distinguished nothing but a feverish reiteration of the phrase: You were right. Then he left the room as abruptly as he had come.

What luck Mr. Perkins had always had! Even now when he brought to bear all his American determination and broke into the gardens of the forbidden Villa, what guardian angel arranged that he should see the Villa at its most characteristic? Surely a rich old Italian villa is at its most characteristic when a dead prince lies among the rosebushes. When Frederick Perkins of Detroit leapt the wall in the crystal airs of seven in the morning, he discovered at his feet the body of Marcantonio d'Aquilanera, 14th prince and 14th duke of Aquilanera and Stoli, 12th duke of Stoli-Roccellina, marquis of Bugnaccio, of Tei, etc., baron of Spenestra, of Gran-Spenestra, seigneur of the Sciestrian Lakes; patron of the bailly of the order of San Stephano; likewise prince of Altdorf-Hotten-lingen-Craburg, intendant elector of Altdorf-H-C.; prince of the Holy Roman Empire, etc., etc.; chamberlain of the court of Naples; lieutenant and cousin of the Papal Familia; order of the Crane (f. class); three hours cold, and with a damp revolver clutched in his right hand.

BOOK THREE

ALIX

The Cabalists received the news of Marcantonio's death philosophically. The account of it which the bereaved mother gave to Miss Grier was a miracle of misunderstanding. According to her I had done wonders; in fact it was the suddenness and thoroughness of the boy's reformation that had broken his health. She, *she,* was to blame. She should have foreseen that continence was not to be expected of a mere lad; he had gone insane from an excess of virtue and shot himself from too much sanctity. These things are out of our hands, dear Leda, murmured Miss Grier. The Cardinal made no comment.

The Cabala went back to its usual occupations. Being the biographer of the individuals and not the historian of the group I shall not take up much space here with details of the discomfiture of Mrs. Pole (she had been impudent to Miss Grier), nor of the Renan performance (*L'Abbesse de Jouarre* was effectively not given as a benefit at the Constanzi). From a purely disinterested love of Church tradition they blocked the canonization of several tiresome nonentities that had been proposed to gratify the faithful in Sicily and Mexico. They saved the taxpayers of Rome the purchase of hundreds of modern Italian paintings, and the establishment of a permanent museum for them. They interested public opinion in the faint smell of drains that is wafted through the Sistine Chapel. When an oak forest fell ill in the Borghese Gardens no one but the Cabala had the sense to send to Berlin for a doctor. To tell the truth their achievements were not very considerable. I soon saw that I had arrived on the scene in the middle of the decline of their power. At first they thought they could do something about the strikes, and about the Fascismo, and the blasphemies in the Senate; and it was only after a great deal of money had been spent and hundreds of persons ineffectually goaded that they realized that the century had let loose influences they could not stem, and contented themselves with less pretentious assignments.

I came to see more and more of them. My youth and foreignness never ceased to amuse them and they were made almost uncomfortable by the knowledge that I so liked them. They thought they had outgrown being susceptible to being liked. From time to time they would point their fingers to where I sat staring at them in sheer wonder.

He's like an eager dog with his tongue out of his mouth, Alix d'Espoli would cry. What does he see in us?

He never loses hope that we will suddenly say something memorable, said the Cardinal looking at me musingly,—the look of a great talker who knows that for lack of a Boswell his greatness must die with him.

He comes from the rich new country that will grow more and more splendid while our countries decline to ruins and rubbish heaps, said Donna Leda. That's why his eyes shine so.

Why, no, cried Alix. I believe he loves us. Just simply loves us

in a disinterested new world way. Once I had a most beautiful
setter, named Samuele. Samuele spent all his life sitting around on
the pavement watching us with a look of most intense excitement.

Did he bite? asked Donna Leda who had a literal mind.

You didn't have to give Samuele a sandwich to win his devotion. He liked to like. You won't be angry with me if every now
and then I call you Samuele to remind me of him?

You mustn't talk about him in front of him, muttered Mme.
Bernstein who was playing solitaire. Young man, get me my furs
from the piano until these people remember themselves.

The Princess explained me. What fairer service can one render
another? How could I do other than attach myself to one with so
quick and gracious an interpretation.

The Princess was not really modern. As scientists gazing at
certain almost extinct birds off Australia are able to evoke a whole
lost era, so in the person of this marvellous princess we felt ourselves permitted to glimpse into the Seventeenth Century and to
reconstruct for ourselves what the aristocratic system must have
been like in its flower.

The Princess d'Espoli was exceedingly pretty in a fragile Pari-
sian way; her vivacious head, surmounted by a mass of sandy
reddish hair, was forever tilted above one or other of her thin
pointed shoulders; her whole character lay in her sad laughing eyes
and small red mouth. Her father came of the Provençal nobility
and she had spent her girlhood partly in provincial convent schools
and partly climbing like a goat the mountains that surrounded her
father's castle. At eighteen she and her sister had been called in
from the cliffs, dressed up stiffly and hawked like merchandise
through the drawing-rooms of their more influential relatives in
Paris, Florence, and Rome. Her sister had fallen to an automobile
manufacturer and was making the good and bad weather of Lyons;

Alix had married the morose Prince d'Espoli who had immediately
sunk into a profounder misanthropy. He remained at home sunk in
the last dissipations. His wife's friends never saw or referred to
him; occasionally we became aware of him, we thought, in her late
arrivals, hurried departures and harassed air. She had lost two
children in infancy. She had no life, save in other people's homes.
Yet the sum of her sufferings had been the production of the
sweetest strain of gaiety that we shall ever see, a pure well of
heartbroken frivolity. Wonderful though she was in all the scenes
of social life, she certainly was at her finest at table, where she had
graces and glances that the most gifted actresses would fall short
of conceiving for their Millamonts, and Rosalinds and Célimènes;
nowhere has been seen such charm, such manners, and such wit.
She would prattle about her pets, describe a leave-taking seen by
chance in a railway station, or denounce the Roman fire depart-
ments with a perfection of rendering of Yvette Guilbert, a purer
perfection in that it did not suggest the theatre. She possessed the
subtlest mimicry, and could sustain an endless monologue, but the
charm of her gift resided in the fact that it required the collabora-
tion of the whole company; it required the exclamations, contradictions, and even the concerted shouts as of a Shakespearean mob,
before the Princess could display her finest art. She employed an
unusually pure speech, a gift that went deeper than a mere aptitude
for acquiring grammatical correctness in the four principal languages of Europe; its source lay in the type of her mind. Her
thought proceeded complicatedly, but not without order, in long
looping parentheses, a fine network of relative clauses, invariably
terminating in some graceful turn by way of climax, some sudden
generalization or summary surprise. I once accused her of speaking
in paragraphs and she confessed that the nuns to whom she had
gone to school in Provence had required of her every day an oral

essay built on a formula derived principally from Madame de Sévigné and terminating in a *concetto*.

Such rare personalities are not able to derive nourishment from ordinary food. Rumors of the Princess's strange stormy loves reached us continually. It seems that she was doomed to search throughout the corridors of Rome a succession of attachments as brief and fantastic as they were passionate and unsatisfied. Nature had decided to torment this woman by causing her to fall in love (that succession of febrile interviews, searches, feints at indifference, nightlong solitary monologues, ridiculous visions of remote happiness) with the very type of youth that could not be attracted by her, with cool impersonal learned or athletic young Northerners, a secretary at the British Embassy or Russian violinist or German archaeologist. As though these trials were not sufficient, society had added to them this aggravation, that her Roman hostesses, conscious of this failing and wishing to make sure that at their tables the Princess would display her finest flights, would intentionally include among their guests the Princess's latest infatuation to whom throughout the evening she would sing, like a swan, her song of defeated love.

As a mere girl, if I may presume to reconstruct the growth of her personality, she sensed the fact that there was in her something that a little prevented her making friends, namely, intelligence. The few intelligent people who truly wish to be liked soon learn, among the disappointments of the heart, to conceal their brilliance. They gradually convert their keen perceptions into more practical channels,—into a whole technique of implied flattery of others, into felicities of speech, into the euphemisms of demonstrative affection, into softening for others the crude lines of their dullness. All the Princess's perfection was an almost unconscious attempt at making friends of those who would first be her admirers, yet realizing that if she were too artistic they would be dazzled but repelled, and that if she were less than perfect they would dismiss her as a trivial bright hysteric. For many years she had practiced this babbling speech on her friends, unconsciously noting on their faces which tones of the voice, which appropriate fleck of the hands, which delayed adjectives were more and which less successful. In other words she had achieved mastery of a fine art, the all but forgotten art of conversation, under the impetus of love. Like some panic-stricken white mouse in the trap of a psychologist's experiment she had been seeking her ends by the primitive rules of trial and error, only to learn that at the last one is too bruised by the mistakes to enjoy the successes. The exquisite and fragile mechanism of her temperament had not been able to stand the strain laid upon it, the double exhaustion of inspiration and woe; and the lovely being was already slightly mad. She grew daily more light-headed and could be caught from time to time in moods that were variously foolish and pathetic. But her deepest wound was still to come.

James Blair and his notebooks were staying over in Rome after all. He had come upon some new veins of research. For him ten lifetimes would be all too short to pursue the horizons of one's curiosity. Think, he would say, it would take about ten years to work up the full critical apparatus to attack the historical problems surrounding the life of St. Francis of Assisi. It would take almost as many to get up the Roman road-system, the salt roads and the wheat roads,—God, the whole problem as to how the Rome of the Republic was fed. Another day he would be dreaming about starting on the eight or ten books in French and German on Christina of Sweden and her life in Rome; then one studied up Swedish and read the diaries and the barrels-full of notes; when one knew more about her than did anyone alive one passed on to her father and buried oneself for months in libraries to master the policies and the military genius of Gustavus Adolphus. Thus life stretched . . . bindings . . . bindings . . . catalogues . . . footnotes. One studied the saints and never thought about religion. One knew everything about Michelangelo yet never felt deeply a single work. James spent weeks of fascinated attention on the women of the Caesars and yet could scarcely be dragged to dinner at the Palazzo Barberini. He found all moderns trivial, and was the dupe of the historians' grand style which fails to convey the actuality (for Blair, the triviality) of their heroes. The present casts a veil of cheapness over the world: to look into any face, however beautiful, is to see pores and the folds about the eye. Only those faces not present are beautiful.

The fact is that quite early James Blair had been frightened by life (in a way which the Princess, in a moment of misery and inspiration, was to divine later with the cry: What kind of a stupid mother could he have had?) and had forever after bent upon books the floodtides of his energy. At times his scholarship resembled panic; he acted as though he feared that raising his eyes from the page he would view the world, or his share in the world, dissolving in ruin. His endless pursuit of facts (which had no fruit in published work and brought no intrinsic esthetic pleasure) was not so much the will to do something as it was the will to escape something else. One man's release lies in dreams, another's in facts.

All this resulted in a real unworldliness, which with his youth and learning and faintly *distrait* courtesy especially endeared him to older women. Both Miss Grier and Mme. Agaropoulos hovered about him with mothering delight and sighed with vexation at his obstinate refusal to come and see them. He reminded me of the lions that stare, unwinking and unseeing, at the crowd about their cage, the crowd that grimaces and waves admiring parasols, though the beast disdains to pick up even a biscuit from such vulgar givers.

At the time that the Princess's story begins he was engaged in establishing the exact location of the ancient cities of Italy. He was reading mediaeval descriptions of the Campagna and tracing through place-names, through dried water-courses, through cracked old paintings the exact position of disused roads and abandoned towns. He was learning about the country's former plants and animals: he was quite happy. Sometimes he made notes of all this, but for the most part he preferred to learn the truth and then forget it.

When it began to get cold in his room he serenely made use of mine, covering my tables with his vellum-bound folios, standing his pictures against my wall, and strewing my floors with his maps. He had dazzled one of the librarians at the Collegio Romano with his allusions and had obtained the privilege of bringing the material home.

One day the Princess d'Espoli came to see me. Ottima admitted her. She came in upon James Blair who was kneeling on the floor crawling from city to city on some yellow crested maps. His coat was off; his hair was in a tangle, and his hands were gray with dust. He had never met her and did not like her clothes. He did not want to be drawn into a conversation and stood, handsome and sulky, his glances stealing to the maps on the floor. Explained that I was out. Might not be back before. Would not forget to tell that.

Alix didn't mind. She even asked for some tea.

Ottima had just come in to begin thinking about dinner. While tea was making Alix asked to have the maps explained to her. Now the Princess was more capable of entering into an enthusiasm for old cities than most of the several hundred women of her acquaintance; but short of a doctorate in archaeology one does not enter upon such ground with James Blair. Coldly, haughtily, and with long quotations from Livy and Virgil, he harangued my guest. He dragged her remorselessly up and down the seven hills; he wrung her in and out of all the shifting beds of the Tiber. When I finally returned I found her sitting gazing at him over the edge of her teacup with a faintly mocking expression. She had not known that such a man was possible. Throughout the whole episode Blair had acted like nothing so much as a spoiled boy of seven interrupted in a game about Indians. It would be hard to say what had most captivated the Princess, but it was probably that trace of sturdy spoiled egotism. It might have been, in part, the cold douche of being unwelcome,—she who was the delight of the most delightful people in Europe, who had never entered a door without arousing a whirlpool of welcome, who had never come too early nor left too late,—suddenly she had tasted the luxury of being resented.

As soon as I arrived Blair took a swift and awkward departure.

But he's charming! He's charming! she cried. Who is he?

I told her briefly of his home, his progress through the universities, and his habits of study.

But he's extraordinary. Tell me: is he—shy, is he *boudeur* with everybody? Now perhaps I did something to annoy him? What could I have said, Samuele?

I hastened to reassure her. He's that way with everyone. And most people like him all the more for it. Especially older women. For example, Miss Grier and Mme. Agaropoulos adore him and all he does is to sit on their chairs inventing excuses for not coming to dinner.

Well, I'm not old and I like him. Oh, he is so rude! I could have slapped him. And he only looked at me once. He will have a hard time in life, Samuele, unless he learns to be more gracious. Isn't there anybody he likes, no? besides you?

Yes, he's engaged to a girl in the United States.

Dark hair or light?

I don't know.

Mark my words, he will be very unhappy, unless he learns to be more amiable. But think! what intelligence, what an eye! And how wonderful it is to see such an absence of trickery, you know, such simplicity. Does he live here?

No, he just brings his books in here when it's too cold in his own room.

He is poor?

Yes.

He is poor!

Not very poor, you know. When he really gets down to his last cent he can always find things to do at once. He's happy to be poor.

And he lives quite alone?

Yes. Oh, yes.

And he is poor. (This caused her a moment's astonished reflection, until she burst out:) But you know, that is not right! It is society's duty . . . that is, society should be proud to protect such people. Someone very gifted should be appointed to watch over such people.

But, Princess, James Blair values his independence above everything. He doesn't want to be watched over.

They should be watched over in spite of themselves. Look, you will bring him to tea some day. I am sure my husband's library has

some more old maps of the Campagna. We have the bailiff's reports of the Espoli back into the Sixteenth Century. Wouldn't that
bring him?

Even surprised at herself, the Princess tried for a time to talk of
other things, but presently she returned to praise what she called
Blair's single-mindedness; she meant his self-sufficiency, for while
we are in love with a person our knowledge of his weaknesses lies
lurking in the back of our minds and our idealization of the loved
one is not so much an exaggeration of his excellences as a careful
"rationalization" of his defects.

When next I saw Blair he wasted two or three hours before he
got up courage to ask me who she was. He listened darkly while I
spoke my enthusiasm. At last he showed me a note in which she
asked him to drive with her to Espoli, look over the estate, and to
examine the archives. He was to bring me if I wanted. James
wished greatly to go; but he was suspicious of the lady. He liked
her and yet he didn't. He was trying to tell me that he only liked
ladies who didn't like him first. He twisted the letter about trying
to decide, then going to the table wrote a note of refusal.

Then began what it is merely brutal to call a siege. Driving in
the Corso Alix would say to herself: There's nothing unconven-
tional in my stopping at his room to see if he wants to drive in the
Gardens. I could do as much for a dozen men and it would be
perfectly natural. I am much older than he is, so much so, that it
would merely be an act of . . . thoughtfulness. When she stood
on the platform before his door (for she was not content to send
up the chauffeur) she would experience a moment of panic,
wishing to recall her ring, imagining when no one answered that
he was in hiding behind the closed door, listening, who knows, in
anger or contempt to her loud heartbeats. Or she would debate all
evening among the gilt chairs of her little salon as to whether she

might drop him a note. She would count the days since last she had spoken to him and gauge the propriety (the inner, the spiritual propriety, not the worldly propriety: for the Cabalists the latter had ceased to exist) of a new meeting. She was always coming upon him by accident in the city (she called it her proof of the existence of guardian angels) and it was with these chance meetings that she had generally to content herself. She would attract his attention the length of the Piazza Venezia and carry him to whatever destination he confessed to. No one has ever been happier than Alix on these few occasions when she sat beside him in her car. How docilely she sat listening to his lecture; with what tenderness she secretly noticed his tie and shoes and socks: and with what intensity she fixed her gaze upon his face trying to imprint upon her memory the exact proportions of his features, the imprint that indifference retains so much better than the most passionate love. There was a possibility that they might have become the most congenial of friends, for he dimly sensed that there was something in her that allied her to the great ladies of his study. If she had only succeeded in concealing her tenderness. At the first signs of his liking for her she would become so intoxicated with the intimation of cordiality that she would make some shy little remark with a faintly senti-mental implication; she would comment on his appearance or ask him to lunch. And lose him.

One day he gave her a book that had been mentioned in their conversations. He did not stop to think that it was the first move he had made spontaneously in the whole relation. Hitherto every suggestion, every invitation, had proceeded from her (from her, trembling, presuffering a rebuff, lightly) and she longed for a first sign of his interest. When this book was brought to her, then, she lost her balance; she thought it justified her in pushing the friend-ship on to new levels, to almost daily meetings, and to long comradely lazy afternoons. She never realized that in his eyes she was, first, an enemy to his studies, and second, that strange hedged monster which all his wide reading had not been able to humanize: a married woman. She called once too often. Suddenly he changed; he became rude and abrupt. When she climbed his stairs he *did* hide behind the door and the bell rang in vain and with a menacing sound, though she had her ways of knowing he was in. She became terrified. Again she confronted that cavern of horror in her nature: she seemed always to be loving those that did not love her. She came to me, distraught. I was cautious and offered her philosophy until I could sound Blair in the matter.

Blair came to me of his own accord. He paced up and down the room, bewildered, revolted, enraged. His stay in Rome had become impossible. He no longer dared remain in his room and when he was out he clung to the side streets. What should he do?

I advised him to leave town.

But how could he? He was in the middle of some work that. Some work that. Damn it all. All right, he'd go.

I begged him before he went to come to dinner with me once when the Princess would be present. No, no. Anything but that. I, in turn, became angry. I analyzed the different kinds of fool he was. An hour later I was saying that the mere fact of being loved so, whether one could return it or not, put one under an obligation. More than an obligation to be merely kind, an obligation to be grateful. Blair did not understand, but consented at last on the difficult condition that I was not to reveal to the Princess that he was leaving for Spain on the very night of the dinner.

Of course, the Princess arrived early, so enchantingly dressed that I fairly floundered in admitting her. She held tickets for the opera; one no longer cared to hear *Salome,* but *Petrushka* was being danced after it, at ten-thirty. Blair's train left at eleven. He arrived and played his most gracious. We were really very happy, all of us, as we sat by the open window, smoking and talking long over Ottima's excellent *zabaglione* and harsh Trasteverine coffee.

It was a continual surprise to me to see that in Blair's presence she was always a proud detached aristocrat. Even her faintly caressing remarks were such as would not be noticed if one had let them fall to someone with whom one was not secretly in love. Her fastidious pride even drove her to exaggerating her impersonality; she teased him, she pretended she did not hear when he addressed her, she pretended she was in love with me. It was only when he was not present that she became humble, even servile; only then could she even imagine calling on him unasked. At last she rose: It's time to go to the Russian Ballet, she said.

Blair excused himself: I'm sorry I must go back and work.

She looked as though a sword had gone through her. But surely, three-quarters of an hour with Stravinsky is a part of your work. My car's right here.

He remained firm. He too had a ticket for that night.

For a moment she looked blank. She had never met obstinacy under such conditions and did not know what to do next. After a moment she bent her head and pushed back her coffee-cup. Very well, she said lightly. If you can't, you can't. Samuele and I shall go.

Their parting was grim. During the drive to the Constanzi she remained silent, fingering the folds of her coat; during the ballet she sat at the back of the box thinking, thinking, thinking, with staring dry eyes. At the close scores of friends pressed about her in the corridor. She became gay: Let's go to the cabaret run by the Russian refugees, she said. At the door of the cabaret she dismissed her chauffeur, telling him that her maid need not sit up for her. We danced for a long time in silence, her depression stealing back upon her.

When we left the hall the unfriendliest moonlight in the world was flooding the street. We found a carriage and started towards her home. But falling into the most earnest conversation in all our acquaintance we failed to notice that the carriage had reached her door and had been standing there for some time.

Look, Samuele, do not make me go to bed now. Let me go in and change my clothes quickly. Then let us drive about and watch the sun come up over the Campagna. Would that make you angry with me?

I assured her that it was just what I wanted and she hurried into the house. I paid off the driver who was drunk and quarrelsome and when she rejoined me we strolled through the streets talking and gradually inviting a resigned drowsiness. We had experimented with vodka at the cabaret and the alcohol conferred upon our minds the same mood that the moonlight was shedding upon the icy bubble of the Pantheon. We strayed into the courtyard of the Cancelleria and criticized the arches. We returned to my rooms for cigarettes.

Last night I wasn't at all brave, she said, lying back in the darkness on the sofa. I was desperate. That was before I received your invitation. Could I go to see him or couldn't I? A week had gone by. I asked myself would he feel . . . well, insulted, if a lady knocked on his door at ten o'clock. It was about ten o'clock. Really, there's nothing peculiar about a lady's paying a perfectly impersonal call at about nine-thirty. There's nothing self-conscious, Samuele, about my being here now, for instance. Besides I had a perfectly good reason for going. He asked me what I thought of *La Villegiatura,* and since then I had read it. Now tell, my dear friend, would it have been ridiculous from the American point of view if I had . . . ?

Beautiful Alix, you are never ridiculous. But wasn't your meet-

ing with him tonight all the fresher, all the happier, just because
you hadn't seen him for so long?

Oh, how wise you are! she cried. God has sent you to me in my
trouble. Come by me and let me hold your hand. Are you ashamed
of me when you have seen me suffer so? I suppose I should be
ashamed. You see me without any dignity. You have kind eyes and
I am not ashamed in front of you. I think you must have loved too,
for you take all my foolishness as a matter of course. Oh, my dear
Samuele, every now and then the thought comes over me that he
despises me. I have all the faults that he hasn't. When I have this
nightmare that he not only dislikes me but laughs at me, yes,
laughs at me, my heart stops beating and I blush for hours at a
time. The only way I can save myself then is by remembering that
he has said many kind things to me; that he sent me that book; that
he has asked after me. And then I pray God very simply to put
into his mind just a bit of regard for me. Just a bit of respect for
those things . . . those things that other people seem to like in me.

We sat in silence for a time, her feverish hand plunged deep
into mine and her bright eyes gazing into the darkness. At last she
began speaking again in a lower voice:

He is good. He is reasonable. When I am analytical this way I
unfit myself for his loving me. I must learn to be simple. Yes.
Look, you have done so much for me, may I ask for one more
favor. Play to me. I must get out of my mind that wonderful music
where Petrushka wrestles with himself.

I felt ashamed of playing before her who played far better than
any of us, but I drew out my folios and started right through
Gluck's *Armide*. I had hoped that the inept performance would
awaken an esthetic annoyance and so shake her out of her dejection, but I presently saw that she had fallen asleep. After a long
and adroit diminuendo I left the piano, turned on a shaded light

near her, and stole off into my own room. I changed my clothes and lay down ready for the walk in which we were to see the sun rise. I was trembling with a strange happy excitement, made up partly of my love and pity for her, and partly from the mere experience of eavesdropping on a beautiful spirit in the last reaches of its pride and suffering. I was lying thus, proud and happy in the role of guardian, when my heart suddenly stopped beating. She was weeping in her sleep. Sighs welled up from the depths of her slumber, hoarse protests, obstinate denials and moans followed one upon another. Suddenly her broken breathing ceased and I knew she was awake. There was a half-minute of silence; then a low call: Samuele.

Hardly had I appeared at the door before she cried: I know he despises me. He runs away from me. He thinks me a foolish woman who pursues him. He tells the servant to tell me he is out, but he stands behind the door and hears me go away. What shall I do? I'd better not live. I'd better not live any more. It's best, dear Samuele, that I go out right now, in my own way, and stop all this mistaken, this, this, futile suffering of mine. Do you see?

She had arisen and was groping for her hat. I really have courage enough tonight, she muttered. He is too good and too simple for me to worry him as I do. I'll just slip out . . .

But Alix, I cried. We love you so. So many people love you.

You can't say that people love me. They like to greet me on the stairs. They like to listen and smile. But no one has ever watched under my window. No one has secretly learned what I do every hour of the day. No one has . . .

She lay back on the sofa, her cheeks flushed and wet. I talked to her for a long time. I said that her genius was social, that she was made for the delight of company, that she relieved others of the weight of their own boredom, their disguised self-hatred. I promised her that she could find happiness in the exercise of her gift. I could see by a glimpse of her wet cheek turned away that it calmed her to be told so, for she possessed the one form of genius that is almost never praised to its face. She grew more tranquil. After a pause she began talking in a dreamy tone:

I will leave him alone. I will never see him again, she began. When I was a girl and we lived on the mountains, Samuele, I had a pet goat named Tertullien that I loved very much. One day Tertullien died. I would not be comforted. I was hateful and obstinate. The nuns with whom I went to school could do nothing with me and when it was my turn to recite I refused to speak. At last my dear Mother Superior called me into her room and at first I was very bad, even with her. But when she began to tell me of her losses I flung my arms about her and wept for the first time. As a punishment she made me stop everyone I met and say to them twice: *God is sufficient! God is sufficient!*

After a pause she added: I know that it can be true for other people, but I still wanted Tertullien. When is your patience with me coming to an end, Samuele?

Never, I said.

The windows were beginning to show the first light of dawn. Suddenly a little bell rang out nearby, a tinkle of purest silver.

Hush, she said. That's the earliest mass at some church.

Santa Maria in Trastevere is just around the corner.

Hurry!

We let ourselves out of the palace and breathed the cold gray air. A mist seemed to hang low about the street; puffs of blue smoke lay in the corners. A cat passed us. Shivering but elated we entered the church joining two old women in wadded clothes and a laborer. The basilica loomed above, the candles of our side-chapel picking out reflections in the curious marbles and the gold of the

mosaics in the vast black cave. The service of the Mass was en-
rolled with expedition and accuracy. When we came out a milky
light had begun to fill the square. The shutters of several shops
were being lowered; drowsy passers-by made the diagonals
staggering; a woman was lowering her chickens in a basket from
the fifth story for a long day's scratching.

We walked over to the Aventine, crossing the Tiber which
twisted like a great yellow rope under a delicate fume. We stopped
for a glass of sour blue-black wine and a paper bag of peaches.

For the time at least the Princess seemed to herself to have forever closed her mind to even the remotest hope that she would ever
see Blair again. Sitting on a stone bench on the gloomy Aventine
while the sun shouldered its way up through plunging orange
clouds, we mused. She seemed for a time to have fallen back into
her old despondency; I resumed the arguments that spoke more
glowingly of her gifts.

Suddenly she straightened up. All right. I will try it for you. I
must do something. Where are you going today?

I murmured that Mme. Agaropoulos was giving a sort of a
musicale: that she was introducing a young compatriot who
claimed to have discovered the secret of ancient Greek music.

Write her a note. Telephone her. Ask her if I may come. I too
shall learn about ancient Greek music. I shall be introduced to
everyone there. I shall be asked to everyone's house. Listen,
Samuele, since you say it is my talent I shall get to know everyone
in Rome. I shall die of social engagements: Here lies the woman
who never refused an invitation. I shall meet two thousand people
in ten days. I shall lay myself out to please anybody on earth. And
mind you, Samuele, if that does not nourish me, we shall have to
finish trying, you know. . . .

Mme. Agaropoulos was staggered with joy when she discovered

that the unhoped for, the improcurable Princess was coming to her house. Mme. Agaropoulos was not the slave of social categories, but she longed to frequent the Cabala, as some long for the next world. She assumed that in that company all was wit and love and peace. There one would find no silly people, none envious, none quarrelsome. She had met the Princess d'Espoli once and had ever since taken her as the type of person she would herself have been if she had been better-looking, thinner and had had more time to read, little realizing that all these had been more in her power than in Alix', and that she had spoiled her own progress by a lazy kindliness, great kindliness but lazy.

The Princess called for me in her car at five o'clock. It would be impossible for me to describe her clothes; it is enough to say that she had the most incredible power of supplying new angles, shades, lines, that interpreted her character. This aptitude received added éclat from her residence in Italy, for Italian women, though often more beautiful, lack both figure and judgment. They anxiously spend enormous sums in Paris and achieve nothing but bundles of rich stuffs that bulge or trail or blow about them in effects they half guess to be unsuccessful, and seek to repair with a display of stones.

We pursued the Via Po for a mile or two and alighted at the ugliest of its houses, an example of that modern German architecture that has done so much for factories. As we mounted the stairs she kept muttering: Watch me! Watch me! In the hall we found a host of latecomers standing with their fingers on their lip while from the drawing rooms there issued the sound of passionate declamation accompanied by the plucking of a lyre, the desolate *moto perpetuo* of an oriental flute and a rhythmic clapping of hands. In other words we had arrived too early; our campaign for meeting two thousand souls in ten days was being balked at the outset. Fretted we pushed on into the garden behind the house. Sitting down on a stone bench, with the tragic ode still faintly sounding in our ears we gave our attention to the spectacle in the middle distance of a white-haired gentleman in a wheel-chair overflowing with brightly-colored shawls. This was Jean Perraye; I told the Princess of how Mme. Agaropoulos had found the saintly old French poet at the point of death, wrapt in shawls in a wretched little hotel at Pisa, and how by supplying him with tender interest, whole milk and a group of pet animals she had restored his muse, comforted his last years and effected his entrance into the French Academy. At this moment he was engaged in addressing a circle of attentive cats. These six cats, intermittently licking the fine silk of their shoulders, and casting polite glances at their patron, were gray angoras, the color of cigarette ash. We had read the poet's latest book and knew their names: six queens of France. We practically dozed on the bench—the hot sunlight, the choruses of the *Antigone* behind and Jean Perraye's exordium to the queens of France and Persia before, would have made drowsy even those who had not passed a night of confession and tears.

When we came to ourselves the audition was over and the company, doubly noisy after music, was shouting its appreciation. We re-entered the house, hungry for pastry and encounters. A sea of hats, with scores of self-conscious eyes staring about in perpetual search of new salutations, marking down the Princess for their own; occasionally the large stomach of a senator or an ambassador swathed in serge and bound with a golden chain.

Who's the lady in the black hat? whispered Alix.

Signora Daveni, the great engineer's wife.

Fancy! Will you bring her to me or should you take me to her. No, I'll go to her. Take me.

Signora Daveni was a plain little woman presenting the high

lifted forehead and fresh eyes of an idealistic boy. Her husband was one of Italy's foremost engineers, an inventor of many tremendous trifles in airplane construction and a bulwark of conservative methods in the rising storm of labor agitation. The Signora was on every philanthropic committee of any importance in the whole country and during the War had directed incalculable labors. The consciousness of her responsibilities combined with a touch of brusqueness from her humble extraction had brought her into many a short triumphant struggle with cabinets and senates and there are stories of her having sharply rebuked the vague, well-intentioned interferences of the royal ladies of Savoy. Yet these distinctions had only made her manners the simpler and her quick cordiality was continually deflating the deference that was paid to her. She dressed badly; she walked badly, her large feet pushing before her like those of some jar-carrier in an upland village. It had been rather fine in uniform, but now that she must return to hats and gowns and rings the consciousness of her lack of grace caused her much depression. Her home was in Turin, but she lived a great deal in Rome out among the open lots of the Via Nomentana and knew everyone. The Princess with the unexpectedness that lies in the very definition of genius turned the conversation upon the use of sphagnum moss as a surgical dressing. The diverse excellence of the two women glimpsed one another; the Princess was astonished to find such quiet mastery in a woman without a *de* and the Signora was amazed to find the same quality in a noblewoman.

I drifted off, but presently the Princess rejoined me. She is real, that woman. I am going to dinner with her Friday; so are you. Find me some more. Who is that blonde with the voice?

You don't want to know her, Princess.

She must be important with that voice; who is she?

She is the woman in the whole world who is most your opposite.

Then I must know her. Will she give me tea and introduce me
to a dozen people?

Oh, yes, she'll do that. But you haven't a thing in common. She
is a narrow British woman, Princess. Her only interest is in the
Protestant Church. She lives in a little British hotel. . . .

But where does she get that *authority*—and the Princess made a
gesture of perfect mimicry.

Well, I admitted, she has received the highest honors an Eng-
lishwoman can receive. She wrote a hymn and they made her a
Dame of the British Empire.

You see I must be caught out of myself. I must meet her right
now.

So I led her up to Dame Edith Steuert, Mrs. Edith Foster
Prichard Steuert, author of "Far From Thy Ways, I Strayed," the
greatest hymn since Newman's. Daughter, wife, sister, what not,
of clergymen, she lived in the most exciting currents of Angli-
canism. Her conversation ran on vacant livings and promising
young men from Shropshire, and on the editorials in the latest *St.
George's Banner* and *The Anglican Cry*. She sat on platforms and
raised subscriptions and got names. She seemed to be forever
surrounded by a ballet of curates and widows who, at her word,
rose and swayed and passed the scones. For she was the author of
the greatest hymn of modern times and gazing at her one wondered when the mood could have struck this loud conceited
woman, the mood that had prompted those eight verses of despair
and humility. The hymn could have been written by Cowper, that
gentle soul exposed to the flame of an evangelism too hot even for
Negroes. For one minute in her troubled girlhood all the intermittent sincerity of generations of clergymen must have combined
in her, and late at night, full of dejections she could not understand, she must have committed to her diary that heartbroken

confession. Then the fit was over, and over for ever. It was a telling example of that great mystery in religious and artistic experience: the occasional profundity of nobodies. Dame Edith Steuert on being presented, straightened visibly to show that she was not impressed by the title. With a candor that was another surprise, Alix asked her if she might use her name as reference on her nephew's application for entrance into Eton College. To be sure the nephew was in Lyons, but if Dame Edith would permit the Princess to call upon her some afternoon she would bring some of the boy's letters, photographs and sufficient apparatus to convince her that he was a student recommendable. Friday afternoon was agreed upon, and the Princess rejoined me for new introductions.

So it went on for an hour. The Princess had no method; each new encounter was a new problem. Within three minutes the meeting became an acquaintance, and the acquaintance a friendship. Little did the new friends guess how strange it was to her. She kept asking me what their husbands "did." It delighted her to think that their husbands did anything; she had never guessed that one could meet such people and smiled amazedly like a girl about to meet a real printed poet. A doctor's wife, the wife of a man in rubber, fancy. . . . Toward the end of the afternoon her enthusiasm waned. I feel a little dusty, she whispered. I feel very Bovary. To think that all this has been going on in Rome without my knowing it. I'll go and say goodbye to Mme. Agaropoulos,—*tiens,* who is that beautiful lady. That is an American, isn't it? Quick.

For the only time in my life I saw the beautiful and unhappy Mrs. Darrell who had come to take leave of her Roman friends. As she entered the room a silence fell upon the company; there was something antique, something Plato would have seized upon in the effect of her beauty. She made much of it, with that touch of conceit that we allow to a great musician listening exaggeratedly to his own perfect phrasing, or to the actor who sets aside author, fellow-players and the fable itself, in order to improvise the last excessive moments of a death scene. She dressed, she glanced, she moved and spoke as only uncontested beauties may: she too revived a lost fine art. To this virtuosity of appearing, her illness and suffering had added a quality even she could not estimate, a magic of implied melancholy. But all this perfection of hers was unapproachable; none of her dearest friends, not even Miss Morrow, dared to kiss her. She was like a statue in a solitude. She presuffered her death, and her spirit was set in defiance. She hated every atom of a creation where such things were possible. The next week she was to retire to her villa at Capri with her collection of Mantegnas and Bellinis and to live through four months with their treacherous love-affair and to die. But this day in the serenity of the selfishness that was her perfection and the selfishness that was her illness she effaced the room.

He would have loved me if I had looked like that, breathed Alix into my ear, and sinking into a retired chair covered her mouth with her hand.

Mme. Agaropoulos took Helen Darrell's fingertips a little timidly and led her to the finest chair. No one seemed able to say anything. Luigi and Vittorio, sons of the house, went up and kissed her hand; the American ambassador approached to compliment her.

She is beautiful. She is beautiful, muttered Alix to herself. The world is hers. She will never have to suffer as I must. She is beautiful.

It would not have consoled the Princess if I had explained to her that Helen Darrell, having been admired extravagantly from the cradle, had never been obliged to cultivate her intelligence to retain her friends and that, if I may say it respectfully, her mind was still that of a school-girl.

Fortunately the flautist was still there to play and during the performance of the Paradise music from Orpheus scarcely a pair of eyes in the room left the newcomer's face. She sat perfectly straight, allowing herself none of the becoming attitudes which music suggests to her kind, no ardent attention, no starry-eyed revery. I remember thinking she marked too deliberately the anti-sentimental. When the music was over she asked to be taken to say goodbye, for the present, to Jean Perraye. From the window I could see them alone together, with the gray cats, queens of France, moving meaninglessly about them. One wonders what they said to one another as she knelt beside his chair: as he said later, they loved one another because they were ill.

Alix d'Espoli would not stir until she knew that Mrs. Darrell had left the house and garden. All her suffering had rushed back upon her. She pretended to be sipping a cup of tea while she gathered herself together. I understand now, she murmured hoarsely. God has never meant me to be happy. Others may be happy with one another. But I shall never be. I know that now. Let us go.

Then began what was ever after known to the Cabala as Alix aux Enfers. She would lunch at a tiny pension with some English spinsters; stop in at some studio in the Via Margutta; pass through a reception at an Embassy; dance till seven at the Hotel Russie as the guest of some cosmetic manufacturer's wife; dine with the Queen Mother; hear the last two acts of the Opera in Marconi's box. Even after that she might feel the need of finishing the day at the Russian cabaret, perhaps contributing herself a monologue to the program. She no longer had any time to see the Cabala and it watched her progress with terror. They begged her to come back to them, but she only laughed at them with her bright febrile eyes and dashed off into her new-found whirlpools. Long after when some Roman name arose in their conversation they would all cry: Alix knows them! To which she would reply coolly: Of course I know them, and a roar would arise from the table. The acquaintances she was now pursuing for distraction, I had long since pursued for study or from simple liking; but she soon outstripped me by the hundreds. I went to a few engagements with her, but often enough we would come upon one another in ludicrous situations; whereupon we would retire behind a door and compare notes as to how we got there. Did Commendatore Boni ask a few people to the Palatine? she was there. Did Benedetto Croce give a private reading of a paper on George Sand? we glimpsed one another gravely in that solemn air. She lost a comb in defense of Reality at the stormy opening of Pirandello's *Sei Personaggi in Cerca d'Autore;* at Casella's party for Mengelberg, who had been surpassing himself at the Augusteo, dear old Bossi stood on her train and the sound of ripping satin caught the enraptured ear of a dozen organists.

When the bourgeoisie discovered that she was accepting invitations there was a tumult as of many waters. Most of her hostesses assumed that she would not have come to them were it not for the fact that better doors were beginning to be closed against her, but fair or foul they would accept her. And they had her at her best; the faint touch of frenzy that was driving her on only rendered her gift the more dazzling. People who had spent their lives laughing at tiresome jokes were now given something to laugh at. She would be begged to do this or that "bit" which had become famous. Have you heard Alix do the Talking Horse? No, but she did the Kronprinz in Frascati for us last Friday. Oh, aren't you lucky!

For the first time she was seeing something of artists and among them she was enjoying her liveliest successes. The underpainting of her misery which especially these days rendered her wit so magical was much clearer to them than to the manufacturers. They never failed to mention it and their love led them to paying her the strangest tributes which at the time she was in too great a daze to stop and value.

For a while I thought she was enjoying all this. She would laugh so naturally over some of the accidents of the days. Moreover I noticed that she was forming some very rare attachments and I hoped that the friendship of Signora Daveni or of Duse or of Besnard would be able to comfort and finally reconcile her. But one evening I was suddenly shown how utterly ineffectual this plunging about the jungle was.

After a month's absence James Blair wrote me from Spain that he had to come back to Rome, even if it were only for a week. He promised to see no one, to keep up side streets and to get out as soon as it was possible.

I wrote him back in the strongest profanity that it was impossible. Go anywhere else. Don't fool with such things.

He replied, no less angry, that he could move about the earth as freely as everybody else. Whether I liked it or not he was coming to Rome the following Wednesday and nothing would stop him. He was on the traces of the Alchemists. He wanted to know all that was left of the old secret societies and his search was leading to Rome. Since I could do nothing to prevent his coming I could at least devote my energies to concealing it. I took almost ridiculous precautions. I even saw to it that Mlle. de Morfontaine had Alix in Tivoli over the week-end and that Besnard had her sitting for a portrait most of the mornings. But there is a certain spiritual law that requires our tragic coincidences. Which of us has not felt it? Take no precautions.

The seer whom Blair had returned to visit, Sareptor Basilis, lived in three rooms on the top floor of an old palace in the Via Fontanella di Borghese. Rumor had it that he could make lightning play about his left hand and that when his meditations approached ecstasy he could be seen sitting among the broken arcs of a dozen rainbows; and that as you mounted the dark stairs you fought your way through the welcoming ghosts as through a swarm of bees. In the front room where the meetings were held (Wednesdays for adepts, Saturdays for beginners) one was awed by discovering a circular hole in the roof that was never closed. Under it had been laid a zinc-lined depression that carried off the rain water and in this depression stood the master's chair.

Long meditation and ecstatic trances had certainly beautified his face. His blue-green eyes, not incapable of sudden acuteness, drifted vaguely about under a smooth pink forehead; he had the bushy white eyebrows and beard of Blake's Creator. Except for his long walks he seemed to have no private life, but sat all day and night under the hole in the roof, lending an ear to a whispering visitor, writing slowly with his left hand, or gazing up into the sky. A host of people from every walk of life sought him out and held him in reverence. He gave no thought to practical necessities, for his admirers, spiritually prompted, were continually leaving significant looking envelopes beside him on the zinc-lined depression. Some left bottles of wine and bars of bread, and brown silk shirts. The only human occupation that arrested his attention was music, and it is said that he would stand by the door of the Augusteo on the afternoon of a symphony concert and wait for some passerby, spiritually prompted, to buy him a ticket. If none came, he would continue on his way without bitterness. He composed music himself, hymns for unaccompanied voices which he affirmed he had heard in dream. They were written in a notation resembling our own, but not sufficiently so to allow of transcription. I have puzzled for hours over the score of a certain *Lo, where the rose of dispersion empurples the dawn.* This motet for ten voices, a chorus of angels on the last day, began plainly enough with the treble clef on five staves, but how was one to interpret a sudden shrinkage of the horizontal lines to two in all parts? I humbly approached the master on this subject. He replied that the effect of the music at that point could only be expressed by a radical departure from standard notation; that the economy of staves denoted an acuity of pitch; that the note on which my thumb was reposing was an E, a violet E, an E of the quality of a lately-warmed amethyst . . . music powerless to express . . . ah . . . the rose of dispersion empurples. At first the nonsense in which he moved and thought enraged me. I invented opportunities for provoking his absurdity. I improvised a story about a pilgrim who had come up to me in the nave of the Lateran and told me it was God's will that I should return with him to a leper colony in Australia. Dear Master, I cried, how shall I know if this be my real vocation? His answer was not clear. I was told that destiny herself was the mother of decision, and that my vocation would be settled by events not by consideration. In the next breath I was bidden to do nothing rashly; to lay my ear over the lute of eternity and to plan my life in harmony with the cosmic overtones. During the course of a year thousands of women visited him, of every rank, and in every sort of perplexity, and to each one he offered the comforts of metaphor. They came away from him with shining faces; these phrases were beautiful and profound to them; they wrote them in their diaries and murmured them over to themselves when they were tired.

Basilis was attended by two homely sisters, the Adolfini girls. Lise must have been thirty and Vanna about twenty-eight. They say that he ran across them in the Italian quarter of London where

they were serving as attendants in a ballet school. Penury and
abuse had left them scarcely the human semblance. Every evening
at eleven when they had unlaced the last slipper of the night class,
treated the floor with tallow, polished the bars and tied up the
chandelier, they went around the corner to the Café Roma for a
thimbleful of coffee to sip with their bread. Here Basilis was to be
found, a photographer's assistant with grandiose pretensions. He
was vice-president of the Rosicrucian Mysteries, Soho Chapter, a
group of clerks, waiters and idealistic barbers who found compensation for the humiliations they underwent by day in the glories
they ascribed to themselves by night. They met in darkened rooms,
took oaths with one hand resting on the works of Swedenborg,
read papers on the fabrication of gold and its metaphysical impli-
cations, and elected one another with great earnestness to the
offices of arch-adept and *magister hieraticorum*. They corresponded
with similar societies in Birmingham, Paris and Sydney, and sent
sums of money to the last of the magi, Orzinda-Mazda of Mount
Sinai. Basilis first discovered his power over the minds of women
when he fell into the habit of talking to the two mute sisters in the
café. They listened wide-eyed to his stories of how some workmen
near Rome, breaking by chance into the tomb of Cicero's daughter,
Tulliola, discovered an ever-burning lamp suspended in mid-air,
its wick feeding on Perpetual Principle; of how Cleopatra's son
Caesarion was preserved in a translucent liquid "oil of gold," and
could be still seen in an underground shrine at Vienna; and of how
Virgil never died, but was alive still on the Island of Patmos,
eating the leaves of a peculiar tree. The wonder-stories, the narrator's apocalyptic eyes, the excitement of being spoken to without
anger, and the occasional offer of Vermouth bewitched the sisters.
They became his unquestioning slaves; with the money they had
saved up he opened a Temple where his gift met extraordinary

success. The girls left the ballet school and became doorkeepers in the house of their lord. The new leisure into which they entered, the sufficient food, the privilege of serving Basilis, his confidence and his love, combined to constitute a burden of happiness almost too great to be borne. Happiness is in proportion to humility: the humility of the Adolfini girls was so profound that there was in it no room for the expression of gratitude or surprise; in the face of it food could not fatten them nor love soften their bony features; not even when after some altercation with the London police Basilis and his handmaidens removed to their native Rome. To be sure the master in turn never confessed his indebtedness to the girls for their silent and skillful ministration. Even in love he was impersonal; they merely provided him with that mood of gentle satiety of the senses which is an indispensable element of the philosopher's meditation.

It was under this skylight then that Blair and I sat at about eleven-thirty, waiting for the public séance to begin. We were early, and leaning back against the wall we watched the little group of visitors that one by one moved up to the unboxed confessional that was the master's ear. A clerk with watery eyes and trembling hands; a stout lady of the middle class, gripping a large shopping purse and talking with great rapidity about her *nepote;* a trim little professional woman, probably a lady's maid, stuffing a tiny handkerchief into her mouth as she sobbed. Basilis' eyes seldom strayed to his vistors' faces; while he dismissed them with a few measured grave sentences his glance revealed nothing but its serene abstraction. Presently a younger woman, heavily veiled, crossed the floor swiftly to the empty chair beside him. She must have been there before, for she lost no time in greetings. Under deep emotion she pleaded with him. A little surprised by her vehemence he interrupted her several times with the words *Mia*

figlia. The reproaches only increased her energy, and brushing
back her veil with her hand in order to thrust her face into the
sage's she revealed herself as Alix d'Espoli. Terror went through
me; I seized Blair's arm and made signs that we were to escape.
But at that moment the Princess with a gesture of anger, as though
she had come, not so much to ask the sage's counsel, as to an-
nounce a determination, rose and turned to the door. Unerringly
her eyes met ours, and the rebellious light died out, to be replaced
by fear. For a moment the three of us hung suspended on one cord
of horror. Then the Princess collected herself long enough to
tincture the despairing contraction of her mouth with a smile; she
bowed to us deliberately in turn and passed almost majestically
from the room.

At once I returned home and wrote her a long letter, using the
whole truth as a surgeon in an extremity would resort to a whole-
sale guesswork with the knife. I never received an answer. And our
friendship was over. I had often to meet her again, and we even
came finally to have agreeable conversations together, but we never
mentioned the affair and there was a glaze of impersonality over
her eyes.

From the night she had seen us in Basilis' rooms the Princess
gave up her social researches as abruptly as she had begun them.
Nor did she ever go to the Rosicrucian again. I heard that she was
attempting the few remaining consolations that lie open to afflic-
tion: she took to the fine arts; she climbed up ladders respectfully
placed for her in the Sistine Chapel and stared at the frescos
through magnifying glasses; she resumed the culture of her voice
and even sang a little in public. She started off on a trip to Greece,
but came back without any explanations a week later. There was a
hospital phase during which she cut off her hair and tiptoed about
among the wards.

At last the beating of the wings, the darting about the cage, subsided. She had come to the second stage of convalescence: the mental pain that had been so great that it had to be passed into the physical and that expressed itself in movement, had now sufficiently abated to permit her to think. All her vivacity left her and she sat about in her friends' homes listening to their visitors.

Little by little then her old graces began to reappear. First a few wry sarcasms, gently slipping off her tongue; then some rueful narratives in which she appeared in a poor light; then ever so gradually the wit, the energy, and last of all the humor.

The whole Cabala trembled with joy, but pretended to have noticed nothing. Only one night when for the first time at table she had returned to her gorgeous habit of teasing the Cardinal on his Chinese habits, only once on leaving the table did he take her two hands and gaze deep into her eyes with a significant smile that both reproached her for her long absence and welcomed her back. She blushed slightly and kissed the sapphire.

I, who know nothing about such things, assumed that the grand passion was over and dreaded any moment seeing her interesting herself in some new Northerner. But one little incident taught me how deep a wound may be.

One afternoon at the villa in Tivoli we were standing on the balcony overlooking the falls. Whenever she was left alone with me her charm abated; she seemed to be fearing that I might attempt a confidence; the muscles at the corners of her mouth would tighten. We were joined from the house by a well-known Danish archaeologist who began to discourse upon the waterfall and its classical associations. Suddenly he stopped and turning to me, cried:

Oh, I have a message for you. How could I have forgotten that! I met a friend of yours in Paris. A young American named Blair— let me see, was it Blair?

Yes, Doctor.

What a young man! How many of you Americans are like that? I suppose you never met him, Princess? . . .

Yes, replied Alix, I knew him too.

Such intelligence! He is surely the greatest instinctive scholar I have ever met, and, believe me, perhaps he is all the greater for never putting anything down on paper. And such modesty, Princess,—the modesty of the great scholar that knows that all the learning one human head can hold is but a grain of dust. I spent two whole nights over his notebooks and I honestly felt as though I had brushed against a Leonardo, really, a Leonardo.

We both stood rapt, listening to the waves of happy praise when suddenly I became aware that the Princess had fainted beside me with a happy smile upon her face.

BOOK FOUR

ASTRÉE-LUCE AND THE CARDINAL

There was a vague understanding among the members of the Cabala that I was engaged upon the composition of a play about Saint Augustine. None of my friends had ever seen the manuscript (even I was surprised to come upon it every now and then at the bottom of my trunk), but it was treated with enormous respect. Mlle. de Morfontaine especially kept asking about it, kept walking about on tiptoes and glancing at it sideways. It was to this that she was alluding in the note I received soon after Blair's frightened departure: Try and arrange to come up to the Villa for a few weeks. It is perfectly quiet until five o'clock every afternoon. You can work on your poem.

It was my turn for a little peace. I had so recently passed through the desperations of Marcantonio and Alix. I sat holding the note for a long while, my wary nervous system begging me to be cautious, begging me to make sure that no hysterical evenings could possibly lie behind it. Here was a place where it was perfectly quiet until five o'clock every afternoon. It was five o'clock every morning that I wanted to be reassured about. You can work

on your poem. Surely the only vexation that could proceed from
that wonderful lady lay exactly there,—she would be asking me
every morning about the progress on the Third Act. It would be
good for me to be hectored about my play. And what wonderful
wines she stored. To be sure the lady was mad, indubitably mad.
But mad in a nice way, with perfect dignity; decently mad on a
million a year. I wrote her I would come.

What could have been more reassuring than the first days?
Mornings of sunlight when the dust settled thicker on the olive-
leaves; when the terraced hillside seemed to be powdering away;
when no sound reached the garden but the cry of a carter in the
road, the cooing of doves, stepping high along the eaves of the
gardener's shed, and the sound of the waterfall with its mysterious
retardations, a sound of bronze. I ate luncheon alone under a grape
arbor. The rest of the day was spent in roaming over the hills or
among the high chairs of Astrée-Luce's rich and curious library.

From the middle of the afternoon one sensed the approach of
dinner. One felt the gradual tightening of the chord of formality
until, like the bursting of some pyrotechnical bomb, full of
dazzling lights and fascinating detail, the ceremony began. For
hours there had come a hum as of bees from the wing of the house
that contained the kitchen; there followed the flights of maids and
hairdressers through the corridors, the candle-lighter, the flower-
bearers. The crushing of gravel under the window announces the
arrival of the first guests. The majordomo clasps on his golden
chain and takes his place with the footmen at the door. Mlle. de
Morfontaine descends from her tower kicking her train about to
teach it its flexibility. A string quartet on the balcony begins a waltz
by Glazounov as subdued as a surreptitious rehearsal. The evening
takes on the air of a pageant by Reinhardt. One passes to the
saloon. At the head of the table behind peaks of fruits and ferns,

or cascades of crystal and flowers, sits the hostess, generally in yellow satin, her high ugly face lit with its half-mad surprise. She generally supports a headdress of branching feathers and looks like nothing so much as a bird of the Andes blown to that bleakness by the coldest Pacific breezes.

I have described how Miss Grier brooded over her table and placed herself to hear every word whispered by her remotest guest. Astrée-Luce followed a contrary procedure and heard so little of what was said that her very guest of honor was often obliged to resign all hope of engaging her attention. She would seem to have been caught up into a trance; her eyes would be fixed on some corner of the ceiling as though she were trying to catch the distant slamming of a door. Generally some Cabalist held the opposite end of the table: Mme. Bernstein, huddled up in her rich fur cape, looking like an ailing chimpanzee and turning from side to side the encouraging amiability of her grimace; or the Duchess d'Aquilanera, a portrait by Moroni, her dress a little spotty, her face a little smudged, but somehow evoking all the passionate dishonest splendid barons of her line; or Alix d'Espoli making passes with her exquisite hands and transforming the guests into witty and lovable and enthusiastic souls. Miss Grier seldom came, having festivals of her own to direct. Nor was it often possible to invite the Cardinal, since any company to meet him must be chosen with infinite discretion.

Almost every evening after the last guest had left the hill or retired to bed, and the last servant had finished finding little things to adjust, Astrée-Luce and I would descend into the library and have long talks over a drop of *fine*. It was then that I began to understand the woman and to see where my first judgments had been wrong. This was not a silly spinster of vast wealth nourishing a Royalist chimaera; nor the sentimental half-wit of the philanthropic committees; but a Second-Century Christian. A shy religious girl so little attached to the things about her that she might awake any day and discover that she had forgotten her name and address.

Astrée-Luce has always illustrated for me the futility of goodness without intelligence. The dear creature lived in a mist of real piety; her mind never drifted long from the contemplation of her creator; her every impulse was goodness itself: but she had no brains. Her charities were immense but undigested; she was the prey of anyone who wrote her a letter. Fortunately her donations were small, for she lacked the awareness to be either avaricious or prodigal. I think she would have been very happy as a servant; she would have understood the role, have seen beauty in it, and if her position had been full of humiliation and trials it would have deeply nourished her. Sainthood is impossible without obstacles and she never could find any. She had heard over and over again of the sins of pride and doubt and anger, but never having felt even the faintest twinge she had passed through the earlier stages of the spiritual life in utter bewilderment. She felt sure that she was a wicked sinful woman, but did not know how to go about her own reform. Sloth? She had been on her knees an hour every morning before her maid appeared. So difficult, so difficult is the process of making oneself good. Pride? At last after intense self-examination she thought she had isolated in herself some vestiges of pride. She attacked them with fury. She forced herself to do appalling things in public in order to uproot the propensity. Pride of appearance or of wealth? She soiled her sleeves and bodice intentionally and suffered the silent consternation of her friends.

She read the lessons so literally that I have seen her give away her coat time after time. I have seen her walk miles with a friend who asked her to go as far as the road. Now I was to learn that her fits of abstraction were withdrawals into herself for prayer and adoration, and often caused by almost ludicrous incidents. I was no longer left to wonder why all references to fish and fishing sent her off into the clouds; I realized that the Greek word for fish was the monogram of her Lord and acted upon her much as a muezzin's call acts upon a Mohammedan. A traveller spoke flippantly of the pelican; at once Mlle. de Morfontaine repaired to her mental altar and besought its guest not to grieve at the disrespect paid to one of His most vivid symbols. Strangest illustration of all was shown me a little later. One day she chanced to notice on my hall table an envelope which I had addressed to Miss Irene H. Spencer, a teacher of Latin in the High Schools at Grand Rapids, who had come over to put her hand on the Forum. At once Astrée-Luce insisted on meeting her. I never told Miss Spencer why she had been tendered so amazing a luncheon, why her hostess had listened so breathlessly to her trivial travelogues, nor why on the following day a golden chain hung with sapphires had been left at the pension for her. In fact Miss Spencer was a devout Methodist and would have been shocked to learn that IHS meant anything.

Strange though Mlle. de Morfontaine was, she was never ridiculous. Such utter refusal of self can by sheer excess become a substitute for intelligence. Certainly she was able to let fall remarkably penetrating judgments, judgments that proceeded from the intuition without passing through the confused corridors of our reason. Though she was exasperating at times, at others she would abound in almost miraculous perceptions of one's needs. People as diverse as Donna Leda and myself had to love her, one moment almost with condescension as to an unreasonable child, and the next with awe, with fear in the presence of something of infinite possibility. Whom were we entertaining unawares? Might this, oh literally! be an . . . ?

This then was the being whom I came to know during those late conversations in the library over a drop of *fine*. The talk was leisurely, full of pauses and to no point, but my bruised instinct could no longer escape the conviction that there was some deeply important matter that she wished to submit to me. I soon foresaw that I was not to rest. My dread of the revelation however was heightened by the obvious difficulty Astrée-Luce found in coming to the point. Finally instead of trying to avoid the discussion I tried to provoke it; I thought I could help here and there by opening veins of conversation that might surprise her problem. But no. The happy moment hung off.

One evening, she asked me abruptly whether it would greatly interfere with my work if we were to move to Anzio for a few days. I replied that I should like nothing better. All I knew of Anzio was that it was one of the resorts on the sea, a few hours from Rome, the site of one of Cicero's villas, and near Nettuno. She added a little anxiously that we should have to go to a hotel, a very poor hotel at that, but that it was out of season and there were ways in which she could supply some of the deficiencies of the service. A little foresight could prevent my being too uncomfortable.

So one morning we climbed into the large plain car she reserved for travelling and drove westward. The back seat served as a warehouse. One glimpsed a maid, a prie-dieu, a cat, a real panel by Fra Angelico, a box of wines, fifty books and some window curtains. I found out later that there had been a lavish assortment of caviare, pâté, truffles and ingredients for rare sauces by which, with a discouraging failure to understand me, she intended to supplement the resources of a tourists' hotel. She drove, herself, and in nothing did Heaven's interest in her reveal itself more clearly. First we stopped at Ostia so that I might see the veritable spot where the last scene of my wretched play took place. We read aloud the page of Augustine and I silently vowed to renounce forever any notion of rephrasing it.

On our first evening at Anzio a cold wind blew in from the sea. The vines and shrubs whipped the houses; the lamps of the cafés about the square swung cheerlessly over wet tables; one could not escape the desolate slip-slap of the waves against the sea-wall. But we both had a taste for such weather. We decided at about six o'clock to walk to Nettuno returning for dinner at half-past nine. We wrapped ourselves in rubber and started off, leaning against the wind and spray and feeling strangely exhilarated. For a time we walked in silence, but entering at last that portion of the road that lies between the high walls of the villas, Astrée-Luce began to talk:

I have told you before, Samuele (the whole Cabala had followed the Princess in calling me Samuele), that the hope of my life is to see a king reigning in France. How impossible such a thing seems now! No one knows it better than I. But everything I love most is improbable. And it is the fact that it seems so untimely that will help us most when we come to prepare the Divine Right of Kings as a dogma of the Church. What anger there will be, what sneers! Even important Churchmen will rush down to Rome and beg us not to upset the progress of Catholicism by such a move. There will be controversies. All the newspapers and the reviews will be shouting and weeping and laughing and the whole basis of democratic government, the folly of republics, will be aired. Europe will be cleansed of the poison in its side. We have nothing to fear from debates. The people will turn to God and ask to be ruled by those houses of His choosing.—However, I am not trying to convince you of it now, Samuele; I am only stating it so as to lead up to something else. You are a Protestant; does this make you impatient? Are you tired of me?

No, no, please. I am very interested, I replied.

At that moment our road brought us again to the water's edge. We stood for a moment on a parapet looking down on the loud sea that plunged about on the washing stones of a village. It began to rain. Astrée-Luce was gripping the iron railing watching the steam that rose from the waves; she was crying silently.

Perhaps, she continued, as we returned to our journey, you can imagine the tenth part of my disappointment as I watch the Cardinal getting older, and myself, and the nations falling deeper and deeper into error, and so little done. He can help us. He seems to me to have been especially created to help us. I do not forget his work in China. It was heroic. But what a greater work remains for him in Europe. Year follows year and still he sits up there on the Janiculum, reading and walking in the garden. Europe is dying. He will not stir.

At the time I was deeply moved. The rain and her tears and the puddles and the slapping noises of the water against the sea-wall had begun to affect me. All the voices of nature kept repeating: Europe is Dying. I would have liked to stop and have a good meaningless cry myself, but I had to listen to the voice beside me:

I cannot understand why he does not write. Perhaps I am not meant to understand. I know he believes that the universality of the Church is imminent. I know that he believes that a Catholic Crown is the only possible rule. But he does not stir to help us. All we ask from him is a book on the Church and the States. Think, Samuele, his learning, his logic, his style—but you have never heard him preach? His irony in controversy and his amazing perorations! What would be left of Bosanquet? The constitutions of the republics of the world would be tossed about—you will forgive me if I seem disrespectful to your great country—tossed about like eggshells. His book would not be just a book fallen from the press: it would be a force of nature; it would be the simultaneous birth of an idea in a thousand minds. It would be placed at once in the canon and bound up with the Bible. And yet he spends his day among rose bushes and rabbits and reading histories of this and that. I want to do this in my lifetime; I want to arouse this great man to his task. And you can help me.

I was excited. The air was full of a divine absurdity. Here was someone who was not afraid of using superlatives. This was being mad on a great scale. It would be hard to come down to ordinary living after these intoxicating threats against the presidents of this world and the binderies of the British Bible Society. I tried to think of something to say. I mumbled something about will-ingness.

She did not notice my inadequacy. It seems to me, she continued, that I have at last discovered one of the causes of his reluctance to join us. But first, tell me how he is regarded by the various Romans whom you have met. What is his legend among people who do not know him?

Here I was frightened. Could *she* have heard? How could any of those strange rumors have reached her?

But she would learn nothing from me. I took leave of good faith and told her all the favorable reports I had heard. Simple souls were captivated by the thought that apart from a few major obligations he lived on sixty-five lire a week; that he spoke twelve languages; that he enjoyed polenta; that he visited in certain Roman homes (her own, in particular) without ceremony; that he was translating the Confessions and the Imitation into exquisite Chinese. I knew Romans who so loved the very thought of him that they took walks to the Janiculan Hill solely to peer between his garden gates and lurked about the house in the hope of giving their children an opportunity to kiss his ring.

Astrée-Luce waited in silence. At last she said with only a trace of reproach:

You are trying to spare me, Samuele. But I know. There are other stories about him. His enemies have been at work systematically poisoning his prestige. We know that there is no one in Rome who is kinder, more humble, higher-minded; but among the common people he has almost the reputation of a monster. Some people have been at work spreading such rumors deliberately. And the Cardinal has heard of them: through the whispering of servants or by cries in the road, or by anonymous letters, in all sorts of ways. He exaggerates this attitude. He feels that he is in a hostile world. It has made his old age tragic. And that is why he will not write. Yet it is within our power to save him still.—But look! There is a francobollo shop. Let us get some cigarettes and find some place to sit down. It makes me so happy to talk of this!

Provided with cigarettes we looked about for a wine shop. Our wish evoked one at the next curve in the road, a smoky uncordial tunnel, but we sat down before the glasses of sour inky wine and continued our conspiracy. Astrée-Luce confessed that if the ill-odor had become attached to the Cardinal's name through any real delinquencies on his part, we could not have hoped to dissipate it. Truth in such subtle regions as rumor would be unalterable. But she knew that the aspersions in this case were the result of a clever campaign and she felt sure that a countercampaign could still sweeten his reputation. In the first place our enemies had taken advantage of the Italians' prejudice against the Orient. An Italian enjoys the same delicious shudder at the sight of a Chinaman that an American boy does at the mention of a trapdoor over a river. The Cardinal had returned from the East yellow, unwrinkled. His walk troubled them. It was easy to build upon this, to pass the whisper along the Trasteverine underworld that he kept strange images, that animals (his gardenful of rabbits and ducks and guinea fowl) could be heard shrieking late at night, that his faithful Chinese servant had been seen in all sorts of terrifying attitudes. Next, his frugal life stirred their imaginations. Every one knew he was fabulously wealthy. Rubies as big as your fist and sapphires like doorknobs, where were they? Did you ever go up to the gate of the Villino Wei Ho? Come with me Sunday. If you sniff hard enough you can get the strangest odor, one that will leave you drowsy for days and give you dreams.

We were to change all this. We sat there choosing a committee of rehabilitation. We were to have magazine articles, newspaper paragraphs. His eightieth birthday was approaching. There would be presentations. Mlle. de Morfontaine was donating a Raphael altar piece to his titular church. But most of all we would send out agents among the people, telling them of his goodness, his simplicity, his donations to their hospitals, and ever so faintly his sympathy with socialistic ideas; he was to be the People's Cardinal. We had anecdotes of his snubbing the arrogant members of the College, of his defending a poor man who had stolen a chalice from his church. China was to be re-created for the Trasteverines. And so on. We were to prop up the Cardinal so that the Cardinal could prop up Europe.

When we returned to the hotel that night Astrée-Luce seemed to have grown ten years younger. Apparently I was the first person to whom she had outlined her vision. She was so eager to be at work that she suddenly asked me if I minded packing up again and going back to Tivoli that night. We could the better start work in the morning. What she really wanted was the exhilaration and fatigue of driving (her terrible driving) before she went to bed. So we put back into the car the maid, the Fra Angelico, the ingredients for sauces and the cat, and returned to the Villa Horace at about two in the morning.

The Cardinal was not to know that we were putting up a scaffolding about his good name and freshening the colors; but we were to persuade him not to do some of the things that particularly antagonized the public. The very next morning Astrée-Luce shyly begged me to go and see him. She did not know why, but she had a vague idea that now I knew her hopes my eyes would be open to significant details.

I found him as one could find him every sunny day the year round, seated in the garden, a book on his knee, a reading glass in his left hand, a pen in his right, a head of cabbage and a Belgian hare at his feet. A pile of volumes lay on the table beside him: *Appearance and Reality,* Spengler, *The Golden Bough, Ulysses,* Proust, Freud. Already their margins had begun to exhibit the spidery notations in green ink that indicated a closeness of attention that would embarrass all but the greatest authors.

He laid aside his magnifying glass as I came up the path of shells. *Eccolo, questo figliolo di Vitman, di Poe, di Vilson, di Guglielmo James,—di Emerson, che dico!* What do you want?

Mlle. de Morfontaine wants you to come to dinner Friday night, just the three of us.

Very good. Very nice. What else?

What do you want, Father, for your birthday? Mlle. de Morfontaine wants me to sound you tactfully . . .

Tactfully!—Samuelino, walk to the back of the house and tell my sister you will stay to lunch. I am to have a little Chinese vegetable dish. Will you have that or a little risotto and chestnut-paste? You can buy yourself something solid on the way down hill. How is Astrée-Luce?

Very well.

A little illness would be good for her. I am uncomfortable when

I am with her. There are certain doctors, Samuele, who are not
happy when they are talking to people in good health. They are so
used to the supplicating eyes of patients that say: Shall I live? In
the same way I am ill at ease in the company of persons who have
never suffered. Astrée-Luce has eyes of blue porcelain. She has a
fair pure heart. It is sweet to be in the company of a fair pure
heart, but what can one say to it?

There was St. Francis, Father . . . ?

But he had been libertine in his youth, or thought he had.—
Senta! Who can understand religion unless he has sinned? who can
understand literature unless he has suffered? who can understand
love unless he has loved without response? *Ecc!* The first sign of
Astrée-Luce's being in trouble was last month. There is a certain
Monsignore who wants her millions for his churches in Bavaria.
Every few days he climbs the hill to Tivoli and breathes into her
ear: *And the rich He hath sent empty away.* The poor child
trembles and pretty soon Bavaria will have some enormous
churches, too ugly for words. Oh, you know, there is for every
human being one text in the Bible that can shake him, just as every
building has a musical note that can overthrow it. I will not tell
you mine, but do you want to know Leda d'Aquilanera's? She is a
great hater, and they say that during the Pater Noster she closes her
teeth tight upon: *Sicut et nos dimittimus debitoribus nostris.*

At this he laughed for a long time, his body shaking in silence.

But was not Astrée-Luce devoted to her mother? I asked.

No, she has had no losses. That was when she was ten. She has
poetized her, that is all.

Father, why did not that literal faith of hers carry her to a
convent?

She promised her dying mother she would stay alive to put a
Bourbon on the throne of France.

How can you laugh, Father, at her devotion to . . .

We old men are allowed to laugh at things that you little students may not even smile about. Oh, oh, the house of Bourbon. Would you be surprised if I gave up my life to reviving the royal brother-and-sister marriages of Egypt? Well! It is not more impossible.

Dear Father, won't you write one more book? Look, you have about you all the greatest books of the first quarter of my century . . .

And very stupid they are, too.

Won't you make us one. Such a great book, Father Vaini. About yourself, essays like Montaigne,—about China and about your animals and Augustine . . .

Stop! No! Stop at once. You frighten me. Do not you see that the first sign of childhood in me will be the crazy notion that I should write a book? Yes, I could write a book better than this ordure that your age has offered us (and with a sharp blow he pushed over the tower of books; the Belgian hare gave a squeal as he barely escaped being pinned under Schweitzer's *Skizze*). But a Montaigne, a Machiavelli . . . a . . . a . . . Swift, I will never be. How horrible, how horrible it would be if you should come here some day and find me writing. God preserve me from the last folly. Oh, Samuele, Samuelino, how bad of you to come here this morning, and awaken all the vulgar prides in an old peasant. No, don't pick them up. Let the animals soil them. What is the matter with this Twentieth Century of yours . . .? You want me to compliment you because you have broken the atom and bent light? Well, I do, I do.—You may tell our rich friends, tactfully, that I want for my birthday a small Chinese rug now reposing in the window of a shop on the Corso. It would be unbecoming for me to say more than that it is on the left as you approach the Popolo.—The floor of my bedroom is getting colder every morning, and I always promised myself that when I became eighty I might have a rug in my bedroom.

What went wrong?

The first hour was delightful. The Cardinal always ate very little (never meat) and that with preposterous slowness. If his soup took him ten minutes his rice required half an hour. To be sure the elements of trouble were present merely in these friends' characters. They were so different that just to hear them talking together had an air of high comedy. First, Astrée-Luce made the mistake of referring to the Bavarian Monsignore. She suspected that the Cardinal was out of sympathy with any plans she might have of helping the Church in that direction; she longed to talk over with him the problem of her wealth and its disposition, but he refused to give her the least advice. He had endless resources of ingenuity in evading the subject. As Rome was arranged at that time it was most important that he should exercise no influence on that aspect of his friend's life. Yet he allowed it to be seen that he knew she would handle the matter foolishly. It ailed him to see such an enormous instrument for progress drift down the wind of ecclesiastical administration.

Now we must remember that it was the eve of his eightieth birthday. We have already seen that the event had precipitated a flood of amused bitterness. As he said later, he should have died at the moment of leaving his work in China. The eight years that had elapsed since then had been a dream of increasing confusion. Living is fighting and away from the field the most frightening changes were taking place in his mind. Faith is fighting, and now that he was no longer fighting he couldn't find his faith anywhere. This vast reading was doing something to him. . . . But most of all we must remember his terror at the thought that the people of

Rome hated him. He would leave in dying a memory without affection and without dignity. An anonymous letter had told him that even in Naples children were kept in good behavior with threats that the Yellow Cardinal would skin them. If one were young one would laugh at such a rumor, but being old one grew cold. He was leaving a world where he was shuddered at for a world that was no longer as distinct as it had been, but which might yet have this consolation that he would not be able to look down from it and see the people surreptitiously spitting on the endings in *issimus* that would compose his epitaph.

Before I knew it we were in the middle of a wrangle about prayer. Astrée-Luce had always longed to hear the Cardinal discourse upon abstract matters. She had often tried to draw him into arguments on the frequent communion and on the invocation of the saints. He had once whispered to me that she was trying to extract from him the materials for a calendar, such sweet manuals as she could buy in the Place Saint Sulpice. Every word of his was sacred. She would not have hesitated to put him in a Church window with St. Paul. It was only after a few moments that she became aware that he was saying some rather strange things. Could that be Doctrine? If anything he said was difficult all she had to do was to try hard to grasp it. Truth, new truth. So she listened, first with surprise, then with mounting terror.

He was launched upon the paradox that in prayer one should never ask for anything. His dialectic was doing an incredible work. He had decided to be Socratic and was asking Astrée-Luce questions. He wrecked her on several orthodox assumptions. Twice she fell into heresy and was condemned by the councils. She seized hold of St. Paul but the epistle broke in her hand. She came to the surface for the third time but was struck by a Thomist fragment.

The previous week the Cardinal had been called to the deathbed of a certain Donna Matilda della Vigna, and it was poor Donna Matilda who was now dragged forth to point the argument. Exactly what had the survivors been praying for? Astrée-Luce was easily routed from the more obvious positions. She became frightened. Presently she rose:

I don't understand. I don't understand. You are joking, Father. Aren't you ashamed of saying such things to bewilder me, when you know how I value everything you say.

Look, then, continued the Cardinal. I shall ask Samuele about this. As he is only a Protestant it will be very easy to entangle him. Samuele, may I assume that God may have intended Donna Matilda to die before long anyway?

Yes, Father, for she died that very night.

But we thought that if we prayed very sincerely we might change His mind.

Why . . . there is authority for our hoping that in extremities our prayer may. . . .

But she died. Then we were not sincere enough! Or persevering enough! Good! Sometimes He grants and sometimes He doesn't, and Christians are expected to pray hard on the chance that this is one of the times He might relent. What a notion! Astrée-Luce, what a thought!

Father, I can't stay and hear you talk this way . . .

What a view of these things. Listen. It is incredible that He should change His mind. Because we frightened mortals are on the carpet? Oh! You are a slave to the idea of bargain. The money changers are still in the temple!

Here Astrée-Luce, gone quite white, returned to the arena with one more brave venture: But, Father, you know He answers the requests of a good Catholic. Then she added in a lower voice with tears in her eyes. But you were there, dear Father. If you had deeply wished it you could have altered the . . .

Here he half rose from his chair crying with terrible eyes: Insane child! What are you saying? I? *Have I no losses?*

Now she flung herself upon the floor before him. You have been saying these things to prove me. What is the answer? I will not let you go until you tell me. Dear Father, you know that prayer is answered. But your clever questions have upset all my old . . . old . . . What is the answer?

Come, sit down, my daughter, and tell me yourself. Think!

This went on for another half-hour. I grew more and more astonished. Mere prayer as a problem was soon left far behind. It was the idea of a benignant power behind the world that was being questioned now. For the Cardinal it was an exercise in rhetoric, sharpened by his temperamental scepticism on the one hand and by his latent resentment against Astrée-Luce on the other. It was a kind of questioning that would have had no effect on sound intellectual believers. It was disastrous for Astrée-Luce because she was a woman without a reason who just this once was trying to reason. She would so have liked to have been a deep thinker, and when she fell it was through her desire to be a different person.

It went on and on. At every fresh proposal he would now cry Bargain! A Bargain! and point out that her prayers sprang from fear or the greed for comfort. Astrée-Luce was going to pieces. I moved over behind her chair and pleaded with the Cardinal by gesture. Was he tormenting her out of caprice? Did he realize her devotion to himself?

At last she seemed to have a light:

My head is in a whirl. But I know now what you mean me to

answer. We may not ask for things, or people, or relief from sickness, but we may ask for spiritual qualities; for instance for the advancement of the Church . . . ?

Vanity! Vanity! How many years have we been praying for a certain good thing? What have statistics shown us?—I refer to the conversion of France.

With a cry Astrée-Luce rose and left the room. I took upon myself to protest to him.

She is foolish, Samuelino. You cannot call those convictions deep that were overturned with straws. No, trust me. This is for her good. I have been a confessor too long to go astray here. She has the spiritual notions of a school-girl. She must be fed on some harsher bread. Understand that she has never suffered. She is good. She is devout. But as I told you the other day, just by accident she has never known trouble.

Just the same, Eminence, I know her well enough to know that this very moment she is in her chapel, clinging to the altar-rails. She will be depressed for weeks.

But just at that moment Astrée-Luce returned. Her manner was agitated and artificially gracious. Will you excuse me if I go to bed now? she asked. (She never called him Father again.) Please stay and talk with Samuele.

No, no. I must be going. But before I go let me tell you one thing. The real truths are difficult. At first they are forbidding. But they are worth all the others.

I shall be thinking over what we have said.—I . . . I . . . Excuse me, if I ask you something?

Yes, my child, what is it?

Promise me you weren't joking.

I wasn't joking at all.

Did I really hear you say that the prayers of good men are of no . . . ? However. Goodnight. You will forgive my slipping away now?

So they took their leaves.

I went to bed worried. I was worrying about Astrée-Luce. Was she going to lose her faith? What do bystanders do in such a case? The loss of one's faith is always comic to outsiders, especially when the loser is in fine health, wealth, and a fairly sound mind. The loss of any one or all of these has a sort of grandeur; Astrée-Luce should have the loss of her faith depend on one of the others. It's not a thing one loses in fine weather.

I was wakened from a troubled sleep by a discreet but continuous knocking upon my door. It was Alviero, the majordomo.

Madame says will you please dress and come to her in the library, please.

What's the matter, Alviero?

I do not know, Signorino. Madame have not sleeped all night. She have been in the church hitting the floor.

All right, Alviero, I'll be there in a minute. What time is it?

Three o'clock and one-half, Signorino.

I dressed rapidly and hurried to the library. Astrée-Luce was still in her gown. Her face was white and drawn; her hair was disheveled. She came toward me with both hands extended: You will forgive my sending for you, won't you? I want you to help me. Tell me: were you made unhappy by the strange things Cardinal Vaini said after dinner?

Yes.

Have you Protestants ideas on these things?

Oh, yes, Mlle. de Morfontaine.

Were his ideas new? Is that what everyone is thinking?

No.

Oh, Samuele, what has happened to me! I have sinned. I have sinned the sin of doubt. Shall I ever have peace again? Can the

Lord take me back after I have had such thoughts? Of course, of course, I believe that my prayers are answered, but I have lost . . . the . . . the reason why I believe it. Surely, there is a key here. Perhaps it's just one word. All you have to do is find the one little argument that makes the whole thing natural. Isn't it strange! I've been looking here (and she pointed at the table which was covered with open books, the Bible, Pascal, the Imitation) but I don't seem to be able to put my finger on the right place. Sit down and try and tell me, my dear friend, what arguments there are that God hears us speak and will answer us.

I talked to her for quite a long while, but achieved nothing. Perhaps I even made it worse. I told her that I was sure that she still believed. I showed her that the very fact that she was distressed about it proved that she was furiously believing. After an hour of this wrestling she seemed a little comforted, however, and picking up a fur coat went back to her cold chapel and prayed diligently for faith until the morning.

At about ten she appeared in the garden and asked me to read a note that she was sending to the Cardinal. I was to pass on it. Dear Cardinal Vaini, I will always honor you above all my friends. I think you love me and wish me well. But in your great learning and multiple interests you have forgotten that we who are not brilliant must cling to our childhood beliefs as best we may. I have been inexpressibly troubled since yesterday evening. I want to ask a favor of you: that you indulge my weakness to the extent of not touching upon matters of belief when I am with you. It gives me great pain to have to ask you this. I beg of you to understand it as apart from any personal feelings of unfriendliness. I hope that I may grow strong enough to talk of these matters with you again.

It was a very bad letter, but that was perhaps due to the content. I suggested shyly that she omit the last sentence. So she copied it and sent it off by a special messenger.

Soon the day came for the end of my stay in the Villa. She came up to my room for a last talk.

Samuele, you have been with me during the saddest days of my life. I cannot deny that all interest has gone out of living for me. I still believe, but I don't believe as I used to. Perhaps it was not right that I went through life as I did. Now I know that I rose up every morning full of unspeakable happiness. It seldom left me. I had never thought before that my beliefs in themselves were unbelievable. I used to boast that they were, but I did not know what I was saying. Now hours come to me when I hear a voice saying: There is no prayer. There is no God. There are people and trees, millions of them both, every moment dying.—You will come and see me again, won't you, Samuele? Have I made it very unpleasant for you in the house?

When I reached my rooms in Rome I found three letters from the Cardinal asking me to come and see him at once. As I entered the gate he came toward me eagerly:

How is she? Is she well?

No, Father, she is in great trouble.

Come inside, my son. I must speak to you.

When we entered his study, he closed his door behind him, and said with great emotion: I want to say to you that I have sinned, greatly sinned. I cannot rest until I have tried to repair the harm I have done. Look, look at this letter she has written me.

Yes, I have seen it.

Her letter forbids my explaining what I meant. Is there no way I can reassure her?

There is only one way now. You must regain all her confidence before you touch on such matters again. You must come and go about her house as though nothing had happened—

Oh, but she will never ask me again!

Yes, she is having you all to dinner quite soon, Alix, Donna Leda, and M. Bogard.

Thanks be to God! I thank Thee, I thank Thee, I thank Thee, I thank Thee . . .

May I speak quite boldly, Eminence?

Yes. I am a poor old man, all mistakes. Speak to me as you like.

If you go, take great care not to let slip any remark on religious matters. I beg of you, do *not* try to reinstate yourself with some orthodox comments. She might misunderstand one little word and think you were attacking her faith again. It is very serious. Your ideas are not orthodox, Father, and if you said an orthodox thing it would not sound sincere and that would be worst of all. But if you come and go simply and affectionately, she will lose her horror of you—

Horror of me!

Yes, and very gradually, perhaps after a year, you may be able—

But I may not live a year!

Es muss sein!

This struck him as humorous and ruefully he sang Beethoven's phrase, adding: All the avenues of life lead to that.

Grave   Allegro

Muss es sein?   Es muss sein!   Es muss sein!

Es muss sein. I should have stayed in China. (Here he fell silent for a while, heaving deep sighs and staring at his yellow hands.) God has chosen to take away my reason. I am an idiot, falling into every ditch. Oh, that I had died long ago—and yet I cannot die until I have righted myself. Hand me that red book behind you. There are two plays about old men, Samuelino, that grow dearer every day to an old man. There is your Lear, and—and opening *Oedipus at Colonus* he translated slowly:

Generous son of Aegeus, to the gods alone old age and death come never. But all else is confounded by all-mastering time. The strength of earth decays and the strength of the body. Faith dies. Distrust is born. Among friends the same spirit does not last true . . . and bowing his head he let the book fall to the floor. *Es muss sein.*

I did not go to that dinner. I dined alone with Miss Grier in the city, but at about ten we drove out to Tivoli to sit with the company. As we went I outlined to her discreetly the relations that now existed between two of her best friends: Oh, how stupid he is, she cried. How cruel! What a lot he has forgotten. Don't you see that the whole thing rests, not on the abstract question as to whether her prayers may be answered, but on the question as to whether ONE prayer may be answered? Her prayer for France . . . Doesn't he believe such things are real to other people?

He thinks that a little doubt will be good for her. He describes her as the woman who has never suffered.

He is in his dotage. I am so angry I am ill.

At this moment our car drew aside to let pass another hurrying by towards Rome. This was Mlle. de Morfontaine's great ugly travelling car and the Cardinal was in it.

There he is now, cried Miss Grier. They must have broken up early.

Something's happened, I said.

Yes, something has very likely happened, God forgive us. If

everything were all right, Alix would be driving back with him. Our wonderful company is dissolving. Alix no longer trusts us. Leda is losing her good old commonsense. Astrée-Luce has quarrelled with the Cardinal. I'd better leave Rome and go back to Greenwich.

As we approached the Villa we became aware that something indeed must have happened. The front door was open. The servants were gathered in the hall whispering in front of the closed doors of the drawing rooms. As we entered these opened and Alix, Donna Leda and Mme. Bernstein appeared supporting a sobbing Astrée-Luce. They led her up the stairs to her tower. Miss Grier without questioning the servants as to what had happened, gently urged them to return to their rooms. We passed into the drawing room just in time to see M. Bogard leaving by another door and looking considerably shaken. We sat down in silence, our thoughts full of foreboding. Simultaneously we became aware of a faint odor of powder and smoke and glancing about my eye fell upon a rent near the ceiling beneath which a little pile of white dust had collected on the floor. Mme. Bernstein hurried in and after closing the door carefully behind her, came toward us:

Not a soul must hear of this. Oh, this must be kept so quiet. What a thing to happen! Anything is possible after this. What a blessing that no servants were in the room when . . .

Miss Grier asked her several times what had happened.

I know nothing. I can hardly believe my own senses, she cried. Astrée-Luce must have gone mad. Elizabeth, will you believe me when I tell you that we were sitting here quietly over our coffee— Look, look! I didn't see that hole in the ceiling before!—Isn't it all frightful?

Please, Anna, please tell us what happened!

I am.—There we were sitting over our coffee, talking in low

voices of this and that, when suddenly Astrée-Luce went over to the piano, picked up a revolver from among the flowers and shot at the good Cardinal.

Anna! is he hurt?

No. It didn't even come near him. But what a thing to happen! What on earth could have made her do such a thing! We were friends—we were all such good friends. I do not understand anything.

Try and think, Anna: did she say anything when she fired at him, or before she fired?

That's the strangest of all. You won't believe me. She called out: The Devil is here. The Devil has come into this room. At the Cardinal!

What had he been saying?

Nothing! Merely everyday things. We had been telling stories about the peasants. He had been telling us about some peasants he had come across on his walks outside S. Pancrazio.

Suddenly Alix appeared: Elizabeth, go to her quickly. She wants to see you. She is alone.

Miss Grier hurried out.

Alix turned to me:

Samuele, you know the majordomo better than we do. Will you go and tell him that Astrée-Luce has had a nervous breakdown. That she thought she saw a burglar at the window, and that she fired at him. It is so important for the dear Father's sake that no hint of this gets about.

I went out and found Alviero. He knew the explanation was insufficient, but utterly devoted to the whole Cabala he could be trusted to dress the story at exactly the points that would most convince the other servants.

Alix did not understand what lay back of the shot, but she was able to recall the conversation that had led up to it. The Cardinal had told the following simple story, an incident he had witnessed in one of his walks outside the city wall:

A farmer wished to break his six-year-old daughter of crying. One afternoon he led her by the hand to the center of a marshy waste, thickly grown with wiry reeds well above the child's head. There he had suddenly flung away her hand, saying: Now are you going to cry any more? The child, with a last rush of contrary pride and with a beginning of fear, started to cry. All right, shouted the father, we don't want any bad children in our house. I'm going to leave you here with the tigers. Goodbye. And jumping out of the child's sight, repaired to a wine shop at the edge of the waste and sat down for an hour's cardplaying. The child strayed about from hummock to hummock, wailing. In due time the father reappeared and taking her affectionately by the hand led her home.

That was all.

But Astrée-Luce had never learned, as the rest of us have, to harden her heart slightly before stories of cruelty or injustice. She may have had no losses of her own, but she had always been ready to expose her imagination to the full force of other people's wrongs. Such an anecdote would have drawn from others a sigh, a swift protective contraction of the lips and a smile of gratitude for its safe conclusion. But to Astrée-Luce it was the vividest reminder that the God whose business it was to brood over the world ministering to the discouraged and the mistreated, was no more. The Cardinal had killed him. There was no one left to soothe the horse that has been beaten to death. The kittens that the boys fling against the wall have no one to speak for them. The dog in torment that keeps his eyes upon her face, and licks her hands even while his eyes grow dim, shall have no comforter but her. This was not a casual story the Cardinal was telling: it concealed a covert

allusion to their conversation of the preceding week. It was a
taunt. It was a sort of curse. Look at the world without God, he
was saying. Get used to it. If she had lost God, oh how clearly she
had gained the Devil. Here he was triumphing in this lacerating
story. Astrée-Luce went over to the piano, picked up a revolver
from the flowers and shot at the Cardinal, crying: The Devil has
come into this room!

As the Cardinal drove back that night he kept repeating to
himself the words: Then these things are real! It had required
Astrée-Luce's shot to show him that belief had long since become
for him a delectable game. One piled syllogism on syllogism, but
the foundations were diaphanous. He strained to remember what
faith was like when he had had it. He kept dragging before his
mind's eye the young priest in China exhorting the families of the
Mandarins. That was himself. Oh, to retrace the way. He would
go back to China. If he could look again on the faces that were
serene with a serenity he had given them, perhaps he could steal it
back. But side by side with this hope was a terrible knowledge: no
words could describe the conviction with which he saw himself
guilty of the greatest of all sins. Murder was child's play compared
to what he had done.

The firing of the shot had done as much for Astrée-Luce. On
awaking, her terror lest she had harmed him, later her fear that she
had fallen out of reach of his forgiveness was greater than had
been her misery in a world without faith. It was given to me to
carry from each to the other the first messages of anxious affection.
When Astrée-Luce and the Cardinal discovered that they were
living in a world where such things could be forgiven, that no
actions were too complicated but that love could understand, or
dismiss them, on that day they began their lives all over again.
This reconciliation was never put into words, in fact it remained to

the end merely in a state of hope. They longed to see one another again, but it would have been impossible. They dreamed of one of those long conversations that one never has on earth, but which one projects so easily at midnight, alone and wise; words are not rich enough nor kisses sufficiently compelling to repair all our havoc.

He received permission to return to China, and sailed within a few weeks. Several days after leaving Aden he fell ill of a fever and knew that he was to die. He called the Captain and the ship's doctor to him and told them that if they buried him at sea they would have to face the indignation of the Church, but that they would be fulfilling his dearest wish. He took what measures he could to shift upon himself the blame for such an irregularity. Better, better to be tossing in the tides of the Bengal Sea and to be nosed by a passing shark, than to lie, a sinner of sinners, under a marble tomb with the inevitable *insignis pietate,* the inescapable *ornatissimus.*

BOOK FIVE

THE DUSK OF THE GODS

When my time came to leave Rome I set aside several days for the last offices of piety, piety in the Roman sense. I wrote a note to Elizabeth Grier arranging for a long late talk on the eve of my departure. There are some questions I want to ask you, I said, which no one can answer. Then I went to the Villino Wei Ho and sat for an hour with the Cardinal's sister. The guinea fowl were less vocal than formerly and the rabbits were still hobbling about the garden looking for a gleam of violet. I went to Tivoli and peered through the iron gates of the Villa Horace. Already it looked as though no one had lived there for years. Mlle. de Morfontaine had returned to her estates in France and was living in the closest retirement. They said that she opened no letters, but I wrote her a note of farewell. I even spent an afternoon in the stifling rooms of the Palazzo Aquilanera, where Donna Leda imparted to me in great confidence the news of her daughter's engagement. Apparently the young man was unable to produce any cousins from among the draughty courts of Europe; his family was merely Italian; but he owned a modern palace. At last a bathroom was to make its appearance in the house of Aquilanera. How time flies!

My most considerable observance was a trip to Marcantonio's grave. I found it by the village cemetery near the Villa Colonna-Stiavelli. Consecrated ground had been denied the boy, but in her bewilderment and love the mother had contrived a false wall of stones and briars that seemed to include his grave among those of souls that the Church felt safe in recommending at the Judgment Day. Here I sat down and prepared to think about him. I was perhaps the only person in the world who understood what had brought him there. The last office of friendship would be to think about him. But some birds were singing; a man and his wife were cultivating the ground in the next field; the sunlight was heavy. Hard as I tried I could not keep my thoughts on my friend; it was not difficult to recall his features or to meditate about dissipation; but really elegiac reflection escaped me, Marcantonio. I drove back to Rome ashamed of myself. But it had been a delightful day in the country, unforgettable June weather.

There was one association I could not renew; I could not go to see Alix. Whenever I met her by chance the barrier of her lowered eyelids told me that we would never have long talks again.

Closing the apartment was melancholy enough. Ottima and I spent hours in packing, our heads bent over our boxes and full of our imminent farewells. She was going back to her wine-shop at the corner. Long before I bought a ticket she had begun to pray for those in peril on the sea and to notice the windy days. After an exhausting struggle with myself I decided to give her the police dog. Kurt's affections were equally divided between us; in Europe or in America he would pine for an absent friend. Ottima and

Kurt would grow old together in a life filled with exquisite mutual attentions. I could swear that before I went to the hotel on that last night Kurt knew I was taking leave of him. There was a grandeur I fell short of in the way he faced an inevitable situation. He placed one paw on my knee and looked to the right and left in deep embarrassment. Then lying down he placed his muzzle between his paws and barked twice.

I found Elizabeth Grier at midnight sitting in the library that Blair had catalogued. Her small neat head looked tired and after some desultory conversation I made a move to go. She reminded me that I had intended asking her some questions.

My questions are harder to put than to answer.

Try.

Miss Grier, did you know that you and your friends were called the Cabala?

Yes, of course.

I shall never know such a company again. And yet there seems to be some last secret about you that I've never been able to seize. Haven't you anything to tell me that will show me what you all meant, how you found one another, and what made you so different from anyone else?

Miss Grier took a few minutes off to think this over. She sat smiling strangely and stroking with her fingertips the roots of her hair beside her left temple. Yes, she said, but it will only make you angry if I tell you. Besides it's very long.

It's not long, Miss Grier, but you will insist on making it long because you hate to have your guests leave before dawn. However, I shall listen to you for hours if you promise to throw some light on the Cabala and the dinners at the Villa Horace.

Well, first you must know, Samuele, that the gods of antiquity did not die with the arrival of Christianity.—What are you smiling at?

You're adorable. You have resolved to make your explanation last forever. I asked about the Cardinal and you have gone back to Jupiter. What became of the gods of antiquity?

Naturally when they began to lose worshipers they began to lose some of their divine attributes. They even found themselves able to die if they wanted to. But when one of them died his godhead was passed on to someone else; no sooner is Saturn dead than some man somewhere feels a new personality descending upon him like a strait-jacket, do you see?

Now, Miss Grier!

I told you it would make you angry.

You don't pretend this is true?

I won't tell you whether this is true, or an allegory, or just nonsense.—Next, I am going to read you a strange document that came into my hands. It was written by a certain Hollander who became the god Mercury in 1912. Will you listen?

Has it anything to do with the Cabala?

Yes. And with you. For I sometimes think that you are the new god Mercury. Take some of that claret and listen quietly.

I was born in a Dutch parsonage in 1885. I was the despair of my home and the terror of the village, a little liar and thief in the full enjoyment of my health and wit. My real life began one morning of my twenty-seventh year when I experienced the first of a series of violent pains in the center of my head. This was my deification. Some untender hand was emptying the cup of my skull of its silly gray brains and filling it with the divine gas of instinct. My body too had its part in this; each microscopic cell had to be transformed; I was not to fall sick or grow old or die, save when I chose. As historian of the gods I have to keep record of an accident whereby, through some monstrosity in spiritual law, an Apollo of the Seventeenth Century failed to completely deify: one arm remained corruptible.

It was then that I discovered the first great attribute of our nature, namely that to wish for a thing is to command it. It does not suddenly fall into your hand or descend in a rosy mist upon your carpet. But circumstances start a discreet ballet about you and the desired thing comes your way through the neatest possible imitation of natural law and probability. Scientists will tell you that they have never seen the sequence of cause and effect interrupted at the instance of prayer or of divine reward or retribution. Do they think, the fools, that their powers of observation are cleverer than the devices of a god? The poor laws of cause and effect are so often set aside that they may be said to be the merest approximations. I am not merely a god but a planet and I speak of things I know. So I stole my mother's savings from under her pillow and went to Paris.

But it is at Rome that we were last worshiped under our own names, and it is thither that we are irresistibly called. During the journey I gradually discovered further traits of my new being. I woke up mornings to discover that bits of information had been deposited in my mind overnight, the enviable knowledge for instance, that I had the power of "sinning" without remorse. I entered the Porta del Popolo one midnight in June, 1912. I ran the length of the Corso, leapt the fence that surrounds the Forum, and flung myself upon the ruins of my temple. All night in the fine rain I tore my clothes in joy and anguish, while up the valley came an interminable and ghostly procession singing my hymns and hiding me in a tower of incense. With the coming of dawn my worshipers vanished and wings no longer fluttered at my heels. I climbed out of the sunken ruins and went out into the misty streets in search of some coffee.

Godlike I never reflect; all my actions arrive of themselves. If I pause to think I fall into error. During the next year I made a great deal of money on the races at Parioli. I speculated in motion pictures and African wheat. I went into journalism and the misrepresentations I sowed will have deferred Europe's recovery from the War many scores of years. I love discord among gods and men. I have always been happy. I am the happiest of the gods.

I had been called to Rome to serve as the gods' messenger and secretary, but more than a year had passed before I recognized even one. The Church of Santa Maria sopra Minerva is built over an ancient temple to that goddess and there one day I found her. So impatient was I to discover the others that I disobeyed the laws of my nature and went hunting for them. I spent hours hanging about the station in search of newly arrived divinities. One night I strode the platform waiting for the Paris Express. I was trembling with premonition. I had donned a silk hat and its complements, a coral camellia, and a little blonde moustache. Plumed with blue smoke and uttering splendid cries the train rushed into the station. The travelers descended from their compartments into a sea of *fachini* and relatives. I bowed to a Scandinavian diplomat and a Wagnerian prima donna. They returned my greeting hesitantly; a glance into their eyes showed me that they were brilliant but not supernatural. There was no incipient Bacchus among the Oxford students on vacation; the Belgian nuns on pilgrimage discovered me no Vesta. I scanned faces for half an hour until the length of pavement was deserted and a long line of old women with pails appeared. I stopped by the engine to ask a guard if another section of the train was to follow. I turned to see a strange face looking at me from the small window of the locomotive—mis-shapen, black with coal-dust, gleaming with perspiration and content, and grinning from ear to ear, was Vulcan.

Here Miss Grier raised her head: There follow fifty pages describing his encounters with the others. Have you anything to say? Do you recognize anything?

But, Miss Grier, I've had no headaches! I don't receive what I want!

No?

What am I to understand? You've made it twice as confused. Explain some more.

He goes on to say that the gods were afraid of being laughed at for what they had lost. Flight, for instance, and invisibility, and omniscience and freedom from care. People would forget that they still had a few enviable powers: their strange elation; their command over matter; their ability to live or die when they chose and to live beyond good and evil. And so on.

What became of him?

Finally he decided to die, as they all do. All gods and heroes are by nature the enemies of Christianity—a faith trailing its aspirations and remorses and in whose presence every man is a failure. Only a broken will can enter the Kingdom of Heaven. Finally tired out with the cult of themselves they give in. They go over. They renounce themselves.

I was astonished at the desolation in her voice. It held me back from eagerly demanding of her the application to the Cabala of all these principles. We went into the next room where her musicians were waiting to offer us some English madrigals. The applications still occur to me, especially when I am depressed. They give in. They go over.

On the night that my steamer left the bay of Naples I lay sleepless in my deck-chair until morning. Why was I not more reluctant at leaving Europe? How could I lie there repeating the Aeneid and longing for the shelf of Manhattan? It was Virgil's sea that we were crossing; the very stars were his: Arcturus and the showery Hyades, the two Bears and Orion in his harness of gold. All these passed before me in a cloudless sky and in the water, murmuring before a light wind, the sliding constellations were brokenly reflected.

Mercury is not only the messenger of the gods; he is the conductor of the dead as well. If in the least part his powers had fallen to me I should be able to invoke spirits. Perhaps Virgil could read my mood for me, and raising my two palms I said in a low voice (not loud enough to reach the open port-holes behind me):

Prince of poets, Virgil, one of your guests and the last of barbarians invokes you.

For an instant I thought I saw the shimmer of a robe and the reflection of the starlight on the shiny side of a laurel leaf. I pressed my advantage:

O anima cortese mantovana, greatest of all Romans, out of the eternity of that limbo to which the Florentine, perhaps wrongly, consigned you, grant me a crumb of time.

Now indeed the shade stood in mid-air just above the hand-rail. The stars were glittering and the water was glittering, and the great shade, picked out in sparks, was glittering furiously. But the image must become clearer. There was one title that might avail more with him than those of poet or Roman.

Oh, greatest spirit of the ancient world and prophet of the new, by that fortunate guess wherein you foretold the coming of Him who will admit you to His mountain, thou first Christian in Europe, speak to me!

Now indeed the gracious spirit became completely visible with pulsations of light, half silver and half gold, and spoke:

Be brief, importunate barbarian. Except for this last salutation wherein you have touched my only pride, I would not delay here. Detain me not from the absorbing games of my peers. Erasmus is in debate with Plato, and Augustine has descended from the hill and sits among us, though the air is gray. Be brief, I pray you, and give heed to your Latin.

At this I realized that I had no definite question to put to my guest. In order to mark time and prolong so uncommon an interview, I engaged him in conversation:

Was I then right, Master, in assuming that Dante was not completely in God's confidence?

Indignation infused a saffron stain into the noble figure in silver-gold: Where, where is he, that soul of vinegar, that chose to assign the souls of the dead more harshly than God? Tell him that though a pagan I too shall see bliss. It is nothing that I must first pay the penalty of ten thousand years. Behold this moment I exhibit the sin of anger; where is *he* in pain for the sin of pride?

I was a little shocked to discover that neither genius nor death removed us beyond the temptation to asperity, but said: Master, have you met the poets of the English tongue that have come into your groves?

Let us be brief, my friend.—One came that had been formerly blind and did me much honor. He spoke a noble Latin. Those that stood by assured me that in his lines mine were not seldom reflected.

Milton was indeed your son. . . .

But before him came another, greater than he, a writer of pieces for a theatre. He was proud and troubled and strode among us unseeing. He made me no salutation. Vanity no longer exists among us, but it is sweet to exchange greetings among the poets.

He knew but little Latin, Master, and perhaps had never read your page. Moreover in life he was neither the enemy nor advocate of grace and being arrived in your region his whole mind may well have been consumed with anxiety as to his eternal residence. Is he among you still?

He sits apart, his hand over his eyes, and only raises his head when, in the long green evenings, Casella sings to us, or when on the wind there drifts from Purgatory the chorus that one Palestrina prepares.

Master, I have just spent a year in the city that was your whole life. Am I wrong to leave it?

Let us be brief. This world where Time is, troubles me. My heart has almost started beating again,—what horror! Know, importunate barbarian, that I spent my whole lifetime under a great delusion,—that Rome and the house of Augustus were eternal. Nothing is eternal save Heaven. Romes existed before Rome and when Rome will be a waste there will be Romes after her. Seek out some city that is young. The secret is to make a city, not to rest in it. When you have found one, drink in the illusion that she too is eternal. Nay, I have heard of your city. Its foundations have knocked upon our roof and the towers have cast a shadow across the sandals of the angels. Rome too was great. Oh, in the pride of your city, and when she too begins to produce great men, do not forget mine. When shall I erase from my heart this love of her? I cannot enter Zion until I have forgotten Rome.— Dismiss me now, my friend, I pray thee. These vain emotions have shaken me. . . . (Suddenly the poet became aware of the Mediterranean:) Oh, beautiful are these waters. Behold! For many years I have almost forgotten the world. Beautiful! Beautiful!—But no! what horror, what pain! Are you still alive? Alive? How can you endure it? All your thoughts are guesses, all your body is shaken with breath, all your senses are infirm, and your mind ever full of the fumes of one passion or another. Oh, what misery to be a man. Hurry and die!

Farewell, Virgil!

The shimmering ghost faded before the stars, and the engines beneath me pounded eagerly toward the new world and the last and greatest of all cities.

THE WOMAN OF ANDROS

The first part of this novel is based upon the Andria, *a comedy of Terence who in turn based his work upon two Greek plays, now lost to us, by Menander.*

The earth sighed as it turned in its course; the shadow of night crept gradually along the Mediterranean, and Asia was left in darkness. The great cliff that was one day to be called Gibraltar held for a long time a gleam of red and orange, while across from it the mountains of Atlas showed deep blue pockets in their shining sides. The caves that surround the Neapolitan gulf fell into a profounder shade, each giving forth from the darkness its chiming or its booming sound. Triumph had passed from Greece and wisdom from Egypt, but with the coming on of night they seemed to regain their lost honors, and the land that was soon to be called Holy prepared in the dark its wonderful burden. The sea was large enough to hold a varied weather: a storm played about Sicily and its smoking mountains, but at the mouth of the Nile the water lay like a wet pavement. A fair tripping breeze ruffled the Aegean and all the islands of Greece felt a new freshness at the close of day.

The happiest, and one of the least famous of the islands, Brynos, welcomed the breeze. The evening was long. For a time, the sound of the waves, briskly slapping against the wall of the little harbor, was covered by the chattering of women, by the shouts of boys, and by the crying of lambs. As the first lights appeared, the women retired; as the air was filled with the clangor of the shop fronts being put into place, the boys' voices ceased; and finally only the murmur of the men in the wine-shops, playing at games with ivory counters, mingled with the sounds from the sea. A confused starlight, already apprehensive of the still unrisen moon, fell upon the tiers of small houses that covered the slope and upon the winding flights of stairs that served as streets between them.

The wine-shops stood about the roughly paved square at the water's edge and in one of them the five or six principal fathers of the island sat playing. By the time the moon had risen, two of these, Simo and Chremes, had outstayed their companions. Simo was the owner of two warehouses; he was a trader and had three ships that passed continually to and fro among the islands. The men had finished playing; the counters lay on the table between them and they sighed into their beards as they thought of the long walk through the ghostly olive trees to their homes. Simo was more tired than usual: whereas the law of moderation teaches us that the mind cannot be employed for more than three hours daily over merchandise and numerals without soilure, he had that day spent five hours in argument and traffic.

"Simo," said Chremes suddenly, with the air of a man bracing himself to an unpleasant and long deferred task, "your boy is twenty-five now—"

Simo groaned as he saw the subject arising that he was never able to look in the face.

"It's four years," continued Chremes, "since you first said that a young man mustn't be forced into marriage by his old people. And certainly no one has been trying to force Pamphilus. But what is he waiting for? He helps you in the warehouse; he exercises in the field; he dines at the Andrian's. How many years must that kind of life go on before you agree with me that he would be better off married to my daughter?"

"Chremes, he must come to me of his own accord. I will not be the first one to speak about it to the boy."

"First! It won't be speaking of it first, Simo. It has been understood between our families for years that he will marry Philumena. It's being spoken of all the time. The young people tease him about it from morning to night. He knows perfectly well that my daughter is ready to marry him. It's sheer laziness on his part. It's sheer unwillingness to take on the responsibilities of being a husband and a father and the foremost young householder on the island."

"He's a young man who knows what he means to do. I will not coerce him."

"Then it's settled that he doesn't want to marry my daughter. It's a humiliation for her to be waiting all these years for him to make up his mind, and her mother's been after me to close the matter for a long time. Perhaps I shouldn't say it, but you'll be throwing away a good thing through sheer hesitancy, both of you. Philumena is by far the healthiest and the prettiest girl on any of these islands. And she's clever at everything that is expected of a woman in the home. The uniting of our two families has advantages, Simo, that I don't have to point out to you. But this lapse of time has made it clear that your son is going to wait until his fancy has been caught by some other girl, I suppose. So be it! From this very night my wife is going to start looking about for some other young man."

"Chremes, Chremes, he's only twenty-five. Let him play about a little longer. Why must they become husbands and fathers so soon? He's good and he's happy. So is your daughter. Let them be awhile."

"Grandchildren!—that's what I want to see. There shouldn't be a long step between the generations. It's bad for customs and manners."

"You'll make a greater mistake by hurrying than by delaying."

"Well," Chremes continued, "there's another reason why I want the matter settled soon. And that is this: we don't like the visits that Pamphilus is paying to the Andrian woman. Naturally, Simo, it's hard for me to be severe about it, because my own son goes there too. But it's natural that a father should be more exacting in regard to his son-in-law than in regard to his son."

Simo looked more uncomfortable than ever and remained silent. Chremes went on:

"I don't think you like this resort to foreign women any more than I do. Our islands have always been famous for strict and good behavior. If the devil was in us as boys we could always follow some shepherdess up a dark road. But this Andrian has brought the whole air of Alexandria to town with her, perfumes and hot baths and late hours."

Simo stroked his cheeks a moment and then replied in a low grunting voice: "Well, if it isn't one thing, it's another, I suppose. I don't know anything about this Andrian. The women seem to talk of nothing else from morning to night, but one can't believe what they say."

Thus invited, Chremes launched into his exposition with considerable relish, examining Simo's face from time to time to see if the details were arousing in him the interest they held for himself. "Her name is Chrysis, and I don't know what she means by calling herself Andrian. The island of Andros was never famous for such airs and graces as she puts on. She's flitted from Corinth and Alexandria, you may be sure. She should have stayed in her cities instead of burying herself in our town and reciting poetry to our young men. Yes, yes, she recites poetry to them like the famous ones. She has twelve or fifteen of them to dinner every seven or eight days,—the unmarried ones, of course. They lie about on couches and eat odd food and talk. Presently she rises and recites; she can recite whole tragedies without the book. She is very strict with the young men, apparently. She makes them pronounce all the Attic accents; they eat in the Athenian mode, drinking toasts and wearing garlands, and each in turn is elected King of the Banquet. And at the close, hot towels are passed around for them to wipe their hands on."

Simo did not concede to Chremes the pleasure of his close interest; his eyes were lowered and his face wore the same bored expression that it brought to all island gossip. Chremes decided to be less expansive and added with easy indignation: "As for me, Alexandria is Alexandria and Brynos is Brynos. A few more imported notions and our island will be spoiled forever. It will become a mass of poor undigested imitations. All the girls will be wanting to read and write and declaim. What becomes of home life, Simo, if women can read and write? You and I married the finest girls of our time and we've been happy. We can at least provide one more generation of good sense and good manners on this island before the age arrives when all the women will have the airs of dancers and all the men go about waiting on them."

Simo knew the answer to this, but he repressed it. Chremes, more than any man on the island, was ruled by his wife. In fact from her loom in the shadow, Chremes's wife tried to rule the whole island, using her harassed husband as her legislative and punitive arm. Simo asked:

"What happens after the banquet?"

"Each boy pays for his plate, and pays right smartly too, and from time to time one or another is graciously permitted to stay until morning. That's all I know."

"Is your son at all these dinners?"

"He was quarreling or something,—or perhaps he drank too much, I don't know. At all events, he was expelled for a time. Thrown right out into the street, he was, by the other guests. But he's made his peace with her again."

"Do you talk to him about this . . . this Chrysis?"

"Why, no. I pretend to know nothing about it."

"Is my son always there?"

"They say he's practically always there."

There was a long pause. The boy who attended in the wine-shop went out into the moonlight and started putting up the shutters. Presently he returned and whispered to Simo that an old woman was waiting outside to speak to him and that she had been waiting there for some time. This was unusual on Brynos, but Simo took pride in never betraying any surprise. He nodded slightly and continued staring before him.

"Are there any other women at the Andrian's?" he asked.

"I don't know. Some say there are and some say there aren't. But there's a houseful of some sort. In fact it's a kind of hospital for the old and the lame and the . . . all kind of old battered pensioners. The house is way up at the edge of the town . . ."

"I know where it is."

". . . and the people, whoever they are, never come into town. They never even go out on the road by day. Oh, you can be sure the townspeople talk of nothing else."

Chremes rose and put on his cloak. He saw that Simo was as far as ever from committing himself. "Well, that's how it stands," he said. "I hope that in another ten days you can give me a more definite answer. My wife is after me a good deal, Simo, and she says that I'm to tell you this, that unless Pamphilus stops those visits all idea of a marriage between himself and Philumena is impossible. And that any such marriage must be definitely settled pretty soon or you'll have to start finding some other girl one-tenth as good."

For the first time Simo bestirred himself and said slowly: "You and your wife will be throwing away a good thing too, Chremes. It's precisely because Pamphilus is a great deal more than an ordinary island boy that I can't speak to him as I could to another son. There are more sides to Pamphilus than you imagine."

"Yes, Simo, we know that he's a fine young man. But we also know, if you will forgive me, that there's a strain in Pamphilus of the . . . the undecided, the procrastinating. To do his best and to take his place, Pamphilus must be urged on by someone, like yourself, whom he admires. And he's not as interested in this island and in what it stands for as he should be. Do you know the young priest of Aesculapius and Apollo? Well, there is something of the priest in Pamphilus. Such people aren't interested in putting their foot forward. They haven't yet come to see what life is about."

Chremes went out and plodded home along the rocky road. Simo sat on a minute longer. What a bad ending to a bad day, he thought. The two men had grown up on the island together. For thirty years they had been its leading citizens. They knew one another too well. In their conversation they had let play the faint antagonism that always lay between them. This boasting about their children,—how vulgar, how unhellene. How unphilosophic. Yet that was true: there was something of the priest in Pamphilus.

Simo turned to the old woman who was hiding in the shadow by the door. "You wanted to speak to me?" he asked roughly.

Between fright and suspense—for she had been waiting there for the greater part of two hours—Mysis was barely able to find her voice. "My mistress wishes to speak to you, sir,—Chrysis, the Andrian," and she pointed with both hands toward the water-front.

Simo grunted. Looking up he saw the beautiful woman leaning against the parapet at the water's edge fifteen paces away. Her head and body were wrapped in veils, and she waited calmly and impersonally in the moonlight as though two hours were but a moment in her serenity. Below her in the little protected harbor the boats knocked against one another in friendly fashion, but all else was still under the melancholy and peace of the moon. Simo approached her without deference and said: "Well?"

"I am—" she began.

"I know who you are."

She paused and began again. "I am in an extremity. I am driven to ask a service of you." Simo pushed his lips forward, raised his eyebrows, and lowered his eyes wearily. She continued in an even voice without anxiety or suppliance: "A friend of mine is very ill on the island of Andros from which I come. Twice I have sent this friend money by the hands of various sea-captains going between the islands. I know now that the captains are dishonest and that my money never reaches him. All that I ask is that you put your frank upon the package of money and it will reach him."

Simo did not like to see women carrying themselves, as this Andrian did, with dignity and independence. His antagonism was increased; he asked abruptly: "Who is this friend?"

"He was formerly a sea-captain," she replied, still without servility. "But now he is not only ill; he is insane. He is insane by reason of the hardships he endured in the war. I have put him in charge of some people, but they will only be kind to him as long as I send them money for it. Otherwise they will put him away on a small island nearby with the others. You know such islands . . .

where basins of food are left for them every few days . . . and where—"

"Well," said Simo harshly, "since your friend has lost the use of his reason and since he cannot realize the conditions under which he lives, it is best that you leave him upon the island with the others. Is that not so?"

Chrysis tightened her lips and looked far out over his head. "I have no answer for that," she replied. "It may be true for you, but it is not true for me. This man was once a very famous sea-captain. You may have known him. His name was Philocles. Now I think I am his only friend, unless you choose to help him also."

Simo did not acknowledge having known him, but the tone in his next words was less vindictive. "When would you like this money to go?"

"I . . . I have some money ready now, but I would prefer to send some in ten days."

"What is your name?"

"My name is Chrysis, daughter of Arches of Andros."

"Chrysis, I will do this for you, and I will even add to the sum. In return you will do a favor for me. You will refuse my son entrance into your house."

Chrysis moved slightly to one side and stretching her arm along the parapet looked down into the harbor. "Favors cease to be favors when there are conditions attached to them, Simo. Magnanimity does not bargain with its powers." These maxims were almost murmured; then she raised her head and said to him: "I cannot do that, unless I tell your son that it is because you have ordered it."

Simo's slightly cynical superiority over the rest of the world reposed on the fact that he had gone through life without ever having been surprised as unjust, untruthful, or ungenerous. Angry, but with himself, for having been caught at this disadvantage, he replied: "That is not necessary. It would be quite simple for your servant to tell him that you do not wish him to come into the house."

"I could not do that. There are several young men on the island to whom my door, for one reason or another, is closed. I cannot do that to Pamphilus without giving him a reason. If you understood the spirit of our group you would not wish me to do that; I think that there we are not lacking in respect for one another. I hardly know your son; I have scarcely exchanged twenty words with him; but I know that he is by far the first young man among my guests." Suddenly the image of Pamphilus rose up before her and she was filled with an excitement and joy in praising him, and for that very reason she subdued herself and added in a lower voice: "He is old enough to make decisions for himself. And if I do this, he must understand."

Simo was aware that some strange wise praise of his son hovered between them and his heart almost stopped beating for pleasure, but from his lips there rushed the brutal phrase he had prepared a moment before: "Then you must send your money to Andros some other way."

"Very well," she said.

They stood looking at one another. Simo suddenly realized that he lived among people of thin natures and that he was lonely; he was out of practice in conversing with sovereign personalities whose every speech arose from resources of judgment and inner poise. With his wife, with Chremes, with the islanders one could talk with half one's mind and still hold one's authority, but here in a few moments this woman had caught him twice at a disadvantage. Chrysis saw this and came to his aid; she broke the silence that was leaving him obstinate, angry, and small.

"It is perhaps his younger brother whose life can be arranged for him; your Pamphilus deserves to be better understood than that." And her tone implied: "You and he are of one measure and should stand on the same side."

Simo preferred talking about his sons to any other activity in the world, but his emotions were very mixed as he assembled an answer to this remark:

"Well, well . . . Andrian, I will frank your money for you. I have boats going to Andros every twelve days. One went off today."

"I thank you."

"Could I ask you . . . euh . . . not to mention this to Pamphilus?"

"I shall not."

"Well . . . well, goodnight."

"Goodnight."

Simo trudged home in an unaccustomed elation. It made him happy to hear Pamphilus praised and "probably this woman was an exceptional judge of persons." He had made a fool of himself, but in good hands one does not mind. "Life . . . life . . .," he said to himself, hunting for a generalization that would describe its diversity, its power of casting up from time to time on the waves of tedious circumstance such starlike persons. The generalization did not arrive, but he walked on in a bright astonishment. How he would like to hear her read a play; he used to be interested in such things and when his journeys took him to an island that was large enough to have a theatre he never missed an opportunity to hear a good tragedy.

As he entered the courtyard of his farm he saw Pamphilus standing alone, looking at the moon.

"Good evening, Pamphilus," he said.

"Good evening, father."

Simo went to bed, deeply moved with pride, but for form's sake he repeated anxiously to himself: "I don't know what I'll do with him. I don't know what I'll do with him."

And Pamphilus stood looking at the moon and thinking about his father and mother. He was thinking about them in the light of a story that Chrysis had told. As the banquets drew to a close she liked to move the conversation away from local comment and to introduce some debate upon an abstract principle. (She cited often the saying of Plato that the true philosophers are the young men of their age. "Not," she would add, "because they do it very well; but because they rush upon ideas with their whole soul. Later one philosophizes for praise, or for apology, or because it is a complicated intellectual game.") Pamphilus remembered that on one evening the conversation had turned upon the wrong that poets do in pretending that life is heroic. And a boy from the other end of the island had said, half-mockingly and half-hopefully: "Well, you know, Chrysis . . . you know, life in a family is not in the same world as life in Euripides."

Chrysis sat a moment searching for her answer, then she lifted her hand and said: "Once upon a time——"

The table burst out laughing, but with an affectionate laugh of mock-repudiation, because they knew that she liked to cast her remarks into the form of fables and to begin them with this childish formula. Pamphilus heard again her beautiful voice saying:

"Once upon a time there was a hero who had done a great service to Zeus. When he came to die and was wandering in the gray marshes of Hell, he called to Zeus reminding him of that service and asking a service in return: he asked to return to earth for one day. Zeus was greatly troubled and said that it was not in his power to grant this, since even he could not bring above ground the dead who had descended to his brother's kingdom. But Zeus was so moved by the memory of the past that he went to the palace of his brother and clasping his knees asked him to accord him this favor. And the King of the Dead was greatly troubled, saying that even he who was King of the Dead could not grant this thing without involving the return to life in some difficult and painful condition. But the hero gladly accepted whatever difficult or painful condition was involved, and the King of the Dead permitted him to return not only to the earth, but to the past, and to live over again that day in all the twenty-two thousand days of his lifetime that had been least eventful; but that it must be with a mind divided into two persons,—the participant and the onlooker: the participant who does the deeds and says the words of so many years before, and the onlooker who foresees the end. So the hero returned to the sunlight and to a certain day in his fifteenth year.

"My friends," continued Chrysis, turning her eyes slowly from face to face, "as he awoke in his boyhood's room, pain filled his heart,—not only because it had started beating again, but because he saw the walls of his home and knew that in a moment he would see his parents who lay long since in the earth of that country. He descended into the courtyard. His mother lifted her eyes from the loom and greeted him and went on with her work. His father passed through the court unseeing, for on that day his mind had been full of care. Suddenly the hero saw that the living too are dead and that we can only be said to be alive in those moments when our hearts are conscious of our treasure; for our hearts are not strong enough to love every moment. And not an hour had gone by before the hero who was both watching life and living it called on Zeus to release him from so terrible a dream. The gods heard him, but before he left he fell upon the ground and kissed the soil of the world that is too dear to be realized."

It was with such eyes that Pamphilus now saw his father pass into the house and that he had seen his mother moving about, covering the fire and going about the last tasks of the day. And it was in the light of that story that his eyes had been opened to the secret life of his parents' minds. It seemed suddenly as though he saw behind the contentment and the daily talkativeness into the life of their hearts—empty, resigned, pathetic and enduring. It was Chrysis's reiterated theory of life that all human beings—save a few mysterious exceptions who seemed to be in possession of some secret from the gods—merely endured the slow misery of existence, hiding as best they could their consternation that life had no wonderful surprises after all and that its most difficult burden was the incommunicability of love. Certainly that explained the humorous sadness of his father and the fretful affection of his mother. And now as his father passed him in the courtyard this interpretation shook him more forcibly than ever. What can one do for them? What—to be equal to them—can one do for oneself? He was twenty-five already, that is—no longer a young man. He would soon be a husband and a father, a condition he did not invest with any glamour. He would soon be the head of this household and this farm. He would soon be old. Time would have flowed by him like a sigh, with no plan made, no rules set, no strategy devised that would have taught him how to save these others and himself from the creeping gray, from the too-easily accepted frustration.

"How does one live?" he asked the bright sky. "What does one do first?"

Chrysis's view of human experience expressed itself, as we have seen, in fables, in quotations from literature, in proverbs and in mottoes. Herself she summed up in a word: she regarded herself as having "died." Dead then as she was, the inconveniences of her profession, the sneers of the villagers, the ingratitude of her dependents, no longer had the power to disturb her. The only thing that troubled her in her grave was the recurrence, even in her professional associations, of a wild tenderness for this or that passerby, brief and humiliating approaches to love. These experiences and any others that were able to depress her, she now dismissed as weakness, as pride, as an old, rebellious and unwhipped vanity. The morning after the conversation with Simo at the water's edge she awoke strangely troubled; but she resolved not to examine the new dejection. It floated all day above her head,—a voice repeating: "I am alone. Why have I never seen that before? I am alone." Indeed the profession she followed was one of those that emphasize the dim notion that lies at the back of many minds: the notion that we are not necessary to anyone, that attachments weave and unweave at the mercy of separation, satiety and experience. The loneliest associations are those that pretend to intimacy.

But she had discovered two ways of mitigating this unresponsiveness and instability in the world she lived in. The first was the development she brought to the institution of the hetaira's banquet. She took endless pains over these reunions and to the wide-eyed guests they seemed indeed all that one could conceive of wit and eloquence and aristocratic ease. Great talkers are so constituted that they do not know their own thoughts until, on the tide of their particular gift, they hear them issuing from their mouths. Chrysis gave herself that luxury, the luxury of talking to these young men from her whole mind. Much of it lay beyond their reach; but her refusal to condescend, her assumption that the analysis of ideas and of masterpieces was their natural element, excited them. She knew that apart from her beauty she was not particularly fitted for her calling; she lacked the high spirits that please the customers of middle age; but younger men, who still approach love with a touch of awe, are not so disappointed with those common exercises when they find them invested with melancholy, dignity and literature. Perhaps the maturity of a civilization can be judged by this trait, by observing whether the young men first fall in love with women older or younger than themselves; if in their youth their imaginations pass their time in hallowing the images of prattling unnourishing girls their natures will be forever after the thinner. But even at their best Chrysis's guests seemed remote and immature to her and finally she discovered a second way of making life more stable and her friends more constant: she adopted stray human beings that needed her.

In the inner monologue of her thoughts Chrysis called these dependents her "sheep." And although they were gathered into her shelter from places and moments of fearful extremity, they became accustomed to their new comfort with extraordinary rapidity. In fact their past trials began to take on a romantic color and when anything in the present situation did not suit them they had been known to regret the lost felicities of the slave-markets, the mills and the massacred villages. For Chrysis human nature no longer had many surprises and the manner in which the sheep scolded and even condescended to their shepherd did not deject her. She loved them and was sufficiently repaid by occasional hours of a late afternoon when the odd group would sit in the garden, weaving in amity and humor. Such hours almost resembled life in a home.

There was to be a banquet that evening, so shaking her head at the shadow that hovered above her she descended into the town to do the marketing. She was accompanied by Mysis and the porter, —Mysis carrying a net to hold the fruit and the salad-greens, and the porter a large jar to be filled with salt-water and then with fish

and shell-fish. Chrysis moved slowly down the long twisting flights
of stairs. She was wrapped about by a great scarf of antique finely-
wrinkled material and wore a broad-brimmed Tanagran hat of
woven straw. The one hand that appeared outside the folds of her
scarf carried a small wooden fan. It was her business to be invested
with the remoteness and glamour of a legend, for at that time
Greek taste turned upon a nostalgia for the antique; it was her
business to be as different from other women as possible and to
convert that difference into money. The shops and temporary
booths were all on the open square at the water's edge and there in
the bright sunlight the most excitable and loquacious of races was
enjoying its morning tumult; but as this calm and day-dreaming
figure appeared above them a hush fell upon the bargainers. This
was the very deportment the Greek women lacked and sighed for.
They were short and swarthy and shrill, and their incessant conversation was accompanied by the incessant play of their hands.
The whole race was haunted by a passionate admiration for poise
and serenity and slow motion, and now for an hour the Andrian's
every move was followed by the furtive glances of the islanders,
with mingled awe and hatred. The Brynians, when she appeared,
felt themselves to be provincial and commercial. From time to time
some of the young men who had been guests at her house approached her and spoke to her. Then it was that the unmarried
girls and the young wives of the island gazed with consternation
and fallen jaw at the way she smiled and talked and dismissed
their brothers and their future husbands. Philumena, in the
shadow of an awning, leaned back against a wall and watched the
stranger; turning her head slightly she could see Pamphilus at the
tally-desk in the door of his father's warehouse. Her eyes fell on
her rough gown and her red arms and a long slow blush mounted
to her face. But all the while Chrysis's heart had been growing

heavier. "I have lived alone and I shall die alone," it said, and groaned within her.

As she returned to her house from the market she fell into a feverish monologue. "The fault is in me. It's my lack of perseverance in affection. I know that. Now, Chrysis, you must begin your life over again; you must assemble some plan. You must devote yourself with all your mind to your sheep. You must break down all their coldness and wilfulness. You must make yourself love them again. You must bring back the happiness you felt with each one of them when you first knew them. It is routine, it is the daily contact that has spoiled all that. It's cowardly of me to be able to love people only when they are new. Now, now, Chrysis!—arise!" For the hundredth time she was visited by hope and courage. She would win in this thing. As she approached the house she was all but stumbling in her eagerness; she would create a home. "If I love them enough, I can understand them," she muttered. "One never learns how to live, or one's lights on living arrive too late, when one has spoiled the surrounding situation, spoiled it beyond repair. But I am to be on the earth for fifty years, and I must do it."

Chrysis did not realize what took place in the house during her absences, and that when she left it the house was empty. The personalities of her flock were extinguished. They fretted; they hovered about the gates peering in the direction from which she would return, and their minds ceased to act save in terms of that resentment which is the complement of devotion. She did not realize that this wasting of love in fretfulness was one of the principal activities on the planet. When she was away fear descended upon them; their dependence upon her was so great that even her temporary absences reminded them of the destitution from which they had been lifted,—circumstances so fearful that their conscious minds never revisited them, but which hovered in the distance enriching their present ease and hardening their self-centredness. All this antagonism therefore met her in a flood as she stumbled across the threshold of her home. By the middle of the afternoon she was saying to herself, almost in a panic: "It is impossible. I can do nothing. They even hate me. But fortunately I am dead. It is not my pride that is hurt. I am at peace in the ground. Yet oh! if only we had some help in these matters. If only the gods were sometimes present among us. To have nothing to go by except this idea, this vague idea, that there lies the principle of living!"

During the banquet she looked about her for comfort. "It is also cowardly of me to be happy only at the banquets where I can lead the conversation and display my thoughts and be admired." But tonight even that exhilaration was wanting; her guests seemed younger and remoter then ever, and she in turn was capricious and all but irritable. It was to be expected, therefore, that the conversation would take turns little likely to comfort her.

Niceratus, one of the more assured of her guests, asked her what life would be like in two thousand years.

"Why," she said at once, "there will be no more war."

"I should not wish to be alive in a world where there was no war," he replied. "That would be an age of women."

Now Chrysis was jealous of the dignity of women and lost no occasions to combat such hasty disparagements. She leaned forward and asked encouragingly:

"You wish to serve the state, Niceratus?"

"I do."

"And you admire courage?"

"I do, Chrysis."

"Then go bear children," she replied, turning away.

Niceratus found this remark unseemly and left the house. (He absented himself from the two successive banquets, but later returned and asked her pardon for making a personal grievance out of a difference of opinion. Confessions of error always gave Chrysis great pleasure. "Happy are the associations," she would say, "that have grown out of a fault and a forgiveness.")

The conversation then turned upon the plays concerning Medea and Phaedra which she had read to them at an earlier banquet and upon all manifestations of extravagant passion. The young men declared that the problem was not as complicated as it appeared to be and that such women should have been whipped like disobedient slaves and shut up in a room with a jar of water and a little plain food until their pride was subdued. They then recounted to her, almost in whispers, the story of a girl from a village on the further side of the island whose behavior had thrown her family and her friends into consternation. The girl had continued for a time, glorying in her disorders, until one morning, rising early, she had climbed a high cliff near her home and thrown herself into the sea. A silence fell on the company as all turned inquiringly to Chrysis asking for the explanation of such a reversal.

To herself she said: "Do not try to explain to them. Talk of other things. Stupidity is everywhere and invincible." But their continued expectancy prevailed upon her. She seemed to struggle with herself for a moment, deeply troubled, and then began in a low voice: "Once upon a time the great army of women came together to a meeting. And they invited to this meeting one man, a tragic poet. They told him that they wished to send a message to the world of men and that he was to be their advocate and mouthpiece. 'Tell them,' said the women eagerly, 'that it is only in appearance that we are unstable. Tell them that this is because we are hard-pressed and in bitter servitude to nature, but that at heart, only asking their patience, we are as steadfast, as brave and as manly as they.' The poet smiled sadly, saying that the men who knew this already would merely be ashamed to be told it again, and the men who did not know it would learn nothing through the mere telling; but he consented to deliver the message. The men at first were silent, then one by one they broke out into laughter. And they sent the poet back to the army of women with these words: 'Tell them not to be anxious and not to trouble their pretty heads with these matters. Tell them that their popularity is not dying out, and let them not endanger it through heroics.' When the poet had repeated these words to the women, some blushed with shame and some with anger; some rose with a weary sigh: 'We should never have spoken to them,' they said. They went back to their mirrors and started combing their hair and as they combed their hair they wept."

Chrysis had barely finished this story when a young man who had hitherto taken little part in the conversation suddenly launched into a violent condemnation of her means of livelihood. This youth was of that temper that seeks to mould the lives of others abruptly to certain patterns of its own choosing. He now commanded Chrysis to become a servant or a sempstress. The other guests began to whisper among themselves and to avert their faces from confusion and anger, but Chrysis sat gazing at his flashing eyes and admiring his earnestness. There was a certain luxury in having an external mortification added to an inner despair. She was already troubled by her recent discomfiture of Niceratus and now chose to be magnanimous. She arose and approached the young fanatic; taking his hand she smiled at him with grave affection, saying to the company: "It is true that of all forms of genius, goodness has the longest awkward age."

But these incidents were not of a nature to distract her mind from the protracted oppression of the day. "Vain. Empty. Transitory," the voice within her repeated. But just as she was about to finish the day with the comprehensive summary that she had nothing to lend to life and no place to fill, her eyes fell upon Pamphilus. It was his custom, through lack of self-confidence, to take the last seat at the remote end of the room. The guests acknowledged his preëminence among them, but when one evening they had wished to elect him King of the Banquet he had furtively and savagely intimated to them his refusal and the votes had passed to another. But Chrysis's eyes had often, as now, rested upon that head bent forward to receive her every word and that received each one with so earnest a frown.

"That is something!" she said to herself suddenly and for a moment her heart stopped beating.

She had intended to recite to them *The Clouds* of Aristophanes that evening, but she now changed her mind. She felt the need to nourish her heart and those watchful eyes with something lofty and deeply felt. Perhaps what she called the "lofty" was in this world merely a beautiful form of falsehood, cheating the heart. But she would try again tonight and see whether, after so dejected a day, it woke any stir of conviction. "What shall I read?" she asked herself as the tables were being removed. "Something from Homer?—Priam begging of Achilles the body of Hector? No. . . . No. . . . Nor would they understand the *Oedipus at Colonus*. The *Alcestis?* The *Alcestis?*"

One of the shyer guests, seeing her deliberating over the choice of the evening's declamation, timidly asked her to read the *Phaedrus* of Plato.

"Oh, my friend," she said, "I have not seen the book for several years. I should be obliged to improvise long stretches in it. . . ."

"Could you . . . could you read the opening and the close?"

"I shall try it for you," she replied and rising slowly disposed the folds of her robe about her. The servants withdrew and silence fell upon the company. This was the moment (on happier evenings) that she loved; this hush, this eagerness, this faintly mocking affection. What drives them—she would ask herself—in the next fifteen years to become so graceless . . . so pompous, or envious, or so busily cheerful?

At first all went well. The boys listened with delight to the account of how other young men gathered in the streets and palaestra of Athens to hear the arguments of Socrates. Listening, they agreed that nothing in the world was more to be prized than a beautifully ordered speech. Then followed the description of the walk that Socrates and Phaedrus took into the country. *"This is indeed a rare resting-place. This plane-tree is not only tall, but thick and spreading. And this agnus castus is at the very moment of flowering and its shade and its fragrance will render our stay the more agreeable. These images and these votive-offerings tell us that the place is surely sacred to some nymphs and to some river-god. . . . Truly, Phaedrus, you are an admirable guide."*

From there she passed to the close:

"But let us go now, as the heat of the day is over.

"Socrates: Would it not be well before we go to offer up a prayer to the gods of this place?

"Phaedrus: It would, Socrates.

"Socrates: Beloved Pan, and all ye other gods who haunt this place, grant that I may become beautiful in the inner man and may

whatever I possess without be in harmony with that which is within. May I esteem the wise men alone to be rich. And may my store of gold be such as none but the good may bear. Phaedrus, need we say anything more? As for myself I have prayed enough.

"Phaedrus: And let the same prayer serve for me, for these are the things friends share with one another."

All went well until this phrase. Then Chrysis, the serene, the happily dead, seeing the tears that stood in the eyes of Pamphilus, could go no further, and before them all she wept as one weeps who after an absence of folly and self-will returns to a well-loved place and an old loyalty. It was true, true beyond a doubt, tragically true, that the world of love and virtue and wisdom was the true world and her failure in it all the more overwhelming. But she was not alone; he too saw the long and failing war as she did, and she loved him as though she were loving for the first time and as one is never able to love again. That was sealed; that was forever assigned.

After a few moments she collected herself and quieted the guests who had risen in concern about her. "Sit down, my friends. I am ready now," she said smiling. "I shall read you *The Clouds* of Aristophanes."

But it was some time before the laughter rose among the couches, the laughter that was a just tribute to the divine wit of the poet of *The Clouds*.

Brynos rose with the dawn, and it was not many hours later that the morning's work was over. Several days after the conversation recorded above, Pamphilus, having helped his father in the warehouse and being in no mood for exercising in the field, started out to walk to the highest point on the island. It was early Spring. A strong wind had blown every cloud from the sky and the sea lay covered with flying white-tipped waves. His garments leapt and billowed about him and his very hair tugged at his head. The gulls themselves, leaning upon the gusts, were caught unawares from time to time and blown with ruffled feathers and scandalized cries towards the violet-blue zenith. Pamphilus led his life with much worry and self-examination and all the exhilaration of wind and sun could not drive from his mind the anxious affection with which he now turned over his thoughts of Chrysis and Philumena and of the four members of his family. He was straying among the rocks and the lizards and the neglected dwarfed olive-trees, when his attention was suddenly caught by an incident on the hillside to his left. A group of boys from the town was engaged in tormenting a young girl. She was retreating backwards up the slope through a disused orchard, shouting haughtily back at her pursuers. The boys' malice had turned to anger; they were retorting hotly and letting fly about her a few harmless stones. Pamphilus strode over to the group and with a gesture ordered the boys down the hill. The girl, her face still flushed and distrustful, stood with her back against a tree and waited for him to come toward her. They looked at one another for a moment in silence. Finally Pamphilus said:

"What is the matter?"

"They're just country fools, that's all. They've never seen anyone before who didn't come from their wretched Brynos." And then from rage and disappointment she began to cry uncontrollably and despairingly.

Pamphilus watched her for a time and then asked her where she had been going.

"Nowhere. I was just going for a walk and they followed me from the town. I can't do anything. I can't go anywhere. . . . I wasn't hurting them. I was just going for a walk alone and they called names after me. They followed me way up here; I called names at them and then they started throwing things at me. That's all."

"I thought I knew everyone on the island," said Pamphilus thoughtfully, "but I have never seen you before. Have you been here long?"

"Yes, I've been here almost a year," she replied, adding indistinctly, ". . . but I hardly ever go out or anything."

"You hardly ever go out?"

"No," and she fumbled with her dress and stared at the sea, frowning.

"You should try to know some of the other girls and go out for walks with them."

This time she turned and looked into his face. "I don't know any of the other girls. I . . . I live at home and they don't let me go out of the house, except when I go out for walks nights with . . . well, with Mysis." She continued to be shaken with sobs, but she was adjusting her hair and the folds of her dress. "I don't see why they have to throw stones at me," she added.

Pamphilus looked at her in silence, gravely. Presently he collected himself and said: "There's a big smooth stone over there. Will you go over there and sit down?"

She followed him to the stone, still busy with her hair and drawing her fingers across her eyes and cheeks.

"I have a sister just about your age," said Pamphilus. "You can begin by knowing her. You can go for walks with her and then you wouldn't be a stranger any more. Her name is Argo. You'd like one another, I know. My sister is weaving a large mantle for my mother and she'd like you to help her with it and she could help you with yours. Are you making a mantle?"

"Yes."

"That would be fine," said Pamphilus, and from that moment Glycerium loved him forever.

"I probably know your father, don't I?" he asked.

"I have no father," she replied, looking up at him weakly, "I am the sister of the woman from Andros."

"Oh . . . oh . . .," said Pamphilus, more astonished than he had ever been in his life. "I know your sister well."

"Yes," said Glycerium. Her bright wet eyes strayed over the streaked sea and the blown birds. "She doesn't want anyone to know that I'm there. All day I stay up on the top of the house or work in the court. Only at night I'm allowed to go for a walk with Mysis. Even now I'm supposed to be in the house, but I broke my promise. She has gone to the market and so I broke my promise. I wanted to see what the island and the sea look like by day. And I wanted to look across to Andros where I come from. But the boys followed me here and threw stones at me and I can never come again."

Here she fell to weeping even more despairingly than before and Pamphilus could do nothing but say "Well" several times and "Yes." At last he asked her what her name was.

"Glycerium. Chrysis went away from home a long time ago and I was living with my brother and he died and I couldn't live with him any more. And I had nowhere to go or anything, and one day she came back and took me to live with her. That's all."

"Have you any brothers or sisters?"

"Oh, no."

"Who is Mysis?"

"Mysis isn't Greek. She is from Alexandria. Chrysis found her. All of them in the house,—she just found them somewhere. That's what she does. Mysis was a slave in the cloth mills. Sometimes she tells me about it."

Pamphilus still gazed at her, and bringing back her wandering evasive glance from the sea she looked at him from her thin face and enormous hungry eyes. Even a long glance did not now embarrass them.

"Do you want me to ask Chrysis to let you go about the island by day?" he asked.

"If she doesn't want it, we mustn't change her. Chrysis knows best." She turned away from him and said in a lower voice, dreamy and embittered: "But what can become of me? Am I always to stay locked up? I am fifteen already. The world is full of wonderful things and people that I might never know about. I know it was wrong of me to break my promise; but to live for years without ever knowing new people,—to hear them passing the door all day, and to see them a long ways off. Do you think I did very wrong?"

"No."

"I don't know anyone. I don't know anyone."

"Well . . . well, you'll come to know my sister. That will be a beginning," he said, taking her fingertips thoughtfully and wonderingly in his.

"Yes," she said.

"Everything is beginning over again. I'm your friend. Then my sister. Soon you will have a great many. You'll see."

"But where will I be five years from now and ten years from now," she cried, staring about her wildly. "I don't know. I'm afraid. I'm unhappy. Everyone in the world is happy except me."

The caress of the hands in first love, and never so simply again, seems to be a sharing of courage, an alliance of two courages against a confusing world. As his hand passed from her hair to her shoulder, she turned to him with parted lips and hesitant eyes, then suddenly bound both her arms about his neck. Into his ears her lips wildly and all but meaninglessly repeated: "Yes. Yes. Yes. I can't stay there forever. I should never know anyone. I should never see anybody."

"She will let you come to see me," he said.

"No," said Glycerium. "But I'll come by myself. I mustn't ask her. She would not let me come. She always knows best. And the boys can throw their stones. I don't mind if you're here. What . . . what is your name?"

"My name is Pamphilus, Glycerium."

"Can . . . can I call you by it?"

It was not at this meeting, nor at their next, but at the third, beneath the dwarfed olive-trees, that those caresses that seemed to be for courage, for pity and for admiration, were turned by Nature to her own uses.

These conversations took place in the early Spring. One afternoon in the late Summer Chrysis slipped out of her house and climbed the hill behind it. She was filled with a great desire to be alone and to think. She looked out over the glittering sea. The winds were moderate on that afternoon and before them the innumerable neat waves hurried toward the shore, running up the sands with a long whisper, or discreetly lifting against the rocks a scarf of foam. In the distance a school of dolphins engaged at their eternal games led the long procession of curving backs. The water was marbled at intervals with the strange fields and roadways of a lighter blue; and behind all she beheld with love the violet profile of Andros. For a time she strayed about upon the crest of the hill, making sure that no one was watching or following her, then descending the further side she sought out her favorite retreats, a point of rock that projected into the sea and a sheltered cove beside it. As she drew near the place, she stumbled forward, almost running, and as she went she murmured soothingly to herself: "We are almost there. Look, we are almost there now." At last, climbing over the boulders she let herself down into an amphitheatre of hot dry sand. She started unbinding her hair, but stopped herself abruptly: "No, no. I must think. I should fall asleep here. I must think first. I shall come back soon," she muttered to the amphitheatre, and continuing her journey she reached the furthermost heap of stones and sat down. She rested her chin upon her hand and fixing her eyes upon the horizon she waited for the thoughts to come.

The first thing to think about was her new illness. Several times she had been awakened by a wild fluttering in her left side that continued, deepening, until it seemed to her as though a great stake were being driven into her heart. And all the day the sensation would remain with her as of a heavy object burdening the place where this trouble lay. "Probably . . . very likely," she said to herself, "the next time I shall die of it." At the thought a wave of anticipation passed over her. "I shall probably die of it," she repeated cheerfully and became interested in some crayfish in the pool at her feet. She plucked some grasses behind her and started dragging them before the eyes of the indignant animals. "Nothing in life could make me abandon my sheep, but if I die they will have to fall back on Circumstance as I did. Glycerium, what will become of you? Apraxine, Mysis . . .? There are times when we cannot see one step ahead of us, but five years later we are eating and sleeping somewhere." (It was humorous, pretending that one's heart was as hard as that.) "Yes," she said aloud, to the pain that trembled within her, "only come quickly." She leaned forward still dragging the stems before the shellfish: "I have lived thirty-five years. I have lived enough. *Stranger, near this spot lies Chrysis, daughter of Arches of Andros: the ewe that has strayed*

from the flock lives many years in one day and dies at a great age
when the sun sets." She laughed at the deceptive comforts of self-
pity and taking off a sandal put her foot into the water. She drew
herself up for a moment, asking herself what there was left in the
house for the colony's supper; then recollecting some fish and
some salad on the shelf, she returned to her thoughts. She repeated
her epitaph, making it a song and emphasizing, for self-mockery,
its false sentiment. "O Andros, O Poseidon, how happy I am. I
have no right to be happy like this. . . ."

And she knew as she gazed at the frieze of dolphins still playing
in the distance that her mind was avoiding another problem that
awaited her. "I am happy because I love this Pamphilus,—
Pamphilus the anxious, Pamphilus the stupid. Why cannot someone tell him that it is not necessary to suffer so about living." And
the low exasperated sigh escaped her, the protest we make at the
preposterous, the incorrigible beloved. "He thinks he is failing. He
thinks he is inadequate to life at every turn. Let him rest some day,
O ye Olympians, from pitying those who suffer. Let him learn to
look the other way. This is something new in the world, this
concern for the unfit and the broken. Once he begins that, there's
no end to it, only madness. It leads nowhere. That is some god's
business." Whereupon she discovered that she was weeping; but
when she had dried her eyes she was still thinking about him.
"Oh, such people are unconscious of their goodness. They strike
their foreheads with their hands because of their failure, and yet
the rest of us are made glad when we remember their faces. Pamphilus, you are another herald from the future. Some day men will
be like you. Do not frown so. . . ."

But these thoughts were very fatiguing. She arose and, returning
to the amphitheatre, laid herself down upon the sand. She murmured some fragments from the Euripidean choruses and fell

asleep. She had always been an islander and this hot and impersonal sun playing upon a cold and impersonal sea was not unfriendly to her. And now for two hours the monotony of sun and
sea played about her and wove itself into the mood of her sleeping
mind. As once the gray-eyed Athena stood guarding Ulysses—she
leaning upon her spear, her great heart full of concern and of
those long divine thoughts that are her property—even so, now,
the hour and the place all but gathered itself into a presence and
shed its influence upon her. When her eyes finally opened she
listened for a time to the calm in her heart. "Some day," she said,
"we shall understand why we suffer. I shall be among the shades
underground and some wonderful hand, some Alcestis, will touch
me and will show me the meaning of all these things; and I shall
laugh softly for hours as I do now . . . as I do now."

She arose and binding up her hair prepared to ascend the slope.
But just as she turned to leave the place, there visited her the desire
to do something ceremonial, to mark the hour. She stood up
straightly and held out her arms to the setting sun: "If you still
hear prayers from the lips of mortals, if our longings touch you at
all, hear me now. Give to this Pamphilus some assurance—even
some assurance such as you have given to me, unstable though I
am—that he is right. And oh! (but I do not say this from vanity or
pride, O Apollo,—but perhaps this is weak, this is childish of me,
perhaps this renders the whole prayer powerless!) if it is possible,
let the thought of me or of something I have said be comforting to
him some day. And . . . and . . ."

But her arms fell to her side. The world seemed empty. The sun
went down. The sea and sky became suddenly remote and she was
left with only the tears in her eyes and the longing in her heart.
She closed her lips and turned her head aside. "I suppose there is

no god," she whispered. "We must do these things ourselves. We must drag ourselves through life as best we can."

Chrysis had made the mistake of accustoming the members of her household to her invariable presence and now while she slept they became increasingly indignant at the length of her absence. In twos and threes they hovered about the door peering to the right and to the left with mingled scorn and alarm.

"When she comes in, see that no one says a word to her," directed Apraxine, a tall lame woman whom Chrysis had found beaten and left for dead at the edge of the desert below the terraces of Alexandria.

"Pretend you don't see her."

". . . to go sallying off a whole day without a word to a soul."

"I'm sure I don't wish to stay in a house where I count for nothing."

". . . less than nothing, it seems."

Presently however something happened that distracted their minds from their resentment. A new sheep arrived at the fold.

Simo's frank had carried to Andros the money that Chrysis intended for the support of the stricken sea-captain. But Philocles's guardians had long since tired of their charge and become discontented with the intermittent payments. They decided to take advantage of this sum of money to ship him off to Brynos. It was necessary for this purpose to wait for a lucid interval in the patient's condition. Such a moment finally arrived; they hurriedly made up his bundle, brushed his hair, and led him down to the waterfront, where they found the captain of a boat sailing between the Cyclades who was willing to undertake the commission. And thus it was that on the afternoon of Chrysis's retreat to solitude

Philocles arrived on Brynos. A boy who attended at one of the wine-shops in the town was directed to escort him to her house, and suddenly the childlike sea-captain was thrust into the courtyard among the conspiring pensioners.

Ten years before Philocles had been the greatest navigator on the Mediterranean, first in skill and experience and first in fame. He had been many times to Sicily and to Carthage; he had passed through the Gates of Hercules and visited the Tyrian mines in Britain. He had sailed westward for months across the great shelf of water, seeking new islands, and had been forced to turn back by the visible anger of the gods. In the present age men were captains or merchants or farmers, but in the great age men had been first Athenians or Greeks, and the islanders regarded Philocles as of that order, a belated giant. He was already in middle life when Chrysis first knew him—she had been a passenger on one of his trips to Egypt—and it astonished her to find someone laconic in a chattering world and with quiet hands in a gesturing civilization. He was blackened and cured by all weathers. He stood in the squares of the various ports of call, his feet apart as though they were forever planted on a shifting deck. He seemed to be too large for daily life; his very eyes were strange—unaccustomed to the shorter range, too used to seizing the appearances of a constellation between a cloud and a cloud, and the outlines of a headland in rain. Wind, salt and starvation had moulded his head, and his mind had been rendered, not buoyant, but rich and concentrated by the enforced asceticisms of a prolonged duty and of long sea voyages. He had been one of the persons whom Chrysis had most loved in all her life and it was she who had discovered his secret, the secret that it was neither adventure nor gain that drove him along his adventurous life. He was passing the time and filling the hours in anticipation of release from a life that had lost its savor with the death of his daughter. These two saw in one another's eyes the thing they had in common, the fact that they had both died to themselves. They lived at one remove from that self that supports the generality of men, the self that is a bundle of self-assertions, of greeds, of vanities and of easily-offended pride. Three years before, Philocles had been forced to captain some ships of a city at war. He had been captured and mutilated and what was left of so kingly a person was a timorous child.

The sheep examined the newcomer who had been thrust so abruptly into their midst. They questioned him and amused themselves with his answers. Then they gave him a bench in the sunlight where he might whisper to his heart's content.

The sun set and soon after Chrysis came stumbling through the door, laughing apologetically and pushing back her hair. "Forgive me, O my dear friends, forgive me. I fell asleep on the sand and I'm very sorry I'm so late." (The men and women raised their eyebrows cynically and went on with their work.) "Apraxine, has anything happened?" (Apraxine cleared her throat with Alexandrian hauteur and became absorbed in looking for a thread on the ground.) "Now we must find something particularly rare for supper."

The sheep exchanged pitying glances over all this tawdry artifice and when Chrysis passed into the house they burst into laughter. The laughter was condescending, but the soul had returned to the community. Finally at a signal from Apraxine, Glycerium went to the door and announced to Chrysis that Philocles had arrived from Andros. He had seen her pass and some twinge of memory had set him trembling. He rose and walked unsteadily to the middle of the court. She saw him standing before her, haggard, with hollow puzzled eyes and with untrimmed beard.

She went forward repeating, "My dear friend, my friend!" but as she embraced him a loud voice within her seemed to say: "Something is going to happen. The threads of my life are drawing together."

That night Chrysis was awakened from a light and feverish sleep by the instinctive knowledge that someone was near her. She raised herself on one elbow and peered toward the faint glimmer of the door.

"Who is it? Who is there?" she said.

A figure seemed suddenly to rise from the threshold. "It's I, Chrysis. It's Glycerium."

"Is something the matter? Is someone ill?"

"No . . . it's only . . ."

"Light a lamp, my child. What do you want?"

"Chrysis, are you angry with me for waking you up? I couldn't sleep, Chrysis, and I had to come into your room."

"But why are you crying, my dear, my dove? Come now and sit on the edge of the bed. Of course I'm not angry with you." Glycerium sank upon the floor beside her. "No, no,—the floor is cold. Come sit up here. Your hair is wet! Tell me now, what is making you unhappy?"

"Nothing."

"What? Then you have something to tell me?"

"No . . . I don't know what . . . I just want you to talk to me."

"Well, I have something to tell you." Chrysis was stroking Glycerium's hair, delicately following with her finger-tips the strands as they passed above and behind the ear, when suddenly Glycerium threw her arms about her sister's neck and sobbed uncontrollably. Chrysis continued gravely with her caress, thinking that she was merely dealing with one of the meaningless accesses of despair that descend upon adolescence when the slow ache of existence is first apprehended by the growing mind. "There!" she murmured in a rhythmic undertone, "Sh . . . sh . . . sh . . . sh. . . . We love you. We all love you in this house. Our beautiful Glycerium, our gentle, our very beautiful Glycerium . . . sh . . . sh . . . there! Are you comfortable now? I have some good news for you. (No, no, there is plenty of room.) This is it: Beginning tomorrow you are going to lead an altogether different life. I am going to let you wander all over the island alone. And when Mysis and I go to market you can go with us. You may climb the hills if you like, and you may explore along the water's edge,—I shall even show you the secret of the secrets of my heart,—a beautiful hidden shelter by the sea where one can be perfectly alone. . . . Well? are you pleased? Doesn't this news make you happy?"

"Yes, Chrysis."

"Now! I thought it would make you very happy and all you say is: Yes, Chrysis!"

"Chrysis, tell me: what will become of me?"

Chrysis changed her position and in the dark shut her eyes a moment. "Oh, my dear, my dear . . . that's what everyone asks, everyone on earth. Well, first you tell me: what do you want to become?"

"I want to marry someone and . . . and be in his home. Chrysis, tell me: can I marry someone? Without a father and a mother and without anything, is it possible that I can marry someone?"

"My dear, there is always . . ."

"Chrysis, I'm grown-up now. I'm fifteen. Please tell me the truth. I must know. Don't say something merely to quiet me. I must know the truth. Can a man ever ask me to marry him? Why are you waiting so long to answer me?"

"I have been planning to have a long talk with you about all these things. But not now. Wait a short time; wait until you have had a week, two weeks, of this new life when you will be free to wander all over the island. Then you will be able to understand better what I have to say."

Glycerium paused a moment. "I know, I know," she said, her face against Chrysis's shoulder. "That means that no one will ever be able to marry me."

"No, no, I don't say that. . . ."

Glycerium rose and stood in the middle of the room. "I understand," she said in the darkness.

Chrysis raised herself again on one elbow and said slowly: "We are not Greek citizens. We are not people with homes. We are considered strange, only a little above the slaves. All those others live in homes and everyone knows their fathers and their mothers; they marry one another. They think we would never fit into their life. Although all that is true,—"

"But there are stories," said Glycerium, "of men who even married girls that had been slaves."

"Yes, if a young man should fall in love with you, it is possible that he would take you into his home. That is why I have tried to take such care of you and why I have kept you hidden here in the house. Through the young men who come to the banquets, the island knows that you are here and that you have been carefully protected. And now that you are to walk about the island freely you must be a hundred times more careful than other girls. You are beautiful and you are good, and before all their unfriendly eyes you must show them your modesty and your goodness. That is all there is to say and to hope, my child."

"Perhaps, Chrysis . . . it is best that I do not go about the island freely, after all."

"No, no. You will feel like going out. It will come gradually. But now you must go to bed and to sleep, my darling. All these things will solve themselves as best they can. All you can do for the present is to be yourself, your very self, my Glycerium."

Glycerium moved unsteadily towards the bed: "Chrysis, I must tell you something."

"Yes? . . ."

"You will be angry with me, Chrysis."

"Why . . ."

"May the gods protect me, I . . . I have been talking with Mysis and now I know that I am going to be the mother of a child."

There was silence for a moment followed by the sound of Chrysis putting her feet upon the floor. "Where is Mysis? Let me get up."

"It is true, Chrysis. I broke my promise the times when you were away. I used to go out over the hills."

"Oh, my child, my child!"

"But he loves me. He will marry me. He loves me, I know."

"Who is it? What is his name?"

"It is Pamphilus, son of Simo."

Chrysis grew rigid in the darkness. Then she slowly put her feet back into the bed. Glycerium continued wildly: "He loves me. He will take care of me. He has told me so a hundred times. Chrysis, what shall I do? What shall I do? I am afraid."

A low moan at the door revealed the fact that Mysis had accompanied her younger mistress to this interview and was kneeling outside the door without the courage to enter.

After a moment Chrysis said in a light impersonal voice: "Well, you . . . go off to bed now and go to sleep. Yes. We'll both be catching cold here. It's late. I think it must be almost morning."

"I cannot sleep."

"Everything will be all right, Glycerium. I can't talk any more now. I'm not well. We'll talk about it in the morning."

Glycerium left the room, trembling.

In her darker hours Chrysis carried on what she called a "dialogue with Fate." And now as she turned to the wall she said: "I hear you. You have won again."

Before long the pain in her side became fixed and unremitting, and Chrysis knew that her life was drawing to a close. She took to her bed and her thoughts no longer clung to the world about her. Now when her courage was being undermined by her pain she dared not ask herself if she had lived and if she were dying, unloved, in disorder, without meaning. From time to time she peered into her mind to ascertain what her beliefs were in regard to a life after death, its judgments or its felicities; but the most exhausting of all our adventures is that journey down the long corridors of the mind to the last halls where belief is enthroned. She resigned herself to the memory of certain moments when intuition had comforted her and she quieted her heart with Andrian cradle-songs and with fragments from the tragic poets. She saved her strength to fulfill a last desire, one that may perhaps seem unworthy to persons of a later age. Her mind had been moulded by formal literature, by epics and odes, by tragedies and by heroic biography, and from this reading she had been imbued with the superstition that one should die in a noble manner, and in this high decorum even the maintenance of her beauty played a part. The only terror left in the world was the fear that she might leave it with cries of pain, with a torn mind, and with discomposed features.

The news spread about the island that the Andrian was gravely ill. The young men who had been her guests were confused by the discrepancy between their mothers' sarcasms and the respect that Chrysis had inspired in themselves, but some brought shy offerings of wine and cheese to her door. For such brief interviews she raised herself on one elbow and sought to recover her light-spoken graciousness. But most of the young men stayed away; it required a maturer mind than they could summon to hold side by side their memories of sensual pleasure and their respect due to the dying.

Pamphilus had other reasons for staying away. It seemed more and more unlikely that he would ever be permitted to marry Glycerium. But one morning he appeared at Chrysis's house and asked to see her. He traversed the court, picking his way among her motley and dismayed pensioners, and his eyes fell upon Glycerium. She was seated beside Philocles at her sister's door, silent and without hope. Pamphilus stopped for a moment on one knee before her and took her hands in his. "Do not be afraid," he said in a low voice. "No harm will come to you." She derived no courage from his words; she lifted her eyes and scanned his face. Her mouth trembled, but no words came and her eyes returned to the ground. Pamphilus passed into the room where Chrysis lay; for a moment he could distinguish nothing in the darkness. Presently he became aware of the priest of Aesculapius and Apollo bending over a brazier in the corner, and finally he saw Chrysis smiling at him gravely from the bed. He sat down beside her in silence; each waited for the other to begin.

"We are sorry, all of us are sorry, Chrysis," he said at last, "to hear that you have been so ill."

"Thank you, Pamphilus. Thank them all."

"There . . . there has been so much rain. When the sunlight returns you will feel better at once."

"Yes, it has always been the sunlight that has done me the most good. You are all well on your farm?"

"Yes, the gods be praised."

"The gods be praised. I shall never forget a favor your father did for me."

Pamphilus was struck with amazement. "My father?"

"Oh, forgive me . . . I remember now I promised him not to mention it to you. Oh, my illness has made me forget that. I am ashamed, I am ashamed. But now I had better add that it was a small commission he did for me by one of his boats going to Andros. I would not have him think me unfaithful to my promise. I beg of you earnestly not to tell him that I spoke of it."

"Indeed, I shall not tell him, Chrysis."

There fell another pause between them, while her strengthless hands lightly pressed upon the bed in her self-reproach.

"Yes," said Pamphilus. "When there is more sunlight you will feel better at once. The sky has been overcast for a long time. I cannot remember when it has been overcast so long."

To themselves they both cried: "How shall we ever get out of this?"

"We have missed the banquets. I would like to tell you again, Chrysis, what great pleasure they gave me. I have been looking forward to the next one when you promised to read us I forget what play."

"It was to have been the *Ion* of Euripides."

"Yes."

"This," said Chrysis, glancing toward the priest with a smile, "this is my Ion."

But perhaps the words were ill-chosen. She thought she saw the priest frowning as he bent over his work. "Forgive me," she said to him abruptly, "if I have offended you. I did not mean it ill."

But the tears were rolling down her cheeks. "Life, Pamphilus," she said, "is full of mistakes, but the wrongs we do to those we love and honor are more than we can endure." The priest approached the further side of the bed and adjusted the pillows; he whispered a few words into her ear and went back to his brazier.

"Am I tiring you?" Pamphilus asked.

"No, no. I am very happy that you have come." To herself she thought: "Time is passing, and what are we saying! Is there not something heartfelt that I can find to say to him, something to remember, for him and for me?" But she distrusted the emotion that filled her heart. It was perhaps mere excitement and pain; or a vague and false sentiment. Probably the best thing to do was to be stoic; to be brave and inarticulate; to talk of trivial things. Or was it a greater bravery to surmount this shame and to say whatever obvious words the heart dictated? Which was right?

Pamphilus was thinking: "She is dying. What can I say to her? But I have never been able to place words rightly. I am dull. I am nothing to her but the man who has wronged her sister." Aloud he said in a low voice: "I shall marry Glycerium if I can, Chrysis. At all events you may be sure that no harm will come to her."

"Though I love her dearly," replied Chrysis, finding her words with great difficulty, "I shall not urge you. I . . . I no longer believe that what happens to us is important. You will marry Glycerium or another. The years will unfold these things. It is the life in the mind that is important."

"I shall do what I can for her."

"You have only to be yourself without fear, without doubting, Pamphilus."

"Chrysis, you will forgive me for having spoken to you so little at the banquets . . . and for having sat at the further end and . . . that is the way I am. It was not because I did not respect you. I cannot talk as those others can. I am only a listener. Even now I cannot say what I mean. But I followed all that you said."

The pain in Chrysis's side seemed to increase beyond all endurance. "Oh, friend," she said, "do not distrust. These things are not so unsatisfactory . . . so interrupted as they seem to be." The priest had been watching her; she made a slight sign to him. "I do not wish you to go away," she continued to Pamphilus, almost in a whisper, "but it is best that I sleep now." Then raising herself on one elbow she breathed in anguish: "Perhaps we shall meet somewhere beyond life when all these pains shall have been removed. I think the gods have some mystery still in store for us. But if we do not, let me say now . . ." her hands opened and closed upon the cloths that covered her, ". . . I want to say to someone . . . that I have known the worst that the world can do to me, and that nevertheless I praise the world and all living. All that is, is well. Remember some day, remember me as one who loved all things and accepted from the gods all things, the bright and the dark. And do you likewise. Farewell."

Simo arose early to witness Chrysis's funeral. The Greeks, for reasons that lay deep in their sense of the fitness of things and in their superstition, conducted their funerals in the hour before dawn, and it was therefore still profound night when the little procession of her household prepared to pass through the streets of the town. When Simo arrived at the square he found that many of the men of Brynos had already gathered there and, drawing the folds of their rough cloaks about them, were standing talking together in low voices. The men of his own age had brought their curiosity and contempt with them and were congratulating themselves on the island's happy deliverance from the foreign woman; but the younger men who had known Chrysis stood with sullen faces, their throats rigid with antagonism at the glee of their elders. Simo took his place in silence beside Chremes, but refused to respond to the latter's animated comment. Presently as the sounds of the flute and the mourners were heard approaching he discovered Pamphilus standing beside him, as silent as himself.

Mysis herded the shuffling and stumbling company before her as best she could. Philocles walked with lifted knees, as children do in a procession. In one hand he held some grasses and with the other he clutched the mantle of his companion, the old doorkeeper; but he was continually straying off, or standing still to gaze with wide dazzled eyes at the torches that preceded him or at the laughing by-standers. Behind him the deaf and dumb Ethiopian girl could scarcely be restrained from running forward to walk beside her sleeping friend, Chrysis, whose rebuke had been so terrible when she had done wrong and whose smile had been sufficient compensation for her imprisonment in silence. Glycerium walked with lowered eyes, lost to hope and lost to the decorum that now required of her the wailing and the distraught gestures of a conspicuous mourner. All these passed forward under the bright stars that had received the first intimation of day and shone with a last heightened brilliance, and under the long garlands of smoke that hung above the company in that windless air.

As the onlookers accompanied the procession into the open country, Simo's attention was fixed upon Glycerium, by reason of her condition, which was apparent to all, of her resemblance to her sister, of the dejection that invested her, and of the beauty and modesty of her bearing. And he became aware that his son also was watching the girl. In fact, during the whole journey, Pamphilus bent upon her his burning eyes, trying to intercept her glance and to communicate to her his encouragement and his love. But not until they reached the heaped-up wood whereon the bodies of a goat and a lamb were laid beside that of Chrysis, and not until the fire had touched it, did she raise her eyes. Then as the sound of the wailing increased in shrillness and the sound of the flute floated piercingly above all, she turned to Mysis and began to speak wildly into her ear. But the words of her vehemence were not heard in that din, nor were Mysis's words of encouragement. Glycerium was trying to draw herself away from the supporting arm of the other and the slow faltering struggle of the two women was lighted up by the rising flames. Pamphilus, in the intensity of his concentration upon the suffering of the girl, moved slowly forward, his hands held out before him. And now he heard the words that she was repeating: "It's best. It's best so!" Suddenly Glycerium pushed the older woman away from her and with a loud cry of "Chrysis!" stumbled forward to fling herself upon the body of her sister.

But Pamphilus had foreseen this attempt. Running across the sand, he seized her by her disheveled hair and drew her back and into his arms. The touch of that encircling arm released her tears. She laid her head against his breast as one who had been there before and was returning home.

The scandal of this embrace was felt at once by all the bystanders and chiefly by Chremes, who turned upon Simo with his protest and astonishment. But Simo had moved away and was walking slowly home through the breaking dawn. Now he understood the Pamphilus of the last months.

The islanders discussed interminably the surprising event that had taken place at Chrysis's funeral. They watched with hushed excitement the chill that had fallen across the relations between the families of Simo and of Chremes. Rumor presently asserted that Pamphilus had promised to acknowledge the child, though no one, naturally, even discussed the possibility of a marriage. Readers of a later age will not be able to understand the difficulties that beset the young man. Marriage was not then a sentimental relation, but a legal one of great dignity, and the bridegroom's share in the contract involved not so much himself as his family, his farm, and his ancestors. Without the support of his parents and without a residence in their home a young man was a mere adventurer, without social, economic or civil standing. A marriage was only possible if Simo declared it to be so. The customs of the islands encouraged fathers in the luxuries of blustering and tyranny, but Simo's relations with his son had always been strangely impersonal. He was confused by his own deference for his son, by what he thought was his own weakness. Yet Simo's silence did not have the air of a final refusal; it even seemed to imply that the decision, with all its possibilities of lifetime regret and of a lifetime's contention on the farm, rested with Pamphilus.

One day several months after Chrysis's funeral Pamphilus betook himself to the palaestra for some exercise. He entered the low door and, nodding to a group of friends that sat scuffling under an awning at the edge of the enclosure, he walked across the hot red sand. The old attendant at the door who had won a laurel wreath in his youth came trotting across the burning ring after him and as soon as Pamphilus had seated himself on a marble bench began kneading his calves and ankles. In the centre of the field Chremes's son was going through the motions of hurling an imaginary discus; thirty and fifty times he turned with lifted knee, trying to fix in his muscular memory the perfect synchronization of the gestures. Two other young men were practicing a festival dance, interrupting their work from time to time to criticize one another's slightest deviation from a harmonious balance. The young priest of Aesculapius and Apollo was running around the course. Pamphilus sent the attendant away and lying down on his cloak let the sunlight beat upon him. He did not think about his problem, but left his mind a blank, suffused with a dull misery that identified itself with the drowsy heat. Presently he placed his elbow on the ground and raising his head rested his cheek upon his hand and watched the priest of Apollo.

The priest never entered the competitive games, but he was undoubtedly first upon the island for endurance and second only to Pamphilus in swiftness. Save on the days of festival he appeared for exercise daily and ran six miles. He preserved a perfect temperance: he drank no wine; he lived on fruit and vegetables; he awoke with the sun and unless there was some call to attend the sick he went to sleep with it. He had taken the vow of chastity, the vow that forever closes the mind to the matter, without wistful backglancing and without conceding the possibility that circumstance might yet present a harmless deviation, the vow which, when profoundly compassed, fills the mind with such power that it is forever cut off from the unstable tentative sons of men. His office required his passing so much time among the sick and the distressed that he had become inadequate to the cheerful and the happy and no one on the island knew him very well. But he had a strange power over the sick and the demented and only in their hours of confession and despair was the shutter of his impersonality lifted; such as had known him then followed him ever after with their eyes, in gratitude and in astonishment. He was only twenty-eight, but he had been sent to Brynos by the priests that attended the great mysteries of Athens and Corinth as a signal honor; for the shrine on Brynos was one of particular significance in the legend of Aesculapius and his father Apollo. Pamphilus had never spoken to him beyond the salutations of the field, but he would rather have known him than anyone in the world, and he in turn watched Pamphilus with grave interest. Now Pamphilus lay following him with his eyes and wishing he had his own life to live over again.

Suddenly he became aware that someone was shaking him by the shoulder. It was one of his companions. "Here comes your father," said the boy and went back to the awning. Pamphilus rose to his feet and waited respectfully as Simo approached, preceded by the old attendant.

"Stay where you are. Lie down again," said Simo; "I'll sit here on this bench. I want to talk to you."

Pamphilus lay down, his face turned away towards the track.

Simo wiped his face with the hem of his skirt. "I won't be long, my boy. . . . But we must consider this matter somehow . . . after all." He was not sure of himself. He blew his nose. He coughed several times and roughly adjusted the folds of his gown. He repeated "Very well" and "Now" and waited in vain for Pamphilus to say something. At last he launched forth among his prepared introductions:

"Well now, my boy, I assume you want to marry the girl. Hm . . ."

Pamphilus put his head down between his folded arms as though he were going to sleep. He sighed in anticipation of all the irrelevancies he was about to hear. In his heart he knew he had only to say yes or no and his father would accede to his wish.

"I don't wish to coerce you. I think you are old enough to see the good and the bad for yourself. But for a few moments now I want to talk all around the matter. I want to put the other side of the case in its plainest terms and leave it there for a while. May I do that?"

"Yes," said Pamphilus.

"Well, to begin with, it's only right to face the fact that there is no outward obligation to marry the girl. I've looked into the matter. She is not a Greek citizen. She happens to have been brought up in a sheltered manner, or so I take it. This Chrysis seems to have tried to prevent the girl's falling into her way of life; but that does not alter the fact that she is a mere dancing girl. Now, mind you, I can see that she is modest and well-mannered. She appears to be just such a person as our own Argo. But she could never have hoped for anything above the situation she is now in. The world is full of just such likable stray girls as this Glycerium, but we cannot be expected to welcome them into the fabric of good Greek family life. You may be sure that Chrysis knew perfectly well that Glycerium must some day become a hetaira like herself, or a servant."

Simo paused. He could see the back only of his son's head, but he was able to imagine upon his face the set unhappy expression they had all been obliged to watch there for the last weeks. He coughed again and abruptly flung himself upon another of his openings:

"No doubt you feel yourself fairly bound to her by a promise— but a promise, Pamphilus, in which you failed to consider the rest of us, and especially your mother. If you decided to marry the girl, your mother and sister would try to live with her as peaceably as possible, we know; but it would be a good deal to ask of them. You know them. This girl does not understand the first thing about our island manners. She doesn't know how simple and monotonous our women's lives are. I expect that life with the Andrian and with that strange company at the house on the hill was an odd affair. She'd be unhappy with us. And even if she didn't contradict your mother all day . . . and worse . . . she'd become silent and sullen. Pamphilus, they would never grow fond of one another. It would be better to be cruel to her now and let her alone, than to set up discord, a lifetime of discord on our farm."

For a moment his memory failed him, but he rallied and continued:

"Well, even assuming that your mother and sister came to like her and to accept her cordially in the home, all her life she would have to endure something insulting in the manner of the other women on the island. We men do not take that interest in social discrimination, my son, but women . . . women with their few interests and . . . and so on . . . they enjoy having someone to ignore or to stare down. It warms them. Glycerium is not a Greek citizen. Her sister was a hetaira. All her life she would be obliged to endure their looking at her with straight lips and (I can see them) with half-closed eyes. But even that is not the chief thing."

He hoped that the suspense in this splendid transition would be reflected in some change in his son's position, but the young man lay motionless. Simo's weary eyes turned slowly about the palaestra.

"The girl is not strong. The women of the village seem to know something about it. She's a quick nervous high-strung girl and she'd bring you a series of thin and sickly children. You and I know those homes. She's not unlike our neighbor Douro's wife; isn't she? and the uneven health of such women—even though they're often more likable, yes, more likable, than the Philumenas—takes the shape of complaining and quarrelsomeness. And in their children. One has no right to bring into the world those children that cannot join others in their games, silent children who go through life regularly subject to fevers and coughs and pains. The most important thing in life is a houseful of strong healthy boys. Take Philumena, now. You do not 'love' Philumena, as the poets use the word. Well, when I married your mother perhaps I did not 'love' her in that sense. But I grew to love her and . . . euh . . . now I cannot imagine myself as having been married to anyone else, as satisfactorily married to anyone else. Philumena is handsome. But most important of all, Philumena is strong. So . . . so, Pamphilus, does what I am saying seem to have some truth in it? . . . Pamphilus?"

But Pamphilus had fallen asleep.

His last thought had been the recollection of one of Chrysis's maxims, an ironic phrase which he had chosen to take literally: *The mistakes we make through generosity are less terrible than the gains we acquire through caution.*

Simo was not vexed. He sighed. Looking up he saw the priest of Aesculapius and Apollo running around the course. He recalled the day several months before when he and Sostrata had taken Pamphilus's sister to the temple. For two days and two nights, Argo had been suffering from an ear-ache, and although they knew that the priest was often ungracious when his attention was asked on smaller ills they ventured to present her to him. The hour at which he was accustomed to receive the sick was a little after sunrise and there they found his colony. There were invalids brought to him on beds; there were sufferers from tumors, from protracted languors, from sore eyes; there were the possessed. Simo and Sostrata had passed their lives without ailments. They regarded them, like poverty, like uncleanliness, as mere bad citizenship; they were on the point of returning home, so great was their distaste for such manifestations. The priest required that the guardians who had brought their sick to him should retire to a distance during his interviews, and Simo and Sostrata had withdrawn with an ill grace to a nearby grove. Argo seemed not to share her parents' revulsion from these matters; even before she approached the place (her fingers pressed upon her ear) she had been subdued to awe and when her turn came she told her little story with caught breath. The priest gently touched her ear, recit-

ing a charm. He poured in some oil and looked deeply into her shy
eyes. And gradually as he gazed at her a smile appeared upon his
lips and slowly she smiled in return. True influence over another
comes not from a moment's eloquence nor from any happily
chosen word, but from the accumulation of a lifetime's thoughts
stored up in the eyes. And there is one thing greater than curing a
malady and that is accepting a malady and sharing its acceptance.
The ear-ache did not abate at once, but Argo pretended to her
parents that it did, for the other healing they would not have
understood; and all night long instead of complaining she pressed
against her ear the little bag of laurel leaves he had given her and
talked to herself, rehearsing that interview and that glance. Thereafter she never had any conversation with the priest, but when she
happened to meet him upon the road, her heart was filled with
excitement; she gave him a shy greeting and her eyelids fluttered in
a quick intimate glance and he in turn let fall upon her a faint
allusion to his smile. Her parents were amused by this bond; the
priest had brought out in their daughter a side they had never
known in her, and one that sent messages all along her life.
Henceforth she even stood up straighter. One day a cousin who
lived on the other side of the island came to a meal with them and
let fall a remark in disparagement of the priest, saying that he was
a comfort chiefly to old women who imagined themselves to be ill.
Argo's eyes grew dark and her lips straight with anger. She
refused to eat another mouthful and forever after the poor foolish
cousin could never draw a word from her and never knew why. All
this now returned to Simo's mind as he watched the priest.

"People like that," he thought to himself, "have some secret
about living. Why don't they tell it to us outright, instead of
wrapping it up in mystery and ceremonial? They know something
that prevents their blundering about, as we do. Yes, what am I

doing here," he added, pushing out his lower lip, "but playing the fool? Blundering, advising in things I know nothing about." He looked long at his sleeping son. "Pamphilus has some of that secret, too. And that woman from Andros had it, too. Chremes was right, though he meant it ill: there is something of the priest in Pamphilus, something of the priest trying to make its way in him. Let me get up and go away before I say anything more."

So he arose and a little guiltily left the field.

Pamphilus's mind was all but made up, yet still under the burden of perplexity and self-reproach he decided to seek still more light on his problem and a last reassurance by reviving a custom that had been in frequent use among the Greeks of the great age, but which had fallen off at the time of the events of this story. It consisted merely in abstaining from speech and from food from one sunrise to the next and in either passing the night in the temple enclosure or in arriving there before the dawn that closed the watch. There was not thought to be any particular magic in the practice: it cleared the mind of bodily fumes, it removed it from the commerce of the day and prepared it perhaps for a significant dream. The watcher guarded his fast and his silence, but the Greek mind did not approve of heightening the experience by any further self-denial. One moved about the home as usual, exercised in the palaestra or worked at the loom; one slept. If some uninformed person spoke to the watcher, he drew his finger across his lips and the condition of the vow was understood. Athletes still observed it several days before a race; brides on the eve of their wedding; old ladies who hoped to recover some lost trinket, or to recapture in a dream the features of some all-but-forgotten love; and devout soldiers about to set forth upon an expedition. It was indeed little short of odd that a healthy young man in the even current of life should revive this custom, but the islanders were still sufficiently religious to respect the habits that had expressed the spiritual life of their glorious grandfathers, and made no comment.

By mid-afternoon hunger had gained upon him and his dejection had increased a hundred-fold. Whichever choice he made would involve the unhappiness of others. Under the weight of the alternatives even the memory of Glycerium lost for a time any tender association. He climbed over the remoter parts of the island, gazing absently out to sea and idly plucking the grasses among the rocks where he sat. He came to the spot where he had first seen Glycerium and stood for a time, quiet as the stones about him, asking himself whether the associations in life are based upon an accidental encounter or upon a profound and inner necessity. When he returned to the farm his mother and sister felt the desolation that invested him and moved about with hushed steps. The very slaves went about their tasks on tiptoe and finally withdrew in silence and in alarmed interrogation. During the evening meal Pamphilus sat by the door with closed eyes. His brother, returning, stepped over his feet with awed circumspection (he too had made the watch only a few months before, but in pomp, with twelve other youths on the occasion of their enrollment in the League) and held himself at a distance, rendered uncomfortable by so much seriousness in a good athlete. Of her own accord Argo brought Pamphilus a bowl of water which he drank, smiling the while intimately into her grave eyes; she returned to her place at the table with great dignity and with secret excitement, as though she had done something conspicuous. When Simo finally told her and her brother to go to bed she slipped up to her father and laid her lips against his ear: "What is it, father?" she whispered. "No, tell me, what is the matter?" He took her hands and played with them a moment; he raised his eyebrows wisely and told her to go to bed and sleep well. From her bed in the darkness she noted the movements of the family: that her mother took a cloak and went out into the garden by the cliff, and that later her father did the same. With wide eyes and cautious lifted ear she followed this unaccustomed nocturnal roaming. She was filled with loving excitement; she kissed her doll many times with violence and wept. She became aware that her younger brother was venturing on hands and knees towards the moonlight in the court: she too ventured out and they stared at one another, but Pamphilus suddenly loomed up from the shadows and waved them back to their beds.

Pamphilus wandered about the outer court. Again the moon was at the full, throwing a milky blue mist over the tiers of olive trees that climbed the hill across the road and casting black shadows among the farm buildings. Its serenity contrasted strangely with the mysterious excitement it awakened among the human beings it fell upon. Pamphilus had seen his parents go into the garden, but he saw them now without emotion, without pity. He returned to the house and lay down upon his bed. Never had he been possessed by mood further from illumination. Lying on his face he traced outlines upon the floor with his finger.

The shells gleamed on the path as Simo walked up and down; from time to time he cast a furtive glance at his wife. She was sitting on a bench of chipped and stained marble that had been his mother's favorite seat. It had been placed there generations before, under a fig arbor blown down long since on a night of legendary storm. It stood at the very end of the garden where a cliff broke down to the sea, and from it one could hear forever the long spreading whispers of the ebbing and the rising waves below. From that seat his mother had directed the bringing up of five children, had dried their tears and listened with nodding head to the absurd procession of their shifting enthusiasms. "Viewed from a distance," Simo said to himself, "life is harmonious and beautiful. No doubt the years when my mother smiled to us from that bench were as full of crossed wills and exasperations as today, but how beautiful they seem in memory! The dead are wrapped in love; in illusion, perhaps. They go underground and slowly this tender light begins to fall upon them. But the present remains: this succession of small domestic vexations. I have lived such a life for sixty years and I am still upset by its ephemeral decisions. And I am still asking myself which is the real life: the present with its discontent, or the retrospect with its emotion?" He looked again guardedly at Sostrata, who sat fingering the folds of her cloak and expressing in every line of her position her unfriendliness and her rebellion. "The fault is in me," he continued. "If I were wiser, I could do this thing. As the head of the family I should be firmer. I should say 'yes' or 'no' clearly and let Pamphilus bring in his little girl. I should weed out all these hesitations. Even now she is waiting for me to make up her mind for her; if I spoke distinctly, even against her will, she would adjust herself without great effort. The house would find a way of accepting the new member and things would run on smoothly enough." He was thinking of going toward her with smiling affection, suggesting that at sixty they had earned the right to remain tranquil though the house fell; but he foresaw that her pride would not accommodate itself to any such resignation, and he continued up and down the garden.

Indeed Sostrata did not wish Simo to speak to her. Her mind was filled with one long obstinate exclamation at the stupidity of men. Only a woman's mind could foresee all the harm that would result from such a marriage as the one now being weighed. It was the women of the island that had measured all danger that came with the arrival of the Alexandrian woman; and now she, the first matron of Brynos, was being ordered to receive into her home the last offscouring of that dispersed colony. She had anticipated all her life the rich satisfactions of being a mother-in-law and a grandmother, though what she anticipated was a daughter-in-law of straw. A Greek HOME, she knew, was the only breakwater against the tide of oriental manners, of financial fluctuation, and of political chaos. The highest point toward which any existence could aspire was to be a member of an island family, living and dying on one farm, respected, cautious, and secretly wealthy; of a family stretching into the past as far as the mossy funerary urns could record, and into the future as far as the imagination could reach, that is to one's grandchildren. Society was similarity. These things she repeated to herself, and under the waves of her indignation and self-pity—though the greater part of the time she stood in awe of her husband and her son—all her gracious traits disappeared, her beautiful eyes became harsh that for three days had been bright with the angry tears of her inner monologue.

When after a long stretch of time Simo paused in his walk and approached her with deferential hesitation, she arose abruptly and walked past him into the house, breathing hard and trembling with excitement.

At last Pamphilus arose and throwing his fleece-lined cloak over his shoulder slowly and musingly walked through the little garden in the court and passed through the outer gates of the farm. He was strangely light-headed from hunger and dejection. He paused for a moment to gaze at the rising hillside before him and its silvered olive trees. To his eyes they seemed to be pulsating in even waves of intensity, as though the whole earth and sky were on fire and burning with a pale slow silver flame, the whole earth and sky, unconsumed yet incessantly feeding the countless tongues of flame. He was gazing at this serene conflagration when he became aware of two dim figures in a pool of profound shadow at his right, leaning against the pillar of the gate. Glycerium was pressing her cheek against the stone and breathing her prayer toward the house within and beside her Mysis, distraught and helpless, stood urging her mistress to return home and to leave the ominous vapors of the night and the jealous chill of the moon.

When Glycerium saw that Pamphilus was standing in the road and that he had recognized her, she drew back into Mysis's arms overcome with shame; but slowly collecting herself she stretched forward a hand to him and fixed her great eyes imploringly on his face.

Mysis whispered to her: "We must go home, my bird, my treasure."

"Pamphilus," said Glycerium, "help me!"

His heart contracted within him as he realized the extremity of suffering that had led her thus far. He laid his finger gravely across his lips. He did not smile, but approaching her he looked down into her face with earnest reassurance and beckoned her to accompany Mysis toward the town.

Glycerium pushed back the scarf from her forehead and fell upon one knee before him, babbling incoherently: "I love you. I love you, Pamphilus. You promised me that you loved me. What am I to do? What is to become of me?"

Pamphilus looked at Mysis and again drew his finger across his mouth.

"Hush, my darling," she said. "You see he has taken the vow and cannot speak to us. And we must not speak to him. Look, he wants you to start home with me." She put her arm about the girl's waist and they began to move slowly toward the road.

"He promised me that he loved me," muttered Glycerium,

unable to see for her tears, but permitting herself to be led forward. After a few steps, however, she turned and, pushing Mysis aside, said: "No, no! I wish to see him again." She pressed her scarf against her mouth for a moment and gazed at him, her whole soul in her eyes: "Pamphilus, do not marry me, if it is not right. But do not leave me alone. Do not leave me so long alone. Remember Chrysis. Remember the day you found me being stoned by the boys. No, no, do not marry me, if your father and your mother do not wish it, but let me know that . . . that I am still loved by you."

At last he nodded and smiled and waved to her slowly.

"He is nodding his head, Mysis!" cried Glycerium.

"Yes, my treasure."

"Look, Mysis, he is smiling at me. Can you see? Look very hard, Mysis."

"See, now he is waving to you. Wave to him again."

Glycerium waved eagerly, like a child, until Pamphilus was out of sight. It was a long walk home over uneven stones. Glycerium talked excitedly of the smile, trying to estimate the exact shade of intention and affection that lay in his waving to her and in the nod of his head. They discussed the significance of his taking the vow and they talked in general of the custom of taking the vow and recalled all the occasions they could remember of this usage and the results of each occasion. "All will be well, Mysis," she repeated feverishly. "You will see, believe me, all will be well." But finally they fell silent, and in the silence their fears returned and an overwhelming weariness. As they reached the door of their house, Glycerium paused with tight-drawn lower lip and with fear in her eyes: "There is nothing to hope for," she said. "The gods are angry because I thought for a time that I was happy and that the world was easy to live in. At that time I did not understand anything about life and I said cruel things to Chrysis, because I thought the world was easy to live in. And the gods are right. Oh, if I could speak to her for only one moment and could tell her that now I understand her goodness, her goodness. But Chrysis is dead!" She turned to Mysis, but at these words Mysis had withdrawn from her and, beating upon her forehead with the knuckles of her two hands, had fallen upon the threshold of the house.

Pamphilus continued in the opposite direction. He wandered about the upland pastures as he had done all day, and climbed to the highest point on the island to gaze upon the moon and the sea. He tried to lift his mind out of the narrow situation of his problem by thinking of things not before him. He thought of the ships that under that magical flowing light were making their way from port to port, each one casting aside at its prow two glistening murmurous waves. It was the hour when the helmsman in the security of the course falls into a revery, remembers his childhood or reckons up his savings. Pamphilus thought of the thousands of homes over all Greece where sleeping or waking souls were forever turning over the dim assignment of life. "Lift every roof," as Chrysis used to say, "and you will find seven puzzled hearts." He thought of Chrysis and her urn, and remembered her strange command to him that he praise all life, even the dark. And as he thought of her his depression, like a cloud, drifted away from him and he was filled with a tremulous happiness. He too praised the whole texture of life, for he saw how strangely life's richest gift flowered from frustration and cruelty and separation. Chrysis living and Chrysis dying in pain; the thoughtful glance that his father so often let rest upon him and the weary expression on his father's face when he thought himself unobserved; the shy mystery of Glycerium. It seemed to him that the whole world did not consist of rocks and trees and water nor were human beings garments and flesh, but all burned, like the hillside of olive trees, with the perpetual flames of love,—a sad love that was half hope, often rebuked and waiting to be reassured of its truth. But why then a love so defeated, as though it were waiting for a voice to come from the skies, declaring that therein lay the secret of the world. The moonlight is intermittent and veiled, and it was under such a light that they lived; but his heart suddenly declared to him that a sun would rise and before that sun the timidity and the hesitation would disappear. And as he strode forward this truth became clearer and clearer to him and he laughed because he had been so long blind to what was so obvious. He strode forward, his arms raised to the sky in joyous gratitude, and as he went he cried: "I praise all living, the bright and the dark."

The exhilaration gave place finally to a tranquil fatigue. As he entered the shadowy temple he saw the priest sleeping before the altar he tended. The priest opened his eyes a moment and above the curve of his arm he watched the young man spread his cloak upon the marble pavement and lie down upon it and fall asleep.

Simo was awakened a little before dawn by the sounds of shrill voices and of unaccustomed movement in the outer courtyard. On approaching he discovered that a clamorous old woman had entered the gates and that a number of his slaves were trying in vain to quiet her and to drive her back into the road. He recognized Mysis. With a gesture he commanded the men to release her. "What is the matter?" he asked.

"I must see Pamphilus."

"He is not here."

"I cannot go away until I have seen him," she replied, her voice

rising in feverish insistence. "A life depends upon it. I do not care
what happens to me, but Pamphilus must know what they have
done to us."

Simo said quietly: "I shall have you whipped; I shall have you
shut up in a room for three days, if you continue to make this
noise. Pamphilus will be able to listen to you later in the morning."

Mysis was silent a moment, then she raised her eyes and said
sombrely: "Later in the morning will be too late, and all will be
lost. I beg of you to let me see him now. He would wish it. He
would not forgive you for turning me away now."

"Come, tell me what is the matter and I will help you."

"No, it is you who have done this harm and now he alone can
save us."

Simo sent the slaves back to their quarters. Then he turned to
her again: "In what way have I harmed you?"

"You do not wish to help us," she said. "The Leno's boat has
arrived at the island and my mistress Glycerium and all the household of Chrysis have been sold to him as slaves. We were
awakened in the middle of the night by the herald of the village
and told to gather our clothes together and to go down to the
harbor. Glycerium is not well now; she must not be driven so. I
myself escaped through the rows of a vineyard and have come to
find Pamphilus. It was you who have done this, for it was the
Fathers of the Island who ordered that we should be sold as slaves
to pay our debts."

This was true. He remembered having listened without interest
to a discussion of the matter, assuming that it would be carried out
with sufficient warning and delay to admit of Glycerium's being
separated from the rest of the destitute company. The Leno's boat
visited Brynos so seldom that it seemed to the Fathers of the Island

that it they might yet be under the necessity of providing for the household through many months while awaiting the arrival of this purchaser.

Suddenly a light dawned upon Mysis: "He is at the temple! How could I have forgotten that he was under the vow of silence and that he must be there!" And turning she started to enter the road.

"You must not go to him at the temple," said Simo sharply. "I shall come down to the harbor with you now and buy your mistress from the Leno."

He returned to the house for his cloak, then walked into the town with Mysis hurrying at his heels. Dawn was breaking as he descended the winding stairs to the square. Against the streaked sky he saw the mast of the Leno's boat. The Leno was not only a dealer in slaves; he was a wandering bazaar and sold foreign foods and trinkets and cloths. If an island were large enough he came ashore and conducted a fair and a circus. And now in the first cold light of morning Simo could see on the raised portion of the deck a brightly colored booth, a chained bear, an ape, two parrots, and other samples of the Leno's stock in trade, including the household of Chrysis. Philocles had remained on shore and for two hours had been standing at the parapet uttering short broken cries towards his companions. Being a Greek citizen he could not be sold into slavery and was to be transported later to Andros.

Simo descended the steps of the landing with Mysis and was rowed out to the boat. While he concluded his transaction with the black and smiling Leno Mysis sank upon her knees before Glycerium, telling her of this good fortune. But Glycerium derived no joy from the news. She sat between Apraxine and the Ethiopian girl, amid the bundles of their clothes, and for weariness she could scarcely raise her eyes or move her lips. "No," she said, "I shall stay here with you. I do not wish to go anywhere."

Simo approached them. "My child," he said to Glycerium, "you are to come with me now."

"Yes, my beloved," Mysis repeated into her ear, "you must go with him. All will be well. He is taking you ashore to Pamphilus."

Still Glycerium remained with bent head. "I do not wish to move. I do not wish to go anywhere," she said.

"I am the father of Pamphilus. You must come with me and good care will be taken of you."

At last and with great difficulty she arose. Mysis supported her to the side of the boat and there taking her farewell she whispered to her: "Goodbye, my dear love. Now may the gods bring you happiness. I shall never see you again, but I pray you to remember me, for I have loved you well. And wherever we are, let us remember our dear Chrysis."

The two women embraced one another in silence, Glycerium with closed eyes. At last she said: "I would that I were dead, Mysis. I would that I were long dead with Chrysis, my dear sister."

"You are to come with us too," said Simo to Mysis, who having known even greater surprises obediently followed him. The little group was rowed in silence to the shore. The Leno's oarsmen struck the water, his bright colored sails were raised, and his merchandise left the harbor for other fortunes.

The sun had already risen when Pamphilus returned with swift and happy steps to his home. There he discovered Glycerium sleeping peacefully under his mother's care. There was not a sound to be heard on the farm, for his mother, already invested with the dignity of her new duties as guardian and nurse to the outcast girl, had ordered a perfect quiet. Argo was sitting before the gate, her eyes wide with wonder and pleasure at the arrival of this new friend. Simo had gone to the warehouse and when he returned, for all his happiness, he moved about with lowered eyes, driven by the constraint in his nature to act as though nothing had happened.

In the two days that followed, all their thoughts were centred about the room where the girl lay and all their hearts were renewed under the fragile claims that Glycerium's beauty and shyness made upon them. Simo seemed, after Pamphilus, to have best understood her reticence and to have been understood by her; a friendship beyond speech had grown up between them. This flowering of goodness, however, was not to be put to the trial of routine perseverance, nor to know the alternations of self-reproach and renewed courage; for on the noon of the third day Glycerium's pains began and by sunset both mother and child were dead.

That night after many months of drought it began to rain. Slowly at first and steadily, the rain began to fall over all Greece. Great curtains of rain hung above the plains; in the mountains it fell as snow, and on the sea it printed its countless ephemeral coins upon the water. The greater part of the inhabitants were asleep, but the relief of the long-expected rain entered into the mood of their sleeping minds. It fell upon the urns standing side by side in the shadow, and the wakeful and the sick and the dying heard the first great drops fall upon the roofs above their heads. Pamphilus lay awake, face downward, his chin upon the back of his hand. He heard the first great drops fall upon the roof over his head and he knew that his father and mother, not far from him, heard them too. He had been repeating to himself Chrysis's lesson and adding to it his Glycerium's last faltering words: "Do not be sorry; do not be afraid," and he had been remembering how with the faintest movement of her eyes to one side, she had indicated her child and

said: "Wherever we are, we are yours." He had been asking himself in astonishment wherein had lain his joy and his triumph of
the few nights before: how could he have once been so sure of the
beauty of existence? And some words of Chrysis returned to him.
He recalled how she had touched the hand of a young guest who
had returned from an absence, having lost his sister, and how she
had said to him in a low voice, so as not to embarrass those others
present who had never known a loss: "You were happy with her
once; do not doubt that the conviction at the heart of your happiness was as real as the conviction at the heart of your sorrow."
Pamphilus knew that out of these fragments he must assemble
during the succeeding nights sufficient strength, not only for
himself, but for these others,—these others who so bewilderingly
now turned to him and whose glances tried to read from his face
what news there was from the last resources of courage and hope,
to live on, to live by. But in confusion and with flagging courage
he repeated: "I praise all living, the bright and the dark."

On the sea the helmsman suffered the downpour, and on the
high pastures the shepherd turned and drew his cloak closer
about him. In the hills the long-dried stream-beds began to fill
again and the noise of water falling from level to level, warring
with the stones in the way, filled the gorges. But behind the thick
beds of clouds the moon soared radiantly bright, shining upon
Italy and its smoking mountains. And in the East the stars shone
tranquilly down upon the land that was soon to be called Holy and
that even then was preparing its precious burden.

A Nephew's Note

Thornton Wilder's three short novels, published in four years between 1926 and 1930, established his international reputation as a writer and made him, by his early thirties, a wealthy man.

The Cabala (1926), Wilder's first novel and always one of his favorites, was a stunning critical success. His third, *The Woman of Andros* (1930), became a notable bestseller. Both novels, however, were quickly overshadowed by the staggering critical and popular success of the novel in the middle: the Pulitzer Prize–winning, worldwide-overnight-sensation, *The Bridge of San Luis Rey* (1927).

Thornton was in his midforties when I was born. Ever since I can remember, I was aware that my uncle was "famous"—far better known for his drama than his fiction. All I knew of *The Cabala* and *The Woman of Andros* was that they occupied shelf space in my father's quiet, second-floor study.

My uncle, always of an acquisitive nature, was a potent mixture of the creative, scholarly and entertaining. He had taught French, the Classics (Greek, Roman, and our own), worked easily in four languages, read sheet music as a hobby, was always eager to see how you reacted to his reading of a new play-in-the-making, and even offered to read my term papers (an offer I gently passed up). Family gatherings were infrequent, yet highly anticipated when Thornton was present. His conversation, curiosity, and entertaining stories created an exhilarating buzz in the room. Thornton Wilder *was* theater.

I took over the care of his literary works in 1995. My first priority was to put out-of-print novels back in print. *The Cabala* and *The Woman of Andros* (which Harper & Row had first issued in a single volume in 1968) were on that list. As I learned more about Thornton's works, I decided to add to each of the seven novels Afterwords that explored highlights of the "why, how, and where" of each story, their critical reception and sales, and the record of reader interest through the years. In researching *The Cabala* and *The Woman of Andros*, I discovered the magnificent literary explosion that Thornton experienced between 1926 and 1930. An added dividend of this discovery was having the opportunity to understand how Wilder used his profound knowledge of the classics and his religious questioning. In these early novels there was an artistic well that he would draw from again and again across his six-decade career as an artist.

It has been a great pleasure to live part of my life overseeing my uncle's work, to have known people he touched during his lifetime, and to meet those inspired by his words since. On this journey with Thornton, I have come to recognize many autobiographical elements in the novels, plays, and nonfiction of this buoyant, entertaining, and yet lonely figure. And in the end, while I still wonder if I really knew him, I can always say, as I often do, that he is very good company.

Welcome to *The Cabala* and *The Woman of Andros*, where it all began—with a big bang!

*   *   *

For their defining contributions to this edition, I thank Barbara Hogenson, Thornton Wilder's literary agent, Rosey Strub, manager of his intellectual property, and Patricia Bacon. It is also a special pleasure to salute Jennifer Civiletto who, in her role as Wilder's HarperCollins editor, has led the Wilder novels and major dramas into the Thornton Wilder Library editions as well as their appearance in entrancing audio form. Sadly, Penelope Niven did not live to see this edition. But her invaluable Introduction to its first iteration more than stands the test of time. Dr. Stephen J. Rojcewicz Jr.'s new material in the Readings helps further elucidate Wilder's use of the classics, and I am grateful to him for his addition to this edition. Citations for Dr. Rojcewicz's study, *Thornton Wilder, Classical Reception, and American Literature*, and Niven's definitive biography, *Thornton Wilder: A Life,* are included in the Afterword's bibliographical note.

Tappan Wilder
Sausalito, CA
February 2022

Afterword

THE CABALA

I began writing my first novel [The Cabala] *thirty-one years ago—in a small hotel on the left bank of the Seine, where so many American novels have been begun.*

—Thornton Wilder on receiving the Gold Medal for Fiction
from the American Academy of Arts and Letters, April 1952

Mr. Thornton Wilder's publishers, Albert and Charles Boni, must have been in a fine frenzy of dismay and delight as the successive chunks of The Cabala *made their tardy appearances in the office.*

—Herbert Gorman, Introduction to the Modern Library
edition of *The Cabala*, #155, May 1929

LATE TO HIS PARTY

Deeply impressed with his highly polished literary style, the recently established New York publishing house of Albert & Charles Boni, Inc., published Thornton Wilder's novel *The Cabala* on April 21, 1926. The first printing was reliably reported at the time to have been 3,250 copies. Befitting a debut book, the dust jacket was unadorned with outside testimonials; the publisher's endorsement on the back read:

> It is seldom that publishers find an author whom they may recommend unreservedly. The biting irony and exquisite phrasing in which this young author couches his intimate story of the high aristocratic group in Rome today seems to us of the highest order. It is a book to delight every admirer of the exotic in writing.

It is a time-honored obligation of friends to come to the aid of an author, especially on the occasion of the first book. Whatever lay ahead, Boni had good reasons for believing that future printings of the dust jacket could contain quotable language from the author's notable literary friends and admirers. Boni would not be disappointed. It is no surprise that a Yale tie was the common denominator for this anticipated publicity; Wilder, who had received his undergraduate degree there in 1920, had lit up the sky as an acclaimed prize-winning student author.

What amounted to a Wilder Yale alumni booster club included two of the author's former teachers: William Lyon Phelps, perhaps the best-known popular lecturer on literature in the country during this era; and Henry Seidel Canby, who, in 1924, had traded the classroom for the New York literary scene where he became a founder and editor of *The Saturday Review of Literature*. The club also included such classmates and close friends as John Farrar, editor of *The*

Bookman, an important literary monthly; Briton Hadden and Henry Luce, who cofounded *Time* magazine in 1923, and had garnered a circulation of more than 200,000 readers by 1926; and Norman Fitts, book reviewer for the influential *Boston Evening Transcript.* During his senior year in Yale College in 1919, Fitts had established a recognized "little magazine," *S.4.N.*, on whose editorial board Wilder served and in which he published occasionally until it closed down in 1924.

Wilder referred to his fans collectively as "Gossip Fair," noting that they had been waiting for his literary debut for years. Gossip Fair had grounds for its opinion; so stunning had been Thornton Wilder's undergraduate literary record that although he was only twenty-nine when *The Cabala* was published, he was judged "unacceptably late to his own party." While aware of this view it appears never to have represented a burden for Wilder. As he was frantically pulling together the manuscript of his first book in June 1925, he wrote to his close friend Les Glenn, "My emergence is long delayed, dear Les, but irresistible!" To his brother, Amos, he assigned a hard number: "Excuse me saying that I waited six years beyond the time when Gossip Fair assigned me a debut."

A Rather Sophisticated Literary Curiosity

> *Books from Yale men ornament the spring lists with persistence. Thornton Wilder, whose undergraduate days were marked with brilliance, has written what promises to be a rather sophisticated literary curiosity in "Cabala," which will be his first published book.*
>
> —*The Bookman,* April 1926

Talent and notoriety aside, how did Boni view the marketplace prospects for a novel *The Bookman* hailed "a rather sophisticated literary curiosity"? The answer is no surprise. Despite his publishers' enthusiasm about Wilder's style and faith that friends in high places would work hard for the book, Boni saw its new author's appeal limited to a highly cultivated readership. In short, they assumed that *The Cabala* would not be a bestseller.

The author's background reflected the esoteric. The biographical note on the dust jacket offered this description:

THORNTON WILDER was born on April 17, 1897, Madison, Wisconsin. He spent his early years in China where his father was Consul General, and later prepared for college in California. He was graduated from Yale in 1920, after which he spent two years in Rome. *The Cabala* grew out of that experience of these two years. After this he taught at Lawrenceville and is now devoting his time to studying and writing at Princeton Graduate School.

For the record, Wilder spent a total of two years in China as a boy and only eight months, not two years, in Rome, after college. But give or take a publisher's exaggeration, there did appear to be more than a tincture of the exotic about his life to go along with his educational credentials.

One fact in this biography was accurate: *The Cabala* was inspired by his stay in Rome after Yale, as reflected in Wilder's dedication of the book: "To my friends at the American Academy in Rome, 1920–1921." Although neither his formal training nor vocational interests qualified him for full admission to one of the American Academy's two established programs, his credentials were strong enough for him to obtain a self-paid place, thanks to the Academy's lean times, and empty beds following World War I. This allowed him to participate in the life of an institution with a notable address on a notable hill in Rome to the degree that he wished. Many years after, he recalled his position and the freedom it offered:

The students on the Janiculum Hill were divided into two disparate and even inimical groups. There were on the one hand the Prix de Rome men who had been carefully selected for great promise in architecture, painting and sculpture, and music. In my time there were no women among the artists. And there were the classical students, men and women, also selected from among scores of applicants to work in archeology, Latin literature, and Roman history. With very few exceptions these two groups kept to themselves, sat at meals themselves, and enjoyed parties and excursions by themselves. The two groups were often designated as "geniuses" and the "grinds."

I was neither a prize man nor a qualified classical scholar. I was a fish who swam in both waters.

And we know from letters to friends and home, Wilder not only swam with both geniuses and grinds, but also explored the city on his own, sat at many a non-Academy table, and attended many a party. To his sister Isabel, he wrote in the spring of 1921:

I seem to be living in Italy for the sole purpose of receiving the confidences of ladies in distress. The details of woe, broken engagements, insult and injury I've had to listen to from grand dame to servant-girl would freeze your spine. There's something in the air over here: everyone is unhappily in love every minute of their lives, and only too glad to find a sympathetic eye and ear.

Wilder, pen always at hand, left Rome for Paris, where he stayed for several months in the spring and summer of 1921. Here, in a hotel on the left bank, followed by a cold-water flat on the Rue St. Jacques, Wilder began a work of prose about a group of fascinating and *very unhappy* individuals in Rome, including a prince of the

Church. The writing did not go easily. As he wrote his mother, "I struggle over the descriptive passages in *Romans* and despair of ever writing prose."

Struggle he did. Wilder worked on his "Romans" intermittently from September 1921 to mid-November 1925, a period encompassing his four years as a French teacher and assistant dormitory master at the Lawrenceville School, a private boarding school for boys in New Jersey, and his first semester of graduate study in French Literature at Princeton University. During the Lawrenceville period, a major contributing influence on his work was his reading in classical French literature, anchored by such authors as La Bruyère and Saint-Simon, coupled with a passionate interest in contemporary authors, particularly Marcel Proust. The membership of Wilder's "cabala" were, as he would often say, inventions of his imagination—an imagination fueled by his literary record, tested against the sights, people, and landmarks of post–World War I Rome in fact and memory.

STOP AND GO

The making of the manuscript breaks down into two periods—before and after the Boni firm opened the door to Wilder on March 3, 1925. In the earlier period, we encounter a writer feeling little pressure to complete his "Roman Memoirs" (as he identified them) and endlessly writing and rewriting. Moreover, although he appears to have had a conception of some larger whole, it is clear that his drive for compression of language and theatrical characterization meant that his work-in-progress marched forward as discreet short stories, or "portraits," as he also referred to them.

If Gossip Fair did not understand Wilder's delay with destiny, it is adequately explained by his profession as a resident teacher and dormitory master in a boy's boarding school, a job entailing endless hours that also spilled over into summer tutoring. Still, in addition to many "stolen hours" reading in the nearby Princeton University

Library, there were free nights, off-duty weekends, pieces of long vacations, and, starting in 1924, a month-long writing residency at the MacDowell Colony, an artists' retreat in Peterborough, New Hampshire. His progress on fiction was further complicated by his competing passion for drama and attending theater. Stories of Wilder working on his "Roman Memoirs" in Davis House (the Lawrenceville student dormitory where he lived) remain part of that school's lore. During this time, however, the would-be novelist haunted theaters in New York, Philadelphia, and Trenton, all located within two hours of the school.

It came down to this: until 1924, Wilder was in no particular hurry to publish. He loved teaching and the steady income it provided, as well as the supportive community that Lawrenceville represented—a community that meant a great deal to a young man raised all over the world. What would someday become *The Cabala* moved forward in a stop-and-go fashion. The following excerpt from letters to his family in 1922 suggests his reading and writing style in this period:

> You will grin to hear that I have taken up again my imaginary memoirs of a year in Rome. . . . The memoirs are made up of formal portraits . . . interspersed with every now and then a complete little "conte" dropped into [the] current, told by some character, like Canterbury pilgrims. I have been reading the endless tomes of Saint-Simon.
> —April 11, 1922, from Lawrenceville School

> Just as soon as I get a fair copy made of BOOK I, I look it over and with my blue pencil start indicating alterations; within an hour the whole script is unsightly. My only consolation is that every touch has been an improvement. This has happened five times already and it is about time the thing were perfect, but I still find shell holes. . . .
> —July 20, 1922, from Newport, Rhode Island

Well, a good deal more has been written and almost the whole projected. I am doing a vast amount of reading (I am never able to see afterwards where I found the time to do yesterday's, or where I shall find it tomorrow; but the inveterate reader somehow contrives—in spite of the fact that I am conspicuously faithful in my school duties). For instance my second book is an elaborate satire on the French Royalist party.

—November 5, 1922, from Lawrenceville School

PICTURE TO YOURSELF A STAGE

The year 1924 was a turning point in Wilder's development as an artist. With some money in his pocket from teaching and tutoring, and excitement about being associated with the MacDowell Colony and the recently established Laboratory Theatre in New York, Wilder found himself dreaming of publishing more than just short pieces in the period's "little magazines." In 1923, at *S.4.N.*, Wilder's Yale friend Norman Fitts launched a book publishing subsidiary. As best as can be determined from the evidence, only Fitts's serious illness, which forced him to close *S.4.N.* late in 1924, kept Wilder from making his major publishing debut with the third volume in this new venture. The book was to contain ten of his short-short plays (or "three-minute playlets," as they were known); several other short pieces of fiction; and "Five Roman Portraits." Judging from their titles, these portraits represented most of the subject matter later found in *The Cabala*. And what title did Wilder propose for this volume? His choice honored his allegiance to the dramatic side of his art: *Picture to Yourself a Stage*.

The failure of the *S.4.N.* venture concluded the first chapter in *The Cabala*'s prehistory. But no sooner had that door closed than another opened. A Yale tie again figured in the story. In the summer of 1924, following an apprenticeship of two years with

Alfred A. Knopf, Wilder's Yale classmate Lewis Saunders Baer moved to the position of secretary-treasurer at the publishing firm of Albert & Charles Boni, Inc. Here he learned, no doubt through the Yale grapevine, that his classmate Thornton Wilder might have a manuscript looking for a publisher. Soon after, what appears to have been a version of Book One of *The Cabala* changed hands. After weeks of silence, on March 3, 1925, Wilder received the letter that would-be authors dream of receiving: "I am more than delighted to report," wrote Baer, "that we are all crazy about it. Albert Boni feels so strongly about your style that he is very anxious to see more." With shades of Gossip Fair in the background, Baer went on:

> I knew this would be the result of our reading, because I remember so distinctly how impressed I was at your stories in college. I do hope we will be able to get together a book which can mean the start of your career as an author, in print I mean. No one would be happier than I.

Although Albert & Charles Boni was a new publishing house, its founding brothers were experienced, inventive book men. Albert Boni was a well-known figure in the trade through his role as a founder of the Boni & Liveright Publishing Company and the Modern Library, both in 1917. His brother Charles cofounded Little Leather Library, a publishing venture that succeeded in targeting a market for a series of classic works of literature, and was the predecessor to the Book-of-the-Month Club. In 1923, the brothers joined forces. Albert, who had also played a role in establishing the Theater Guild, was particularly interested in modern European letters. In 1920 he had edited a popular edition of French verse, and he later saw to it that the work of such authors as Proust and Colette were represented among the early titles of his new publishing venture. Given his taste in fiction, it is no surprise that

Albert Boni was attracted to Wilder's prose and "anxious to see more."

Because few early drafts of *The Cabala* survived, we know all too little about how the five Roman Portraits destined for *Picture to Yourself a Stage* evolved into a novel called *The Cabala*. What we do know is that over an eight-month period beginning in March 1925 and ending in late November, Wilder revised existing copy once more and added new material, including Book Five, "The Dusk of the Gods." The title *The Cabala* dates from this period, at the end of which, in November, Wilder finally received a book contract. Why did the Boni firm withhold this document until the last minute? The answer has to be that until they were confident they had enough material to make a book from an author practicing compression with an all but religious fervor, the Boni brothers did not wish to offer a contract.

The history of *The Cabala* as a legal entity began on November 19, 1925, the day Wilder signed a book contract for a novel identified in Article 1 as *The Caballa,* as it was often spelled at the time. As noted, the transformation of a series of portraits into a novel had taken place during his last semester of teaching at Lawrenceville, a summer job, and much of the first semester of his year of graduate studies at Princeton. Wilder burned the candle at both ends to accomplish his mission, as suggested by these excerpts from letters to his mother:

> I am still on the Alix d'Espoli story. I hope it will move people as it does me. I sit at the foot of my bed writing until I am—prevented.
>
> —June 10, 1925, Lawrenceville School

> I am sending you Book Four today. It is terminated but not finished. . . . "It will have to do." I never thought I should have to say that of anything of mine, but I am frantic to

finish this five-year thing and get back to my plays. . . . But first I must finish the Epilogue to the Memoirs.

—November 2, 1925, Graduate College,
Princeton University

THE DEBUT OF AN AMERICAN STYLIST

The Cabala was published on April 20, 1926, by Boni in the United States, and in October of the same year in England by Longmans, Green & Co., Ltd., using a Longmans cover and Boni-supplied pages. Any fair reporting on the book's reception must treat the two editions as one.

Reviewers were almost uniformly enthusiastic about the novel. While the occasional notice pointed to elements of wisdom and insights about human nature in Wilder's story, critics above all praised his style, a viewpoint expressed in the lordly *New York Times* that has followed the book ever since: "The appearance of Thornton Wilder's *Cabala* marks the debut of a new American stylist." That many others agreed, picking up on the novel's satire, irony, wit, and epigrammatic style, is suggested by this collage of phrases from the dailies: "[The] prose is exceptionally beautiful; its texture has a rare consistency of distinctive weaving." (*New York Post Literary Review*); "The writing is beautiful in the extreme." (Sheffield, U.K., *Independent*); "It has the cool sparkling quality of a champagne cocktail." (*New York Tribune*); "A remarkable maturity and sureness of its style." (Yorkshire, U.K., *Post*); "To students of style it is well worth careful perusal." (Portsmouth, U.K., *Evening News*)

Wilder's friends from Gossip Fair joined the parade, as expected. William Lyon Phelps wrote in *Scribner's*, "An exquisite work of art, written with beauty, grace and charm." *Time* called *The Cabala* "one of the most delectable myths that ever issued from the hills of Rome."

Something akin to a fanfare appears to have occurred when

Wilder returned to the American Academy in Rome in late October 1926. As he wrote his family about the novel's reception in this special place,

> I went up [to] the Academy, had tea with the prizemen in my beloved halls, was taken home to dinner by the director and around the faculty for brief calls. The book has been read by all with a sort of scandalous delight. Even old Romans take it as the hot stuff from the secret circles.

Finally, as the good news rolled in, Wilder found himself compared favorably to a remarkable range of successful and popular authors of the period, among them James Branch Cabell, Walter Pater, George Moore, Carl Van Vechten, Anatole France, Norman Douglas, Elinor Wylie, Max Beerbohm, and Aldous Huxley.

While no novel is immune to negative press, what is unusual about *The Cabala* is how few outright knocks Wilder's first book received. In England the august *Times Literary Supplement* put the American in his place by observing that "the book . . . has a certain deceptive brilliance, an aggravating air of 'knowingness' and familiarity with European culture that may have helped its American popularity." When arrows arrived, they typically did so as comments on technical matters, such as Wilder's choice to avoid quotation marks and the numerous typos in the first printing. One feature of the first printing of *The Cabala*, well known to book collectors, is the more than two dozen errors it contains, due to inadequate proofreading by the author and the apparent resetting of the book at the last minute to increase its page size. Dorothy Bacon Woolsey in the *New Republic* found the otherwise "excellent suggestive writing marred by inexcusable typographical errors, misspelling, total omission of words, and astonishing inaccuracies in punctuation."

All in all, *The Cabala* enjoyed remarkable critical success. If its sales kept it from the bestseller status that other Wilder novels would achieve, the numbers were nonetheless impressive. It appeared that the market for the exotic was larger than anticipated. In its first year, Wilder's first novel sold 5,357 copies in the United States, probably more than twice what Boni needed to sell to break even, and as many as another thousand in Great Britain. His debut may have been delayed, but from the beginning, it exceeded expectations, as suggested by the author's happy words to his friend Les Glenn in September, six months after *The Cabala*'s initial appearance:

> Our book is now well through the third printing. We thought it was intended for a restricted circle of reflective sophisticates but all sorts of people are reading it, understanding little, but driven on by the faintly snobbish feeling that it's high-brow and "beautiful" and modern.

And the novel kept selling. By the eve of the appearance of Wilder's second novel, *The Bridge of San Luis Rey,* in November 1927, sales of *The Cabala* totaled some seven thousand, and the book was in its fourth printing. Its strong reception naturally registered quickly on that sensitive barometer of literary fortunes, the dust jacket. By the summer of 1926, the book was festooned with no less than eight blurbs—four on the front and four on the back. Sales were strong enough for Boni to justify advertising the novel in *Publishers Weekly* and *The Saturday Review of Literature*. On the outside, no member of Gossip Fair was more active on the book's behalf than John Farrar, editor of *The Bookman*. Besides an enthusiastic review ("a talent so authentic and so startling") and several tidbit stories (among them that Wilder pronounced "Cabala" with the emphasis on the first syllable), Farrar highlighted the novel with the only triple star in a 1926 list of fifty recommended books for summer reading.

"Also by Thornton Wilder"

In the end, a first book can do an author no greater service than guaranteeing publication of the second. From the moment of *The Cabala*'s appearance, his publisher was urging Wilder on. Twenty months later, on November 3, 1927, *The Bridge of San Luis Rey* was published. There was nothing naked about the dust jacket this time: "AUTHOR OF THE CABALA," appeared under the title, and the back of the jacket featured five *Cabala* blurbs under the header "ALSO BY THORNTON WILDER." Although expecting to do better with *The Bridge*, Boni still viewed Wilder's readership as limited, and guardedly published a first printing of 4,000 copies, 750 more than the first printing of *The Cabala*. "Once more," read the dust jacket, "it may be prophesied that this book will stir the most sophisticated reader."

The appearance of *The Bridge of San Luis Rey* did not stir the few; rather, it ignited one of the great explosions in American twentieth-century literary history. By 1929, more than 300,000 copies had been sold in the United States and England, the novel had been serialized in the Hearst newspaper chain, a film version had been released, and Wilder had received the 1928 Pulitzer Prize for fiction. In September 1930, in *The Delineator*, Professor William Lyon Phelps wrote of the impact on Boni, "[*The Bridge*] was accepted by the publishers because they thought so fine a book ought to be printed, but they had no belief in its success with the public, and they have not yet recovered from the shock."

How did *The Cabala* weather this extraordinary success? Very well indeed. Seeking to understand the phenomenon of *The Bridge*, critics and readers turned back to Wilder's first novel. This led to a fresh crop of thoughtful reviews, especially in England, where a new Longman's Green originated edition of the novel appeared in March 1928. Thanks to the power of *The Bridge*, *The Cabala*'s Second Coming was capped by its publication as Number 155 in the Modern Library in May 1929. By then, total sales of *The Cabala* stood at nearly 19,000 copies in the United States alone, and negotiations were far advanced for the first foreign-language editions, of which there have been eleven through the years.

Because of its inevitable comparison with *The Bridge of San Luis Rey*, *The Cabala* has long been judged a *succès d'estime*. But even in its infancy, as this account suggests, the novel was something more than that. With an eye on its subsequent history, we cannot forget that besides its many foreign editions (fourth in number only to *The Bridge*, *The Ides of March*, and *The Eighth Day*), *The Cabala* has been in print almost continuously.

Wilder always reserved a special place in his artistic heart for his first novel. He even considered the idea of adding new chapters for it in 1940. In 1962 he read a selection from it as part of "An Evening with Thornton Wilder," a gala event arranged at the State Department Auditorium by members of President John F. Kennedy's cabinet. The author remained grateful to a tale marked, as he later put it with bemused affection, by a "frequent display of far-fetched information."

Finally, there is the author's last and greatest compliment to his first book: *Theophilus North*, his final novel, published in 1973, two years before his death. In this story, an all-seeing young man moves in and out of the houses of the mighty and not so mighty in Newport, Rhode Island, in the summer of 1926, in much the same way Samuele visits palazzos in Rome in 1921. *Theophilus North* is Thornton Wilder's American *Cabala*, the former his evening light, the latter his morning.

READINGS

READING 1: THORNTON WILDER, COLLEGE GRADUATE

A. B., Yale Class of 1920, English major, Latin minor.

"The plan is for him to sail September first . . . to Naples—
and attend the American Classical School at Rome for a year.
He is going to study Latin, Italian and the usual archeology."
— Thornton Wilder's mother, Isabella Thornton Niven
Wilder, to Bruce Simonds, her son's Yale classmate,
August 15, 1920

READING 2: CHARLES MALLISON'S YEAR IN ROME: "THE PROFOUND IMPRESSION THAT A YEAR IN ITALY CAN MAKE"

The "Memoirs of Charles Mallison: The Year in Rome," is a 4,200-word manuscript dating possibly from Wilder's year in Rome. The kernel of *The Cabala* story is here: an American innocent abroad meets James Blair and Miss Grier and is soon caught up in the occult. Like Samuele and Thornton, Mallison and Wilder share many similarities, among them a common birth year (1897), ties to China, the authorship of many unpublished plays, and, of course, a memorable year in Rome at an impressionable age. In fact, Mallison and Wilder arrived in Rome the same month and year after spending time in Sorrento.

This excerpt includes the opening lines and four of the footnotes Wilder added to this playfully ambitious "memoir," the earliest known pass at what would someday be *The Cabala*. Up to publication, as he informed his brother, Wilder was removing "notes of burlesque, smartalecisms and purple-rhetoric."

The Memoirs of Charles Mallison: The Year in Rome

In an earlier series of memoirs I have described my life through my twenty-first year.

In a previous series of memoirs[1] I attempted to describe the changing matter of a boy's mind, written by the boy himself during the changes.[2] With the completion of the Boy Sebastian, I thought my studies in introspection were over and set about the composition of plays and novels. Although the present book discovers me again describing my life, the interval that separated the two works saw a certain change in the temper of my mind. In this book I record as tirelessly what I discovered about me, as in the previous book I recorded what I saw passing in my mind. The profound impression that a[3] year in Italy can make upon a youthful spirit prepared by wide reading and a habit of reflection opens as great an opportunity for the subjective method of my first manner as, surely the school years which served as background for the Boy Sebastian; but the novelty of European manners, the multiplicity of things seen and above all the rapid acquisition of an extensive circle of acquaintance inevitably and perhaps wholesomely belied the anticipations of study and self-examination. I am become a genre painter and a portrait painter rather than the water-colorist of subjective fancies.

---

1 *The Boy Sebastian:* by Charles Mallison. Published by the Soochow Press, Soochow, China, 1913 in six unbound folio volumes. These interminable sheets describe in diary form, the events of the author's life from his first recollections to the middle of his sixteenth year. They are written in a less disciplined style than the present work. An American publication would not be possible as a great deal of the matter would be bound to offend the censors of this country; but a one-volume selection is being prepared. Portions of the earlier work that illustrate the present memoirs will be quoted extensively in these footnotes.

2 Charles Mallison was born Sept. 24, 1897. The portion of the Boy Sebastian in diary form covers the years 1909 to 1912, or from the author's twelfth to his fifteenth year. The main revision and expansion of the diary took place in the year preceding the publication.

3 Charles Mallison arrived in Rome on Oct. 4, 1920, after spending a month at Sorrento. [Wilder arrived in Rome October 14, 1920.]

The very first day of my life in Rome showed how completely I had outgrown the old taste for self-analysis. My first evening's walk with its view of the Colliseum and the Forum of the Cancelleria and the Massimi Palace, the river and the bridges, the Veneto and its hotels and embassies stirred in me the determination to saturate myself with the legends and tradition, ancient and old and recent and modern of Rome. There and then I invested myself in nothing but curiosity. The event showed me that my intention had been too ambitious, that I had gradually to sacrifice the Romes—those superimposed cities of contrasting epochs—to the Romans. Archaeological and historical studies gradually gave way to personal encounters. Moreover when I had restricted my study to the living Romans, I had to restrict it still further to what must be called Roman Society and Distinguished Transients. . . .

By chance I was taken on my third day to see the two people in Rome who were most able to create rich opportunities for further acquaintance. James Blair took me to tea on that Tuesday afternoon in the apartments of Miss Grier at the Palazzo Barberini; and in the evening to one of the Saretor Basilis' demonstrations of the occult, 13 Via Fontanella di Borghese.

[Placement of footnote number not indicated in text]

The author is undoubtedly overmodest here. The reader may judge for himself of the erudition that enters, always as a secondary interest, into these pages. Friends who knew him at the time affirmed that his store of rather gossipy historical information was most extensive. Especially in the Old Rome between the Corso and St. Peters', he overflowed with allusions and associations for every church and palace. To please himself however he knew far too little and in the monologue of discouragement that appears toward the middle of this volume he wonders whether it would not have been better for him to have retired to the labyrinths of the library of the Collegio Romano and devoted himself to the histories of the Popes.

Reading 3: On to Paris

Lawrenceville School

This picture, dated May 1921, shows Wilder, book in hand, with a fellow resident of the American Academy in Rome at the Rome Railroad Station. It shows him on the day of his departure from Rome for Paris via Florence. In Paris, Wilder worked on *The Cabala*.

I take long walks in this priceless city, and I actually stay home in this nasty little room and write as I haven't written for years. The fact that I write is the most important item in this envelope. . . . I stroll the quais, roam about Notre Dame, eat in the sidewalk before little dining restaurants, go to my worshipped Théâtre du Vieux-Colombier, and come home and write delicious things for Amos' and Charlotte's grandchildren. [Reference to his brother and sister.]

—Thornton Wilder to his father, June 27, 1921, from Paris

READING 4: DENIZENS OF DAVIS HOUSE

Wilder did significant work on *The Cabala* in Davis House, the Lawrenceville School dormitory where he served as assistant housemaster for four years and housemaster his final year, 1927–1928. This photograph shows Wilder that last year sitting among the thirty-two boys who boarded in Davis House. The teacher-author had recently abandoned his middle initial and added a mustache.

"The whole week is passed in the company or earshot of boys. The dyer's hand is tinctured to what it works in, and at length even I begin to think in terms of football scores, Victrola records and feeble jokes. At least seventeen meals a week I eat at a narrow table with eight of them; twenty-two times a week I unlock a classroom door and admit a band of reluctant learners; four evenings I supervise their study of two-hours-and-a-half and with a flashlight coaxingly persuade them to retire and sleep.... It is pure accident that I happen to like them, and that all this does not turn my stomach."

—Thornton Wilder to his mother, circa September 1922

READING 5: AT DUSK—IN HIS HAND

This reading shows a draft of the opening lines of Book V of *The Cabala*, "The Dusk of the Gods." Excised language is shown with the strike. Readers wishing to compare these words with the final text will observe many changes made by an author seeking, as he wrote his brother at the time of publication, "to achieve a restrained Grand Style."

When my time came to leave home I set aside a few days for visits of piety, piety in the Roman sense. A strange urgency arose within
me to finish the year with care. I went to Tivoli and strayed about
the locked Villa Horace. I sat a while in Santa Maria in Trastevere.
~~And I took two days off to visit Marcantonio's grave. A strange ur-~~
~~gency arose in me to finish off carefully the year. Yet even after these~~
~~observances (and many more)~~ I called on Miss Grier and on Donna
Leda; I even sat for a while with Jean Perraye; I had a photographer
make me an impression of Besuard's portraits of Alix and Cardinal
Vaini. Yet even after these observances something told me that my
debt of affection was not paid.

READING 6: A NOTE ON WILDER'S USE OF THE CLASSICAL TRADITION IN *THE CABALA*

With its evocation of "Rome," "Virgil's country," and "a long Virgilian
sigh," the first paragraph of *The Cabala* signals to classicists that they are
in the presence of a work inspired by the great Latin poet, Publius Ver-
gilius Maro (70–19 BCE). Virgilian resonances are prominent, including
legends about whether Virgil has not died but is still alive. Wilder evokes
the classical world by alluding to Latin and Greek literature, portraying

contemporary Latin scholars, quoting Horace in Latin, and depicting landscapes and architecture suggesting antique Rome. Wilder combines Latin themes with allusions to Greek, biblical, medieval Italian, and English literature. The opening pages, for example, refer to Greek mythology (3), Renaissance artists (3, 6), and Dante (5–6).

On his first night in Rome, as another example, the narrator visits a dying English poet, based on John Keats, whom he comforts by praising poetry, including works of Sappho, Euripides, and Terence, as well as of Villon and Milton. The narrator's attempts to comfort the Englishman with Greek, Latin, medieval French, and English poetry highlight the persistence and the value of great poetry through the ages, prefiguring Wilder's integration of multiple literary sources throughout his work.

An aristocratic Roman coterie, known as the "Cabala," welcomes the narrator into their privileged circle, eventually giving him the nickname "Samuele." Often obsessed with power and past glories and beset with cynicism and hypocrisy, the members of the Cabala cause Samuele to question his puritanical tendencies, and to understand the risks of fanaticism, and of excessive devotion to the powerful or wealthy. Samuele, destined to be a writer, will not become pedantic and dry like James Blair who, although brilliant, responds to a woman's love by haranguing her with long quotations from Livy and Virgil. Samuele will also not become contemptuous and nonempathetic like Cardinal Vaini, although the Cardinal is "the only person living who could write a Latin that would have enhanced the Augustans" (37–42).

With evocations of Dante's *Inferno* and *Purgatorio*, the spirit of Virgil appears at the conclusion of the novel, in a dialogue that also embraces Dante, Shakespeare, Milton, and other creative artists. The words of Virgil to Samuele are strong echoes of the words of Creusa, who appears as a spirit to Aeneas in Virgil's *Aeneid*. Creating an overall atmosphere of sadness and beauty, the Virgilian references, especially Virgil's last words (134), underline Wilder's reinterpretation of Virgil's famous phrase, *sunt lacrimae rerum et mentem mortalia tangunt* ["here are the tears of the world, and human matters touch the heart," *Aeneid* 1.462]. Virgil anoints the narrator as his American successor, one who will become a writer in the classical tradition. While the narrator will follow Virgil's advice: "give heed to your Latin" and "in the pride of your city . . . do not forget mine" (*Cabala,* 133), he will also be true to his own American background. Unlike the Cabala, Samuele will not be enslaved to the European past. Inspired by Greek and Roman authors, the narrator (and Wilder) will incorporate classical learning into his writings without being rigidly tied to the past. He will become a writer who will focus on Virgil's own theme of "the tears of the world" to represent the shortcomings and brevity of human existence in all its wonder.

—Dr. Stephen J. Rojcewicz Jr.

THE WOMAN OF ANDROS

> *We don't at the moment know the date of publication, but a new book by Wilder is a genuine literary event.*
> —"The Phoenix Nest," *The Bookman*, September 7, 1929

> *When a situation is more than a human soul can be expected to bear, what* then?
> —Interview with Thornton Wilder in *Fashions of the Hour*,
> Chicago, Spring 1930

Thornton Wilder conceived the idea for *The Woman of Andros* at the Lawrenceville School in New Jersey in the spring of 1928 in the midst of a literary explosion titled *The Bridge of San Luis Rey*. The fallout from this event would determine how and where *The Woman of Andros* would be written, and how it would be designed and marketed by its publisher, Albert & Charles Boni. It would also help to shape its reception by critics and the public and give Wilder the necessary leverage for publishing drama, his other literary passion which was very much on his mind.

EXPLOSION

Before *The Bridge of San Luis Rey* transformed his life, Wilder had taught and served as a dormitory master at Lawrenceville School from 1921 to 1925. During a two-year leave of absence from Lawrenceville, Wilder completed *The Cabala* and received a graduate degree in French Literature from Princeton University. Because he did not earn enough royalties from his first novel, *The Cabala,* to stake himself for at least another year of writing, he returned to teach at the school in the fall of 1927, three months before *The Bridge* was published. By the end of 1928, sales of *The Bridge* had reached more than 300,000 copies in the United States and England. After one of the most celebrated debuts in twentieth century American literature, Wilder found himself the toast of the English-speaking world, the recipient of the Pulitzer Prize, and a wealthy man.

The stunned author also found his stunned publisher at his side, reminding him of a significant new fact of life: now that Wilder was an author with an enormous following it was his obligation to feed it with the next novel, and as quickly as possible, please. The acclaimed author of *The Bridge of San Luis Rey* appeared to see his duty. In February 1928, amid the madness of trying to teach, run a dormitory, handle the phone calls, correspondence, and visits generated by his newfound fame, Wilder informed Boni that the next novel would be entitled *The Woman of Andros*. He appears to have described it with no more detail than he gave his mother in a brief and harried note: "The Woman of Andros—after play by Terrence—Aegean island. Paganism with premonitions of Xianty."

AN ANGEL APPEARS

The Woman of Andros would be Wilder's next work of fiction, but not his next book. In October 1928, the recently established New York publisher Coward McCann published a handsome trade edition of 2,000 copies of *The Angel That Troubled the Waters*, along with an expensive companion boxed edition of 750 signed copies. This first published book of drama by Wilder contained sixteen three-minute playlets, each featuring three actors, the dramatic form Wilder had practiced passionately since high school. All but four of these short-short plays had been written and appeared initially in student publications during his undergraduate years at Oberlin and Yale; the final four were composed after 1926. Wilder himself viewed these plays as "belle lettres" designed to be read aloud among family and friends or enjoyed on the page in a comfortable chair next to a roaring fire, beverage in hand. The playlet's contents represented brief excursions into what one student has usefully summarized as "the grand themes of life and death, faith and reason, creation and love." Wilder, in his introduction to these playlets writes, "The art of literature springs from two curiosities, a curiosity about human beings pushed to such an extreme that it resembles love, and a love of a few masterpieces of literature so absorbing that it has all the richest elements of curiosity."

This detour into a curious corner of drama was no surprise to his publishers, and they were not happy about it. Soon after *The Cabala* appeared in 1926, Wilder had approached Boni about publishing his playlets. Prospecting for the gold to be found in fiction, Boni had no interest in throwing away a contractual claim to one of the author's next two novels on a bizarre book of drama. In April 1927, they gave Wilder permission to publish his playlets elsewhere "in some kind of limited edition."

Wilder was not blind to the marketplace risks involved. As early as April 1926 he had put the matter this way to Boni's secretary treasurer Lewis Baer:

> My thought was that they [the playlets] were so frail that even if you did bring them out during the next two years it would probably be bad for "my booksellers" and even perhaps for most of "my readers." And yet I should love to get those little things out somewhere, quietly and even unprofitably.

Thanks to the leverage provided by *The Bridge of San Luis Rey*, there was nothing quiet or unprofitable about the *Angel* in print. The dust jacket language of the *Angel* nailed to the mast showed the relationship between the play collection and *The Bridge*: "[These playlets] should prove of exceptional interest as showing the development of a talent that has astonished the critical world." The volume was widely and thoughtfully reviewed on both sides of the Atlantic, although a number of critics were puzzled by its purpose and wondered whether it was really necessary to read the playlets which they identified as Wilder's juvenilia. *Angel* earned some gold, returning royalties to the author of more than $5,000 over two years, a modest sum compared to the success of *The Bridge*, which garnered more than $100,000 for Wilder in its first two years of shelf life, but a remarkable amount for a book of playlets.

THE ANGEL AND AN ISLAND

It is helpful to view *The Woman of Andros* as a novelistic successor to the playlets. First, there is the novel's brevity, only 23,000 words, barely qualifying it as a short novel. Drawing on a few masterpieces of literature, it also reveals the author exploring human beings in extreme situations as they search for meaning. The title playlet *The Angel That Troubled the Waters*, written in June 1928, was just when Wilder was beginning to write *Andros*. The play was inspired by the story of the Bethesda Pool in the Gospel of John. In it, an angel informs a newcomer to the pool that his time for healing at the sacred waters has not yet arrived. "In love's service," the angel says, "only the wounded soldiers can serve." In a similar way in *The Woman of Andros*, Chrysis, a slave and courtesan, is not allowed to be healed, therefore dramatically depicting questions of virtue and forgiveness. We know from Wilder's later interviews that one of Wilder's first three novels began as a play. Surely it is *The Woman of Andros*, based on Terence and the lost plays by Menander.

In addition to attracting significant attention to his curious little playlets, *The Bridge* also provided Wilder with the means to write as he would for the rest of his career; his pattern was to sequester himself in hotels, apartments, or pensions throughout the United States and abroad for stays of a few days, a few weeks, months, or even more than a year. His notations on the manuscript of *The Woman of Andros* open the door on the creative process of a writer on the move:

> *The Woman of Andros*. Idea first came spring of 1928. First two conversations written at Axeland House, Horley, Surrey; and much of the later parts clearly planned during church attendances at Red Hill, Outwood, etc. The copying out of already completed portions begun into this book Oct 11, 1928. Pension Saramartel, Juan-les-Pins. A lot (Towards Chrysis monologue in the cove) done in The Law Dorm's 76 Wall St New Haven April 1929. Then Sept-Oct Oxford-Paris-Munich.

The notation includes two locations where he had in fact worked earlier on *The Bridge*—the pension in Juan-les-Pins, and a short-term rental in a Yale Law School dormitory. This list, however, is incomplete. We know from letters and records that Wilder also did considerable work on the manuscript in London's Hotel Savoy, and at the MacDowell Colony in Peterborough, New Hampshire. Wilder also discovered that he worked well on ships crossing the Atlantic. ("Baby does best on boats," he was later fond of saying.) As a result, the ocean liners *Adriatic*, *Lapland*, and *Cedric* are part of the making of *Andros*. The manuscript's peripatetic journey ended at the legendary Biltmore Hotel in Los Angeles, for it was here, on or about January 4, 1930, only six weeks before publication, that Wilder completed the last lines of his third novel. (His publishers had been setting type as he submitted pieces of the manuscript.)

These excerpts from letters offer a glimpse of Wilder's study of classic religious works as he was writing *The Woman of Andros*:

> Have you read much of Abbé Bremond's Histoire Litt du Sentiment Religieux? I'm working thru the first volume because Francis de Sales has always been one of my favorites

(Sainte Chantal, her sister-in-the-Lord, was Mme de Sévigné's grandmother. But I first got to know him through your Abbé Huvet.)

—Thornton Wilder to his brother, Amos (an ordained minister), October 25, 1928, from Juan-les-Pins

It's still [*The*] *Woman of Andros*, my *hetaita*, developing into a sort of Dr. Johnson. Her sayings and parables and her custom of adopting human strays is weighing down the book. But die she must and with unhellenic overtones, an *anima naturaliter christiana* [a Christian spirit by nature]. I love to think that Terence's play on which, ever so inexcusably, I base the *novella* was a favorite with Fénélon and John Henry Newman.

—Wilder to Lady Sybil Colefax, July 24, 1929, from MacDowell Colony

Whenever he moved about, the celebrated Pulitzer Prize–winning author attracted reporters. The recurring question was predictable: What are you writing now, Mr. Wilder? In response the author was usually brief and guarded, typically saying that his new novel involved the ancient world, a play by Terence, and a Greek Island. He also commonly said he would write plays after completing the novel. Occasionally he offered further detail.

In addition to working on his novel, as early as the fall of 1928, Wilder turned to the question of the design of the book and how it would be presented to the public. Assuming that lightning does not strike twice in the same place, he cared about these practical questions for two reasons. First, he felt that the Boni firm inappropriately exploited *The Bridge of San Luis Rey* by serialization and careless handling of subsidiary rights, and second, he recognized that his story about life and death on an obscure Greek island was very different from *The Bridge*. His terminology for how he wanted his new novel presented to the world was "conservative arrangements." He did not want to see it serialized in newspapers (there were offers), as had happened with *The Bridge*, and he wanted to prohibit limited editions such as those for *The Cabala* and *The Bridge* that had turned into objects of frenzy in the collectors' market.

That Wilder could address these questions in the first place was another significant result of the success of *The Bridge*. His new status gained him an agent in all but name to help him wield power, his trusted new attorney, J. Dwight Dana of New Haven, Connecticut. As a result of the shifting relationship with his publisher, the Wilder-Boni contract for *Andros*, signed on December 18, 1929, contained special provisions forbidding any "first edition . . . sold at a special price nor restricted to a relatively small number of copies," and no "cheap edition . . . to be published nor any republication or repro-duction rights granted by publisher except upon the request of the Author communicated to the Publisher by said J. Dwight Dana." Wilder also asked his publisher a month before publication, to "send wrapper to me and blurb material as soon as it is done," reminding Boni "to be sure that because of the very subject-matter no faint color of Hearst-Cosmopolitan enters into the format or publicity."

"Simple Village Dwellers"

The novel greeted the public on February 21, 1930, with an an-nounced prepublication printing of 30,000 copies and another 20,000 on the day of its birth, numbers illustrating how popular Wilder had become since *The Bridge*'s first printing of 4,000 copies and *The Cabala's* first printing of 3,250. The book's design reflected Wilder's desires for dignity and simplicity of appearance. The dust jacket contained not a single blurb about the new novel or any of Wilder's previous books. Instead of the testimonials that filled the dust jackets of *The Bridge* and *The Cabala*, the back of the *Andros* jacket contained only a list of seven current Boni books, each with a short tagline description. *Andros* led the list with this announcement:

"The long-awaited successor to *The Bridge of San Luis Rey*. It is a study in the inner life of a few characters passing through circumstances that are common to domestic life in all times and places." The inside front flap repeated this language word for word, with an additional sentence alerting readers not to expect another *Bridge*: "In contrast to Mr. Wilder's earlier novels the characters in *The Woman of Andros* are simple village dwellers."

The remaining space on the front flap was filled with a brief tribute from *New York Herald Tribune* critic Isabel Paterson, saluting Wilder's "classical temper" and his signature theme of "the ageless problem of love and death." The back flap was devoted to a 200-word extract from an article by Norman Fitts in the *Boston Evening Transcript*. It told the now obligatory story of how an "obscure prep-school teacher" in less than two years had become one of the "most discussed figures in the English speaking world," an author who wrote about a subject that was "the one . . . favored by great writers—the human soul."

Lightning did not strike twice when *The Woman of Andros* appeared. But sales were strong enough through the first six months to judge the novel a partial strike in the marketplace. Wilder's third novel was a bestseller for twelve weeks between April and June 1930, reaching the number one position at least once. By the end of June it had sold 65,994 copies in the United States and was selling well in England. American sales fell off dramatically after June, and at year's end stood at approximately 70,000, arrested by the onset of what proved to be the Great Depression. *The Woman of Andros*'s numbers were nonetheless strong enough to place it third on the year's list of the ten best-selling novels and earn Wilder royalty income of more than $16,000, a notable figure in 1930.

Is Beauty Enough?

Much favorable press undergirded this success. While several critics were frank to say that they were not sure they understood Wilder's contemplative novel, they were, as with his first two novels, enthusiastic about its style, praising the novel's "craftsmanship" and "workmanship." No word was more employed than beauty: "Beauty is the key-word of this new novel." (*Saturday Review*, London); "In every page, one feels that Wilder is writing for the ages-a creation of beauty." (*New York Telegram*); "Vivid beauty" (*Dominion News*, Morgantown, West Virginia); "efficient beauty" (*Boston Evening Transcript*); "the fire of beauty" (*Bristol Times*, U.K.). Isabel Paterson wrote in the *New York Herald Tribune*, "Mr. Wilder's prose is as clear and as pure as the Castilian spring from which he has drawn its present inspiration." Mary Lamberton Becker in *The Saturday Review of Literature* threw up her hands: "Nothing one can say about it is so convincing as to quote it," she observed, joining other critics in citing especially the opening lines of the book.

Wilder's novel also received many mixed reviews. Some critics faulted him for an affected style: "Mr. Wilder's fine writing has just the whiff of the self-conscious beauty of Ye Gifte Book." (*The New Yorker*); "Too sophisticated." (*New York Sun*); "Artificial and bloodless." (*The Saturday Review*). But these negatives about taste and technique amounted to quibbles compared to a small but determined and highly vocal body of critical opinion about whether Wilder's subject matter was relevant. Here we remember that *Andros* appeared in print during the Great Depression, an entirely different era from the 1920s. Influenced by the rising social and political tensions of the time, critics granted that Wilder was employing an ancient setting from which to write about timeless issues and pose questions about human existence and meaning but wondered if it was enough. "One reads with edification and pleasure whatever Wilder chooses to write," Edmund Wilson reflected in *The New Republic* in March 1930, "but precisely because he is evidently very much a first-rate man, one wishes one saw him more at home."

Lorine Pruette, in the establishment *Book League Monthly*, made an obligatory bow to the novel as "a minor example of the exquisite," but also wondered about the relevance of Wilder's story for contemporary readers. Pruette wrote in April 1930:

Paganism passes, doubting, troubled, seeking; Christ is born. But is this enough for us today? Mr. Wilder's fable is concerned with the doubts and difficulties of to-day, while his answer lies two thousand years in the past. It is possible to suspect that in literature the utilitarians have had their day and that any affirmative writings will be hailed with a certain relief. When the fun has gone out of the study of offal, for the time being, men may very likely return to a contemplation of the stars, an age of faith may well be just ahead but faith in what? It scarcely seems that we shall find the answer in a backward glance. . . . The present trend in *The Woman of Andros* is clear enough. It has reverence and pity, tenderness and flashes of beauty, but it lacks the terror and the agony that would seem to have a rightful place in any story of a man's life, it lacks strength as does the ineffectual figure of Pamphilus. And as the fourth in the uncounted series of productions, it makes the future unfolding of a serious artist distressingly suspect.

Mike Gold, the Communist editor of the *New Masses*, harbored no doubts about Wilder's worth. In a review of *Andros* in April in his journal, he described Wilder as a "fairy-like little Anglo-American curate." Gold wasn't finished: "Yes, Wilder writes perfect English but he has nothing to say in that perfect English. He is a beautiful, rouged, combed, well-dressed corpse, lying among the sacred candles and lilies of the past, and sure to stink if exposed to sunlight." This was too much even for one of Gold's colleagues, J. Q. Neets, who defended Wilder the next month in the same publication: "Perfect English is not such a bad thing. Why object to a subtle use of words, to a splendidly organized prose?" Neets asked. He admired Wilder's "superb structure, his economy of means, his crystalline style," and observed that "A wise proletarian writer does not pooh-pooh the very real technical achievements of the bourgeois writers."

Gold would have none of it. Offered space in the October 1930 fall book issue of *The New Republic*, he assaulted all of Wilder's published work in a 2,200-word essay titled "Wilder: Prophet of the Genteel Christ." He painted the Pulitzer Prize winner as a poster boy for a genteel bourgeois literary tradition devoted to hiding from society's "real problems." Gold accused Thornton Wilder of cultivating a "museum . . . not a world," and identified *Andros* as "a still further masterly retreat into time and space." "Where are the modern streets of New York, Chicago, and New Orleans in these little novels?" Gold asked of an author whose work he summarized as a "synthesis of all the chambermaid literature, Sunday school tracts and boulevard piety there ever were." He concluded his diatribe with a challenge: "Let Mr. Wilder write a book about modern America. We predict it will reveal all his fundamental silliness and superficiality, now hidden under a Greek chlamys."

Gold's challenge was met by an outpouring of letters, the majority of them favoring Wilder. In all, twenty-seven letters were published in six issues of the magazine before the editors drew the curtain on the controversy "on account of darkness." By that time this lively literary food fight had spread into the journals and weeklies, where it occasioned a broad debate about the relationship and responsibilities of writers to contemporary society. Thornton Wilder did not respond to Gold in print. Privately, he found it a "wretched affair" and appears to have let it go. In any case, by the fall of 1930, as he had been saying publicly for several years, he had moved on to writing plays. After 1931 his one acts, including *The Happy Journey to Trenton and Camden* and *The Long Christmas Dinner* were soon being produced on amateur stages throughout the country.

THROUGH THE DECADES

Compared to the fireworks of the early 1930s, *Andros* has lived a quiet life down through the decades, despite nibbles by fans to adapt it for the stage, screen, and opera. Saint Louis composer John Kessler wrote an opera version of the novel in the mid-1930s from which famed Metropolitan Opera soprano Helen Traubel (1899–1972), a fellow Saint Louis native, apparently sang at least one song as part of her repertoire. Nothing further came of it. Actress Lillian Gish wrote to Wilder in 1947 inquiring about a film adaptation. Wilder's lively response underscored the novel's lack of dramatic tension, not to mention the challenges of the period costumes ("Modern man cannot wear that dress and appear real"). (See Reading 4.)

The novel, however, lives on. Most famously, *Our Town*, as the playwright often pointed out, was inspired in part by the story related by Chrysis to the young men on the island of Byrnos. Zeus seeks a favor that the King of the Dead cannot deny, much as he would like to. Here we find an all but word-by-word foreshadowing of the scene when Emily returns from the dead in a no-less-mythical place on her twelfth birthday.

No novel lives in an historical vacuum, and changes in culture cast light on once overlooked attributes of Wilder's storytelling. For example, students and practitioners of Wilder's works increasingly point out the centrality of leading female characters in his novels and plays, and the sensitivity with which he depicts gender roles. Here, to start a long list, Chrysis and Glycerium in *The Woman of Andros* join hands with the Marquesa de Montemayor and the Abbess in *The Bridge of San Luis Rey,* Clodia Pulcher and Cleopatra in *The Ides of March,* and the central figures in Wilder's dramas: Alcestis in *The Alcestiad,* Emily Gibbs in *Our Town* and, at the head of the line, the irrepressible Dolly Gallagher Levi in *The Matchmaker.* In 1999, classicist Jennifer Haycock noted, "*The Woman of Andros* anticipates the re-thinking a new unfettered idea of gender will require: an exploration of the limits and an understanding of the far-reaching structures of thought that rest on gender definitions," an observation that applies to Wilder's large cast of women.

READINGS

READING 1: THORNTON WILDER ON PARADE

This caricature of Wilder appeared in *On Parade,* a collection of forty-two caricatures of "Prominent Authors" published in 1929 by the German artist Eva Herrmann. Each drawing is accompanied by the author's list of works and a self-selected descriptor. The cosmopolitan Wilder chose language he was using in public lectures and interviews: "I think of my work as being French in form and manners (Saint-Simon and La Bruyère); German in feeling (Bach and Beethoven); and American in eagerness." Magazines and journals used this illustration at the time of the publication of *The Woman of Andros.*

READING 2: CARVING CHERRY STONES—APHORISMS

The aphorism, defined variously as a "terse saying embodying a general truth" or "a short, pithy maxim," lies at the heart of Wilder's search for style in the 1920s. With the indicated exception, the aphorisms here are drawn from two unpublished sources in the Wilder Archive from the period when *The Cabala* and *The Woman of Andros* were written: a two-page typed manuscript identified as "Aphorisms" (Mss), and Wilder's unpublished journal (J). Wilder credited his reading and writing in the Princeton University Library as his laboratory for sharpening this rhetorical form.

❦

Gossip is the art of telling someone else's tragedy as though it reflected credit on oneself. [Mss]

It is true that of all forms of genius, goodness has the longest awkward age. Chrysis in *The Woman of Andros.* [With slight variations, this aphorism appeared earlier in Wilder's journal and manuscript, and later as the epigraph for *Heaven's My Destination,* his fourth novel, published in 1935.]

We bend with pitying condescension over past civilizations, over Thebes, Ur and Babylon, and there floats up to us a murmur made up of cries of war, cruelty, pleasure and religious terror. Even as our civilization will some day exhale to its observers the same cries of soldiers, slaves, revellers and suppliants. [Mss]

Literature is the orchestration of platitudes. The revival in religion will be a rhetorical problem-new persuasive words for defaced or degraded ones. [J] [The first sentence appears in the Mss, and in Wilder's foreword to *The Angel That Troubled the Waters.*]

EDUCATION: True influence over another comes not from anything said or done, but from the accumulation of a lifetime's thoughts stored up in the eyes. [Mss] [This aphorism appears in *The Woman of Andros* as follows: "True influence over another comes not from a moment's eloquence nor from any happily chosen word, but from the accumulation of a life-time's thoughts stored up in the eyes."]

A great age of the theatre: when the play is more interesting than the talk about the actors. [J]

READING 3: INTERVIEWS—BEFORE AND AFTER PUBLICATION OF ANDROS

BEFORE ...

A reporter in London found the celebrated author in a talkative mode as he prepared to leave for the United States after a long stay in Europe. The subject was the usual question: What is your next novel about, Mr. Wilder? Slightly cut, this is the piece that appeared in the London *Sunday Times* on October 20, 1929. Wilder visited Greece for the first and only time in 1966—a day trip to Athens during his ship's brief layover in Piraeus.

❦

The book, [Wilder] explained, is based on Terence's comedy "Andria," ("the girl from Andros"), which in turn is based on two lost Greek plays—Menander's "Andria" and the same poet's "Perinthia."

Terence's comedy concerns the adventures of a young Athenian gentleman who falls in love with the sister of a *hetaira* [a cultured courtesan], and who by a series of stratagems, in which a nimble-witted slave is involved, succeeds in gaining his father's consent to the match.

"The action in my book," said Mr. Wilder, "passes before the curtain rises in Terence's comedy. It is the retrospective action of the story. In fact, it might serve as an introduction to Terence—but with certain facts changed."

"In what ways have you changed the facts?" he was asked.

"Well," replied Mr. Wilder with a laugh, "I have actually changed the lives, marriages and deaths of certain of the characters to suit my purposes. But there is more than this. There is a discrepancy in mood between Terence's play—which is really a farce—and my novel.

"My book is really a study of a pagan soul. The background is Greece after the great age—Greece in 200 BC—a Greece in which some vestiges of past glories remain. And against this background I have shown a human soul in circumstances which are really more than the human soul can bear. Christianity has not yet come into the world, and the pagan, under the stress of fate, has nothing outside the world to cling to.

"My principal character is a *hetaira* who has lived in Corinth and other centres of civilization. And although it is as yet two centuries before Christianity, there is in her a strange, groping humanitarianism which leads her to fill her house with helpless folk, with the lame and the one-eyed, so to speak.

"Has the story a happy ending? Well, yes, in the sense that the 'Bridge' has a happy ending. And there is a plot which—just as in Terence—hangs on the efforts of a young man to get married."

In conclusion, Mr. Wilder remarked that he had still two chapters to write—and that he had never been to Greece, the scene of his tale.

AFTER . . .

The Woman of Andros was the bestseller in the Book Department at the Marshall Field & Company store in Chicago when Wilder, now a part-time teacher at the University of Chicago, made an obligatory author's visit in early spring 1930. As department store sales in this era accounted for twenty-nine percent of all book sales, we can assume that the author autographed many copies of his new novel after his talk and a reported "volley of questions." This piece was published in the spring issue of the store's house organ, *Fashions of the Hour,* with this accompanying note: "Some of the comments which Mr. Wilder made . . . are published here with his special permission."

"Thornton Wilder Discusses His Latest Novel"

The scene of *The Woman of Andros* is laid on an imaginary island, Brynos, in the Aegean Sea, at about 200 BC—that is, in the decline of the Great Age of Greece. I did not write this book nor my others continuously day by day. I carry books about with me or keep them near at hand while I go about my ostensible profession, which is teaching. This one was begun at the Lawrenceville School in New Jersey. Some of it was written at the MacDowell Colony at Peterborough, New Hampshire. Pages have been composed in hotel rooms in Munich and London.

It is even shorter than *The Bridge.* The habit of compression seems to be growing on me, and I begin to wonder whether I shall ever be able to write a long novel. As to the theme of the book, there are a number of themes on all levels. Some of the lesser themes are, I suppose: the difference between the matter-of-factness and almost the triviality of daily life as we live it and the emotion and beauty of the same life when we remember it, looking backward from years later.

Another theme is the wistfulness and bewilderment of the pagan soul and the elements of sincerity and faith even in superstition.

Perhaps the principal theme is the theme of all my books: namely, when a situation is more than a human soul can be expected to bear, what then? *The Cabala* was a series of three such extremities, three such "nervous breakdowns." *The Bridge* said that there lay an intuition at the heart of the major attachments of life that offered a last sufficient strength for such crises.

Someday soon I hope to do a book for children with overtones for adults. For the present I shall try to write some plays.

If I work while teaching at the University, it will only be at great intervals. Time is always a notebook lying around with fragments of future pieces. One takes a long walk and without intending it one returns with new paragraphs to add to some project.

READING 4: A LETTER

New Orleans, La.
April 1. 1947

Dear Lillian:

It's a joy to get a letter from you and to think about you.

Now as to this proposal, I don't say yes or no, but I call your attention to the following points:

A. The plot-lines have no real tension. The novel combines famous well-tried plot motives: the Magdalene-Thaïs story (or Fallen woman with heart of gold) and Camille (Fallen woman barred by social opinion from achieving a happy union). But my novel has robbed both of these stories of their popular pull. Chrysis is helplessly silent and dies having won a success only in her mind. And Glycerium-Pamphilus story is a matter of waiting helplessly and then coming to very little. All the characters are externally passive and engaged in waiting.

B. Have you ever noticed that the one costume that always looks phoney and corny on the screen is the Graeco-Roman? Modern man cannot wear that dress and appear real. Think of the "Passion Plays" and the De Mille *Quo Vadis, Ben Hur,* and *The Sign of the Cross.* The only way to get away with it is by extreme "character" types, like Charles Laughton as Nero or Claude Rains as Caesar. Otherwise, everybody looks like dead chromo illustrations of ancient history.

C. Readers of *Andros* write me all the time. The things they like about the book are the descriptions of nature, and the "thoughts" of the characters. Now there's certainly room for thoughts on the screen, sure, but they only live on the screen when they are carried by strong situations and strong emotions. Now *The Woman of Andros* from the point of view of action is pale, muted, and passive. In a novel characters can suffer and meditate, but on the screen wouldn't it all look dreary and spineless?

D. Suppose you hopped up the plot for the screen. Contrived real clashes between the characters. Then I think you'd run into another danger, in those unconvincing costumes, no one would believe it. Lots of action and crisis but all looking like wax-works charades or a Sunday School pageant. To bring any vitality to *Ben Hur* they have to work up a vast spectacle and was there any real vitality? And to make *Quo Vadis* come alive don't they crown the picture with a mighty orgy? (In Hollywood I used to have lunch with the script writer who was trying to think up a sensational item to "top" the orgy. I think he ended up with naked women bound to the backs of bulls. All concerned knew that the "story" wasn't holding the audience, so that they had to inject sensation and spectacle).

But dear Lillian, I don't say yes or no. I've always believed that you have a magnificent sense of all aspects of movie and theatre. At various times Pauline Lord and Blanche Yurka approached me about a play from it; an opera for Helen Traubel was written from it (she sang from it at concerts, but the opera was never put on).[1] I feel that it was just about material for a short novel, some word-landscapes, and some semi-philosophic reflections: to expand it would break its back; to transfer it to the stage would reveal the fact that none of the characters really pull themselves together to do anything until it's too late; and to picturize it would reveal that it falls into a series of melancholy tableaux.

All this is merely subject to your judgment and intuition. And it comes with

devotedly
Thornton

---

1 Wilder is referring to the opera *The Woman of Andros* composed by John Jacob Kessler, held by the John Jacob Kessler archive, Gaylord Music Library Special Collections, Washington University in Saint Louis Libraries, Saint Louis, MO.

Reading 5: In His Hand

This holograph, of which the typed version appears below, depicts the next-to-final draft of one of the most admired paragraphs in twentieth-century American literature. Reading it has been said to turn people into writers on the spot. Readers here are invited to compare this version with the final text. The arrow points to the penultimate version, not shown here. in which only one minor change was made before it was set in type.

Transcription:

I Chrysis

The earth sighed as it turned in its course and Asia was left in darkness. Black night crept gradually along the Mediterranean. Triumph had passed from Greece and wisdom from Egypt, but with the fall of night they seemed to have regained their lost honors, and the land that was soon to be called holy prepared more richly its wonderful burden. A fair tripping breeze ruffled the Aegean and all the islands of Greece felt the new freshness at the close of day. The caves that surround the Neapolitan gulf fell into a profound shadow, but each continued to give forth its chiming or its booming sound, or its sound of applause. A storm played about Sicily and its smoking mountains, but at the mouth of the Nile the sea lay like a wet pavement. The great cliff that was one day to be called Gibraltar held for a long time a brilliant gleam of red and orange while across from it the mountains of Atlas began to show deep blue pockets in their shining sides.

READING 6: A NOTE ON WILDER'S USE OF THE CLASSICAL TRADITION IN *THE WOMAN OF ANDROS*

The classical tradition permeates *The Woman of Andros*, not only in the novel's descent from Greek and Latin comedies, but also as the inspiration for the many changes Wilder incorporated. The author's note immediately calls attention to the classics: "The first part of this novel is based upon the *Andria*, a comedy by Terence who in turn based his work upon two Greek plays, now lost to us, by Menander." Writing in Latin, Publius Terentius Afer (*circa* 195–159 BCE), known as Terence, was a Roman slave of North African background who produced *Andria* in 166 BCE. Terence's own prologue indicates the play's origin in the Greek comedy writer Menander (*circa* 342–290 BCE). The fourth century CE commentator Aelius Donatus tells us that Terence made changes to his Greek antecedents by combining two separate plays of Menander, rewriting the first scene, introducing new characters, and adding a subplot.

Wilder's revisions echo those of Terence in that he too included new plot elements and new characters while eliminating other *dramatis personae*, but his numerous transfigurations result in a re-interpretation of the *Andria*, and a guidepost for much of Wilder's future work. Wilder made changes in the setting (the fictitious island of Brynos, a Greek community, but not Athens), the time of the action (although the novel does not specify the time, in later discussions Wilder usually referred to it as occurring *circa* 200 BCE), and the genre (from dramatic comedy to narrative tragedy). Moreover, Wilder provides us with the full development of his characters, allusions to a wide range of classical tragedies and philosophy, and the inclusion of contemporary social issues. For example, the novel explores the themes of women's education, women's rights, immigration, and citizenship, motifs that were implicit in Terence but not fully explored in the Latin comedy, leading to a true conversation between texts.

The most striking modifications that Wilder has introduced into Terence's comedy are the expansion of Chrysis's character and her impact on others. Not simply a courtesan without intellectual attainments, she is now an educator and a sage, using elegant dinner parties to awaken the love of beauty, literature, and humanity in young men through her recitations of literature and Platonic dialogues. She instills in the protagonist Pamphilus an awareness and acceptance of earthly joys and sorrows, "the bright and the dark." In developing the character of Chrysis, Wilder relies on the poet Sappho and two characters from Platonic dialogues—Aspasia, who teaches rhetoric to Socrates and composes speeches, and Diotima, who instructs Socrates in the progression of love from physical attraction to the love of the beautiful soul. The full appreciation of everyday life, its joys and its sorrows, is the message not only of Chrysis but also of many of Wilder's later characters, including Dolly Levi and Julius Caesar. Chrysis's fable about a dead hero granted his wish to return to earth for one day, but who soon asks to return to the grave because the world "is too dear to be realized," will find its immortal expression in Emily Webb's graveyard experience in *Our Town. The*

Woman of Andros represents Wilder's lifetime oeuvre in miniature: learned, poignant, beautifully written, and relevant to contemporary life. Rooted in the classics, with its changes inspired by other Greek and Roman examples, it transforms our understanding of the original works.

—Dr. Stephen J. Rojcewicz Jr.

SOURCES

Unless otherwise indicated in the narrative and readings or noted below, the back matter of this volume is constructed largely from Thornton Wilder's words in unpublished manuscripts and letters in the Wilder Family Archives held in Yale's Collection of American Literature (YCAL) in the Beinecke Rare Book and Manuscript Library. Silent corrections in spelling and punctuation have been made when deemed appropriate. Use has also been made of the Yale Library's holdings of undergraduate, alumni, and *Yale Alumni Weekly* records. I hope that readers find that this approach brings these two novels, and the artist who wrote them, into view in an intimate fashion. Any errors in the afterword are my responsibility and I welcome corrections.

My definition of a short novel as falling between 20,000 and 60,000 words is adopted from the schema Edward Weeks set forth in his selection of *Great Short Novels*, published in 1941 by the Literary Guild of America. I have also drawn for background on O. H. Cheney's classic study of publishing, *Economic Survey of the Book Industry*, published originally in 1931 by R.R. Bowker Company, as reprinted in 1960. The Thornton Wilder Library afterwords in Wilder's second novel, *The Bridge of San Luis Rey* (2021) and his fourth, *Heaven's My Destination* (2020), contain, respectively, additional material about the relationship between *The Cabala* and *The Bridge,* and Mike Gold's attack on Wilder in 1930.

QUOTATIONS AND PUBLICATIONS

The Cabala: Herbert Gorman's lively Introduction to *The Cabala* is found in Modern Library Vol. 155 (May 1928), pp. v–xiii. His quotation appears on p. v.

The Woman of Andros: Dr. Edyta Oczkowicz' description of the playlets is taken from her critical essay: "'Carving Some

Cherry Stones': Disparities in *The Angel That Troubled the Waters and Other Plays*," *Thornton Wilder/New Perspectives*, Jackson R. Bryer and Lincoln Konkle, eds. (Northwestern University Press, 2013), pp. 360–377, with quoted language on p. 361. Jennifer Haytock's view of Wilder and gender appears in her essay "Woman, Philosophy, and Culture: Wilder's Andrian Legacy," *Thornton Wilder New Essays*, Martin Blank, Dalma Brunauer, David Garrett Izzo, editors (Locust Hill Press, 1999), pp. 207–216, quoted on p. 115. Thornton Wilder's April 1, 1947, letter to Lillian Gish collected in *The Selected Letters of Thornton Wilder*, edited by Robin G. Wilder and Jackson R. Bryer (HarperCollins, 2008), is quoted on pp. 454–456. The original document is held in the Billy Rose Theatre Collection, New York Public Library, and used with permission.

IMAGES

Unless credited herein, the images in this volume are in The Wilder Family Archives in YCAL and appear with the permission of the Wilder Family LLC. The Eva Herrmann caricature was published in *On Parade: Caricatures by Eva Herrmann* edited by Erich Posselt (Coward-McCann, 1929), p. 168, and appears here with permission of the Artists Rights Society. The three photographs from the Lawrenceville School appear with permission of that institution and the helpful assistance of Jacqueline Haun, school archivist.

GENERAL BACKGROUND

Important new works for a general audience interested in learning more about Thornton Wilder's life and works have become available since the first edition of this book was published. Key titles include the definitive biography *Thornton Wilder: A Life* by Penelope Niven

(HarperCollins, 2012) and *The Selected Letters of Thornton Wilder*, edited by Robin G. Wilder and Jackson R. Bryer (HarperCollins, 2008). Wilder's playlets in *The Angel That Troubled the Waters and Other Plays* (1928) are conveniently found today in *The Collected Short Plays of Thornton Wilder Vol. II* (Theater Communications Group Press, 1998); *Collected Plays & Writings on Theater* (Library of America, 2007); *Thornton Wilder's Playlets: Short, Short Plays for 3–5 Actors* (Concord Theatricals, 2022).

SPECIALIZED STUDIES

Readers interested in greater depth about Wilder's use of classical and religious themes are referred to *Thornton Wilder, Classical Reception, and American Literature* by Stephen J. Rojcewicz, Jr. (Abingdon, UK: Routledge Press, 2022), *Thornton Wilder & Amos Wilder: Writing Religion in Twentieth-Century America* by Christopher J. Wheatley's (University of Notre Dame Press, 2011).

❦

Two websites feature extensive information about all of Wilder's major works: www.thorntonwilder.com and www.thorntonwilder society.com

Tappan Wilder
February 2022

ACKNOWLEDGMENTS

The back matter of this volume is constructed in large part from Thornton Wilder's words in unpublished letters, manuscripts, and journals, and publications not easy to come by, among them the undergraduate and alumni records of the Yale College Classes of 1919–1921, and issues of the *Yale Alumni Weekly* from 1920–1931. I hope readers will find that this approach brings these two novels, and the artist who wrote them, into view in a personal way. Those interested in further information about Thornton Wilder are referred to standard sources and to the bibliography available at www.thorntonwildersociety.org. Widely available sources on certain topics addressed in this volume deserve special mention. The collection of Wilder's playlets, *The Angel That Troubled the Waters,* first published in 1928, is found in *The Collected Short Plays of Thornton Wilder*, Volume II (1998), a volume also graced by a deeply informed introduction by the playwright A. R. Gurney. The afterword to Wilder's fourth novel, *Heaven's My Destination* (1935), contains in this HarperCollins series additional information about the Michael Gold attack and Wilder's response to it. My definition of a short novel as falling between 60,000 and 20,000 words is adopted from the schema Edward Weeks set forth in his selection of *Great Short Novels*, published in 1941 by The Literary Guild of America. I have cited information found in O. H. Cheney's classic study of book publishing, *Economic Survey of the Book Industry*, published originally in 1931 by R. R. Bowker Company, as reprinted in 1960.

J. D. McClatchy, Robin Wilder, Jackson Bryer, and the staff of Yale's Beinecke Rare Book and Manuscript Library have provided unwavering support for this book and the project it is part of. Noa Wheeler and Ellen Wilhite helped with many a practical task. Two individuals deserve a special salute: Hugh Van Dusen for his faith in these novels and the larger project of which they are a piece, and Penelope Niven, the Thornton Wilder biographer, for her wisdom and encouragement from beginning to end and for providing a Foreword that is a model of the art. Any errors in the Afterword are my responsibility, and I welcome corrections.

SOURCES AND PERMISSIONS

With the exception of sources noted below, all excerpts quoted from unpublished sources are from Thornton Wilder's correspondence, manuscripts, and related records in the Thornton Wilder Collection in the Yale Collection of American Literature (YCAL) in the Beinecke Rare Book and Manuscript Library, or from the Wilder family's own holdings, including many of Thornton Wilder's legal and agency papers. Silent corrections in spelling and punctuation have been made when deemed appropriate. The Sibyl Colfax letters are held in the Thornton Wilder Collection, Fales

Manuscripts, Fales Library, New York University, and Marvin J. Taylor's assistance is gratefully acknowledged. Dr. Eve Katz provided the English translation of Ernst Renan's words.

PUBLICATIONS

Wilder's Foreword to *The Angel That Troubled the Waters* is reprinted in *American Characteristics & Other Essays* (New York: Harper & Row, 1979; Authors Guild Backinprint edition, 2000), 95–99. Unless otherwise noted, all rights for all published and unpublished work by Thornton Wilder are reserved by the Wilder Family LLC. *Thornton Niven Wilder: The Memorial Service* was privately printed in 1976 by Yale University. Passages from his works read at this service appear on pages 14–19.

IMAGES

Unless otherwise credited herein, the images in this volume are taken from material in the Wilder Archives at Yale or are held by the Wilder family. The Eva Hermann caricature appears with the permission of the Artists Rights Society. The three indicated photographs, including the author picture probably dating from 1924, appear with the permission of the Lawrenceville School and were provided by the helpful Jacqueline Haun, Archivist of that institution.

About the Author

In his quiet way, Thornton Niven Wilder was a revolutionary writer who experimented boldly with literary forms and themes, from the beginning to the end of his long career. "Every novel is different from the others," he wrote when he was seventy-five. "The theater (ditto). . . . The thing I'm writing now is again totally unlike anything that preceded it." Wilder's richly diverse settings, characters, and themes are at once specific and global. Deeply immersed in classical as well as contemporary literature, he often fused the traditional and the modern in his novels and plays, all the while exploring the cosmic in the commonplace. In a January 12, 1953, cover story, *Time* took note of Wilder's unique "interplanetary mind"—his ability to write from a vision that was at once American and universal.

A pivotal figure in the history of twentieth-century letters, Wilder was a novelist and playwright whose works continue to be widely read and produced in this new century. He is the only writer to have won the Pulitzer Prize for both Fiction and Drama. His second novel, *The Bridge of San Luis Rey,* received the Fiction award in 1928, and he won the prize twice in Drama, for *Our Town* in 1938 and *The Skin of Our Teeth* in 1943. His other novels are *The Cabala, The Woman of Andros, Heaven's My Destination, The Ides of March, The Eighth Day,* and *Theophilus North.* His other major dramas include *The Matchmaker,* which was adapted as the internationally acclaimed musical comedy *Hello, Dolly!,* and *The Alcestiad.* Among his innovative shorter plays are *The Happy Journey to Trenton and Camden* and *The Long Christmas Dinner,* and two uniquely conceived series, *The Seven Ages of Man* and *The Seven Deadly Sins,* frequently performed by amateurs.

Wilder and his work received many honors, highlighted by the three Pulitzer Prizes, the Gold Medal for Fiction from the American Academy of Arts and Letters, the Order of Merit (Peru), the Goethe-Plakette der Stadt (Germany, 1959), the Presidential Medal of Freedom (1963), the National Book Committee's first National Medal for Literature (1965), and the National Book Award for Fiction (1967).

He was born in Madison, Wisconsin, on April 17, 1897, to Amos Parker Wilder and Isabella Niven Wilder. The family later lived in China and in California, where Wilder was graduated from Berkeley High School. After two years at Oberlin College, he went on to Yale, where he received his undergraduate degree in 1920. A valuable part of his education took place during summers spent working hard on farms in California, Kentucky, Vermont, Connecticut, and Massachusetts. His father arranged these rigorous "shirtsleeve" jobs for Wilder and his older brother, Amos, as part of their initiation into the American experience.

Thornton Wilder studied archaeology and Italian as a special student at the American Academy in Rome (1920–1921), and earned a master of arts degree in French literature at Princeton in 1926.

In addition to his talents as playwright and novelist, Wilder was an accomplished teacher, essayist, translator, scholar, lecturer, librettist, and screenwriter. In 1942, he teamed with Alfred Hitchcock to write the first draft of the screenplay for the classic thriller *Shadow of a Doubt,* receiving credit as principal writer and a special screen credit for his "contribution to the preparation" of the production. All but fluent in four languages, Wilder translated and adapted plays by such varied authors as Henrik Ibsen, Jean-Paul Sartre, and André Obey. As a scholar, he conducted significant research on James Joyce's *Finnegans Wake* and the plays of Spanish dramatist Lope de Vega.

Wilder's friends included a broad spectrum of figures on both sides of the Atlantic—Hemingway, Fitzgerald, Alexander Woollcott, Gene Tunney, Sigmund Freud, producer Max Reinhardt, Katharine Cornell, Ruth Gordon, and Garson Kanin. Beginning in the mid-1930s, Wilder was especially close to Gertrude Stein and became one of her most effective interpreters and champions. Many of Wilder's friendships are documented in his prolific correspondence. Wilder believed that great letters constitute a "great branch of literature." In a lecture entitled "On Reading the Great Letter Writers," he wrote that a letter can function as a "literary exercise," the "profile of a personality," and "news of the soul," apt descriptions of thousands of letters he wrote to his own friends and family.

Wilder enjoyed acting and played major roles in several of his own plays in summer theater productions. He also possessed a lifelong love of music; reading musical scores was a hobby, and he wrote the librettos for two operas based on his work: *The Long*

Christmas Dinner, with composer Paul Hindemith, and *The Alcestiad,* with composer Louise Talma. Both works premiered in Germany.

Teaching was one of Wilder's deepest passions. He began his teaching career in 1921 as an instructor in French at Lawrenceville, a private secondary school in New Jersey. Financial independence after the publication of *The Bridge of San Luis Rey* permitted him to leave the classroom in 1928, but he returned to teaching in the 1930s at the University of Chicago. For six years, on a part-time basis, he taught courses there in classics in translation, comparative literature, and composition. In 1950–1951, he served as the Charles Eliot Norton Professor of Poetry at Harvard. Wilder's gifts for scholarship and teaching (he treated the classroom as all but a theater) made him a consummate, much-sought-after lecturer in his own country and abroad. After World War II, he held special standing, especially in Germany, as an interpreter of his own country's intellectual traditions and their influence on cultural expression.

During World War I, Wilder had served a three-month stint as an enlisted man in the Coast Artillery section of the army, stationed at Fort Adams, Rhode Island. He volunteered for service in World War II, advancing to the rank of lieutenant colonel in Army Air Force Intelligence. For his service in North Africa and Italy, he was awarded the Legion of Merit, the Bronze Star, the Chevalier Legion d'Honneur, and honorary officership in the Military Order of the British Empire (M.B.E.).

From royalties received from *The Bridge of San Luis Rey,* Wilder built a house for his family in 1930 in Hamden, Connecticut, just outside New Haven. But he typically spent as many as two hundred days a year away from Hamden, traveling to and settling in a variety of places that provided the stimulation and solitude he needed for his work. Sometimes his destination was the Arizona desert, the MacDowell Colony in New Hampshire, or Martha's Vineyard, Newport, Saratoga Springs, Vienna, or Baden-Baden. He wrote aboard ships, and often chose to stay in "spas in off-season." He needed a certain refuge when he was deeply immersed in writing a novel or play. Wilder explained his habit to a *New Yorker* journalist in 1959: "The walks, the quiet—all the elegance is present, everything is there but the people. That's it! A spa in off-season! I make a practice of it."

But Wilder always returned to "the house *The Bridge* built," as it is still known to this day. He died there of a heart attack on December 7, 1975.

WORKS BY THORNTON WILDER

THEOPHILUS NORTH
A Novel

"An extremely entertaining array of American life in a bygone era."
—*New Yorker*

THE BRIDGE OF SAN LUIS REY
A Novel

"One merely has to consider the central question raised by the novel, which, according to Wilder himself, was simply: 'Is there a direction and meaning in the lives beyond the individual's own will?' It is perhaps the largest and most profoundly personal philosophical inquiry that we can undertake. It is the question that defines us as human beings."
—Russell Banks, foreword to *The Bridge of San Luis Rey*

THE CABALA and THE WOMAN OF ANDROS
Two Novels

"No matter where and when Wilder's novels take place, his characters grapple with universal questions about the nature of human existence."
—Penelope Niven, author of *Thornton Wilder*

THE EIGHTH DAY
A Novel

"We marvel at a novel of such spiritual ambition."
—John Updike, foreword to *The Eighth Day*

HEAVEN'S MY DESTINATION
A Novel

"If John Steinbeck's mighty *The Grapes of Wrath* is the tragic novel of the Great Depression, then *Heaven's My Destination* is its comic masterpiece."
—J. D. McClatchy, foreword to *Heaven's My Destination*

THE IDES OF MARCH
A Novel

"Full of the wisdom of the ages—as well as satirical observations on man's political instability, loves, joys and terrors."
—*Chicago Tribune*

HARPER PERENNIAL

OUR TOWN
A Play in Three Acts
"Our Town is probably the finest play ever written by an American."
—Edward Albee

THE SELECTED LETTERS OF THORNTON WILDER
"A remarkable collection. . . . What emerges from these pages is a new and sometimes surprising self-portrait of a great American artist."
—Marian Seldes

THE SKIN OF OUR TEETH
A Play
"For an American dramatist, all roads lead back to Thornton Wilder."
—Paula Vogel, foreword to *The Skin of Our Teeth*

THREE PLAYS
Our Town, The Skin of Our Teeth,* and *The Matchmaker
"These plays are a gift." —John Guare, foreword to *Three Plays*

THE MATCHMAKER
A Farce in Four Acts
"Loud, slap dash and uproarious . . . extraordinarily original and funny."
—*New York Times*

THORNTON WILDER: A LIFE
by Penelope Niven
"The best kind of literary biography, one likely to send the reader back (or perhaps for the first time) to the author's works." —*Washington Post*

HARPER ⬤ PERENNIAL